*The Most Amazing
Department Store*

The Most Amazing Department Store

Sharon Neiss-Arbess

TORONTO 2023

RE:BOOKS

Copyright © Sharon Neiss-Arbess.

All rights reserved.

www.rebooks.ca

Published in Canada by RE:BOOKS.

ADDRESS:
RE:BOOKS
Brookfield Place
181 Bay Street
Suite 1800
Toronto, Ontario
M5J 2T9
Canada

www.rebooks.ca

No portion of this publication may be reproduced or transmitted, in any form, or by any means, without express written permission of the copyright holder.

First RE:BOOKS Edition: October 2023

ISBN: 978-1-7389452-4-5
eBook ISBN: 978-1-7389452-5-2

RE:BOOKS and all associated logos are trademarks and/or registered marks of RE:BOOKS.

Printed and bound in Canada.

1 3 5 7 9 10 8 6 4 2

Cover Design By: Chloe Faith Robinson and Jordan Lunn
Typeset By: Karl Hunt

For Lillian z"l
And her great-granddaughter Liv

There are no coincidences

ELIE WIESEL z"l

Times change, people change, thoughts about
God and evil change, about true and false.
But what always remains fast and steady is the
affection that your friends feel for you.
Those who always have your best interest at heart.

MARGOT FRANK z"l

PROLOGUE

1950s—Somewhere in Montreal

There's nothing like a visit to a department store.

As you see the grandiose mecca in the distance, your heart beats a little bit faster, from the quicker pace of your step, of the anticipation of getting closer. As you reach the marble tiles that frame the entrance way and grasp the elaborate handle, you pull the framed glass doors toward you while a delicious yet prominent scent makes its way to your senses. It's your mother's perfume, the maid's arrival, and a present wrapped in the fanciest wrapping paper and topped with a shiny silver bow that all welcomed you with open arms to the place you had been looking forward to all day.

"I'm here," you mutter under your breath while your eyes dart around as you know your surroundings like the back of your hand. You feel comfortable here. You belong here.

But what about the places where you were encouraged to belong but you really didn't feel like you did.

There were days when the nature lover guided you and held a sturdy branch as a symbol of strength and guidance while hearing the loon in a nearby body of water calling to its mate.

"Listen!" she whispered. "Can you hear that?"

You nod while letting your eyes expand to show how impressed you are.

Because you are, right?

Let's continue the scene.

The distinct tap of the woodpecker making its mark on a tree. The inhaled scent of the wet leaves and fresh-cut wood. You are told to admire this God-given beautiful nature, as it is breathtaking. But let's be honest. Do you really like it here? Among the birds, spiders, snakes, and other creatures that may be crawling up your neck right now. Where do you really want to be? I know. It's okay. You can say it. Oh, all right, if you don't, I will.

You would much rather be standing in the middle of a department store and purchasing a fresh new mascara! As you hold the new glistening tube of plastic and gently twist it to release the wand from its nest to reveal a row of minuscule fibers that are coated in the formula of your dreams that will caress and hug each of your lashes to make them expand like a peacock's tail. Ah, Yes! You know it. Amazing right? Meditate that manufactured-made beauty goodness and close your eyes to breathe it all in deeply.

Hail to the fashionista who stands in the center of the department store aisles, holding the statement purse in one hand and the tattooed lipstick coffee cup in the other, which is the fuel for the *hunt du jour.*

"Listen!" she heavily whispers. "Can you hear that?" You nod while letting your eyes expand to show how impressed you are. BECAUSE YOU REALLY ARE. BECAUSE THIS PLACE. THIS DEPARTMENT STORE IS AMAZING!

The sound of the perfected engineered click from a brand-new monogrammed powder compact has closed. The feel of the glossy cellophane wrapped box of hand cream just waiting to be opened and drunk by your sandpaper skin that wears the scars from the daily abuse. The aroma of that new perfume that smells like a vacation.

1950s—Somewhere in Montreal

Like the nature lover, the fashionista knows where the best views are and what to be careful of—because it's a jungle out there, even if it's framed with marble that glistens, mirrors that shine, and the most beautiful things.

The elegant perfume bottles that sparkle from the fluorescent lights that hang from above and the perfectly stacked cashmere scarves in a rainbow of colors on a nearby shelf are waiting for you to run your fingertips along their fine and delicate fibers that are silky and soft to the touch. The glass countertops are gleaming enough for you to see your reflection, while you *tap tap tap* on the glass that houses the face cream that you want to buy that promises to erase all your worries.

The cosmetician who knows your name, your shade of blush, what skin cream gives you the best glow, and what perfume gives you a headache is waiting for you with more patience than your psychologist. There is also the shoe salesperson who not only knows your size but also your style and how high of a heel you can wear. What would look best with that skirt you just bought? And how are you doing with your wedding list, do you have to invite them?

Bonds of all kinds can blossom at the department store, but the real magic happens beyond what you see. It's where the employees push the merchandise out from the meticulously designed displays into your hands. There is a bond of their own that developed spending countless hours together in the inventory trenches, holding each other's hand after a conversation that needed a tissue. While some may be on their mark to outrun, there are a chosen few would not know what they would do if they never met each other.

This is the story of two women, Lilly and Vivian, who share a most unique friendship that went through a journey during a time that was incredibly challenging, yet full of hope, in *The Most Amazing Department Store.*

Vivian: Fashionista Fury 1934, Montreal

At a small school in a neighborhood called Outremont, Vivian Steiner sat at her student desk, cross-legged, with her hand beneath her chin, staring out of the classroom window completely bored out of her mind, save for a daydream about being in a fashion shoot. No, she wasn't a model in this dream but was taking charge of the model and all that surrounded her. Like a maestro conducting a symphony, she gave directions to the photographers to do this and the lighting crew to do that as she placed a light blue silk scarf around a model's neck that brought out the thin turquoise stripes in the charcoal gray trousers that she wore.

"Vivian . . . Vivian?"

Vivian regained her focus and felt peeved at her teacher, who interrupted such a superb scenario that she thought up all on her own.

"Wha—"

Vivian responded in a semiconscious trance to her teacher, who was trying to bring her attention to the arithmetic question on the chalkboard. She clearly didn't understand what her teacher wanted her to do.

Vivian sighed, completely ignoring both what was on the chalkboard and her very loud teacher, who was desperately trying to drill the process of fractions into her brain. There she was, with her tall and skinny wooden stick hitting the chalkboard on a mathematical problem, repeatedly with such force. And she yelled so loud that her explanation was lost and felt like a different language. The language of noise.

How could Vivian concentrate on the task while an atrocious vision stood right in front of her? What a dreadful sight, she thought.

Her shoes. The teacher was wearing a pair that looked like they have been through a war. They were also outdated, covered in scuff marks, and had at least two holes at the toes. Vivian realized that new shoes were not a priority for a teacher, but the scuff marks were inexcusable. *Why wasn't this matter taken care of?* she thought. Any twit could get a quick shine with some shoe polish and an old rag. And what about those stockings? Why was there a run up the side? Couldn't she have stashed an extra pair in her purse for moments like these?

And why couldn't they teach how to dress properly instead of silly fractions?

Day after day, these thoughts ran through Vivian's head. She couldn't look anyone in the eye or simply carry on a conversation without analyzing what they were wearing first. Anyone who was in Vivian's presence was either unapologetically scrutinized or showered with praise for how they looked. At home and to all who knew her, she was the first to be asked if something looked right . . . or wrong. Nothing got by her keen fashionista eye and talent for detail. Most of them took advantage of this interesting and unique gift, which she had developed at such a young age.

Six years ago, when Vivian was a toddler, she spent hours playing with all the different fabrics that hung in her mother Miriam's closet. Her eyes expanded with keen interest as her chubby little hands reached for a pair of shoes, followed by an embrace similar to holding a doll, while she thought about her next move. After scanning the wardrobe like a detective looking for clues, she matched a pair with the proper dress and/or skirt and then squirmed a few inches away to view her creation with great satisfaction.

Toddler Vivian knew when her mother was going out, as she would smell her Chanel No. 5 from her bedroom. As fast as her little legs could carry her, she ran down the hall into her mother's boudoir, so she could watch her get dressed from stepping into her stockings to watching her dip the mascara wand into the dark pressed powder to gently brush her eyelashes with.

Back to nine-year-old Vivian, stretched out on the living room sofa, as *The Guiding Light* played on the living room radio. She hardly missed an episode, as she adored this new radio drama so much. She was interrupted by familiar footsteps one floor above that she knew so well. The corners of Vivian's mouth slowly raised, knowing what was coming—her older sister Marsha—as she barged into the room and posed in her outfit.

"How's this, Viv?" Marsha asked in anticipation on one such occasion.

Vivian had turned her head away from the radio. "Very nice. Don't care for the scarf. Borrow Mom's pearls instead." Marsha zoomed up the stairs to change, no questions asked.

After the radio program was over, Vivian moved from the living room sofa to her favorite place in the world. The middle of the hallway in her home, where she was beckoned for another consultation, by her mother.

"Vivian! I'm so glad you're home!" Miriam Steiner said as she entered through the front door just before 5 p.m. That moment—where she was and what she was doing—was Vivian's absolute favorite pastime. The Steiner's had a large, vibrant emerald-green rug with a gold trim that was laid out on the wood-paneled floor. It added so much brightness to the hallway. Vivian loved to lie down on it and caress the fluffy fibers.

But what the heck did she do on this coveted rug? After a hard day at school, Vivian would dump her books on the floor and collapse like a boxer after the 18th round. Do her homework—or at least try to—and witness all the excitement that was happening around her. Like a train station, everyone was coming and going, and Vivian loved to be smack in the middle of it all while lying on something warm, soft, and beautiful.

But the one emerald-green-rug activity that Vivian looked forward to the most each month was the delivery of her *Vogue* magazine. She knew exactly when it arrived, as she counted down the days until the glossy and glamorous magazine was delivered to her doorstep.

Studying all the pretty models who wore the latest designers sucked Vivian's attention in like a vacuum cleaner. She found the articles to be quite interesting too. Of course, help was needed to read the bigger words that weren't a part of a nine-year-old's vocabulary, which Marsha or her parents were more than happy to help with; but the beautiful, photographed pictures spoke for themselves, and she related to the significance of them with ease—especially the new trend of bringing in casual pajama-like pants into a woman's daily wardrobe. How could one just wear dresses and skirts all day long?

The Steiner family was a safe place for Vivian to express her thoughts, and Miriam and Henry were doing the best that they could to shelter their children from what was going on in the world and how they were treated in their very own city of Montreal.

"Vivian, what do you want to be when you grow up?" Miriam and Henry would ask their daughter, full of hope now that they were safe in Canada. "I want to work for *Vogue!*" Vivian would exclaim, with her hands up in the air for extra drama, fully aware that she had no interest in making pies and changing diapers. Being in charge of who wore what was right up her alley, and at the age of nine, she was only getting started.

Vivian decided to keep the details of her career aspirations to herself, as she knew it would cause quite a stir with her parents and sensed that they seemed more uptight than usual. Her mother didn't smile as often, but when she did, it was forced. Her father kept rubbing his chin and squinting his eyes. The last time her parents acted like this was when Vivian had a high fever and a doctor had to come to the house. They behaved that way because they were worried, as they told her so when she recovered.

But Vivian wasn't sick. However, the state of the Jewish people was, and her parents were trying to protect her from knowing this. But Vivian knew that something was wrong—especially because her father began to remove his *kippah* when he left the house for work.

Just the other day, Miriam was out shopping for cheese at the market. Standing in line and waiting for her turn, she asked the sales lady for the Havarti in a half pound of slices. The sales lady waited a few moments and then made a quick turn to the back of the store. Miriam waited in anticipation, wondering why the fresh block of Havarti was not taken out of the display case and sliced for Miriam to take home so that Henry could devour his favorite cheese on toast.

"Here you are!" the woman said, handing her a package that clearly revealed green fuzz.

"Excuse me, ma'am, but this cheese is spoiled. Can you please sell me the fresh one that you keep right here?" Miriam pointed to the block of cheese in the window."

"The cheese is spoiled, just like you! You are not welcome here!"

At the Steiner home, where Vivian wore her fashion police badge, life felt safe, but didn't go so well once headed outside.

Back to 5 in the afternoon, in the center of the hallway, where Miriam had requested her daughter's advice: "Ta dahhh!" Miriam pointed to her shopping bag, which she placed on a nearby chair.

She then slipped out of the dress she was wearing and threw it on the floor.

"Maaa!" Vivian yelled.

"It's no big deal. It's only us."

"No, that's not it—you don't throw your good dress on the floor! It will wrinkle and get dirty.

It's better to pick it up and drape it gently on that chair," Vivian pointed.

Miriam shrugged her shoulders and did what she was told and then reached into her bag to put on her new purchase, which was a skirt. "Whaddya think!" she sang as she modeled the skirt.

Vivian knew within seconds that this was not a look for her mother. It just didn't suit her hip frame properly. Vivian's impulse to speak her mind rushed quickly to her brain, even though she had been scolded countless times before to *think* before speaking, as what came out of her mouth was not always kind, "Please save that for my Halloween costume."

"What did we say about speaking kindly?" Miriam asked sternly.

"Mother, it's the truth. I cannot tell a lie!"

Marsha, who was sitting in the kitchen, made sure everyone heard her sigh, loudly.

"Really?" Miriam asked.

"Really," Vivian said.

"I'll return it tomorrow."

Vivian smiled as she dropped her head back into the pages of her magazine.

Vivian's father, Henry, walked into the hallway.

"That skirt is awful, Miriam. It's all bunched up at your waist."

"See?" Vivian said. "Mom, you can do so much better." She held up a page from her magazine and pointed to a skirt that was designed by Madeleine Vionnet. "Perhaps consider a skirt that cuts on a bias. You have beautiful hips, and you should show them properly."

"She's right!" Henry said. Miriam nodded, forced a smile and grabbed her dress from the chair and went upstairs to change.

***

"Why are you wearing that awful dress?" Vivian blurted out.

A week later, the Steiner family was at a family gathering for a cousin's birthday when Vivian showed no mercy.

That fearless yet rude question was asked without a thought, across the hall, to a young woman whom she didn't know and who was wearing an orange polka-dot dress with puffy sleeves two sizes too big for her tiny figure.

"Excuse me?" the young woman asked, aghast by the comment.

"VIVIAN!" her father scolded her.

"VIVIAN!" her mother yelled to the ceiling with her arms extended.

"You're such a pill!" Marsha yelled toward her feet.

All three comments felt like slaps on her face. What was their problem? The dress was atrocious. Why couldn't anyone see that? Why couldn't this young woman see that?

Vivian just stood there and said, "I *needed* to tell her."

"She's right. I wasn't sure about this frock when I put it on this morning, and I should have left it in my sister's closet, as it is clearly too big for me," the young woman had said.

"And ugly," Vivian said under her breath, smiling.

"That's enough, young lady," her mother whispered to her.

"Yes, Mom," Vivian obediently said while trying her best to learn proper etiquette.

***

Back in the classroom, where Vivian's mind was not where it needed to be, her teacher with the torn stockings and shoes that deserved a purple heart continued to yell and hit the chalkboard with her skinny wooden stick until the chalkboard developed scratches. "Vivian, can you solve this mathematical problem?!"

The question tried to enter Vivian's mind, but the state of her teacher's wardrobe blocked any processing that her brain could master. She couldn't help it; she just had to say it because it was the truth that was staring right at her, and she had to share it before she thought she would just burst. Ah! The opportunity to teach how to dress presented itself. *Take that, meaningless math and get a load of what I can teach you.*

"No, but I can solve the problem that's happening below your knees."

Each child went home from school to report the spectacle of the day to their families.

They could have sworn they saw smoke coming out of the teacher's ears. However, there wasn't enough time to fully observe the reaction, because before you could say "horsefeathers," the teacher grabbed the ruler from her desk drawer, marched right up to Vivian's desk, and motioned for her to expose her palms.

"You're lazy and spoiled!" the teacher yelled, as she whipped her ruler across Vivian's hands.

Vivian came home from school that day; she placed her red hands in front of her mother's face and announced that it happened again. Miriam certainly felt the pain her daughter was feeling—and not just the physical kind.

"Again?" her mother asked as she held her daughter's hands.

"Again," Vivian admitted.

"You've got to start to keep your opinions to yourself. Not everyone wants or needs your advice, Viv."

"Yes, but they need to know," Vivian said as she looked up at her mother with eyes full of tears. "They need to know."

Lilly—1934

Daylight couldn't come soon enough. In a home a few streets away from the Steiner house in Outremont, nine-year-old Lilly Krovchick lay in her bed, staring out the window, waiting for the sun to rise.

The fifth child of Sarah and Norman Krovchick, she was a feisty and determined young girl with a mop of curly, light brown hair who wanted to take a bite out of everything. Living in Canada since she was a baby, she and her family fled from Russia, ten years prior. Lilly's father, Norman, fought and perished in World War I in Russia, which left Sarah to stand on her own, holding five children in her arms.

When an opportunity to own a small grocery store three blocks from home came up, Sarah jumped at the chance. Lilly and her other four siblings helped at different hours of the day. Her eldest sister, Anna, was there most days, as at eighteen, she had already graduated from high school. The rest came to help when they were able, mainly after school. Whatever was in season was put on the shelves, which wasn't a huge variety, but there were many canned goods to choose from.

Lilly lay on her bed and held onto her stuffed elephant while she stared out the window, searching for a speck of daylight to burst through the darkness. Not an owner of a clock or a wristwatch, but she knew that once she saw light, it was safe for her to get up and start her day. It was Monday, her favorite day of the week, which meant she could go to her favorite place in the world for five days in a row: school.

Finally, Lilly threw the sheets off her legs and placed her bare feet on the floor. Wincing from the cold, she shoved the uncomfortableness away because she got what she was waiting for: daylight.

"It's morning," Lilly announced to Anna, who lay in her bed, three steps away. She knew it was three steps because each night before she went to bed, she would sing "One-two-three! I'm coming to kiss you goodnight—See?" as she would plant a kiss on her sister's cheek while she was reading in bed. A smile quickly framed Lilly's young face as she thought of her conversation with Anna the evening before.

"Aw, Lilly, how can I even think of going to sleep without that ritual?" she would say with a wink. "Hey, did you study for that math test that you have tomorrow?"

"Study? You bet your sweet *tuchas* I studied. I am so prepared for that test; when mother was making a pie last night, I looked at her cookbook and shouted out the measurements while multiplying, subtracting, and dividing them—all in my head—without a pencil and paper."

"Impressive," Anna squinted. A trick she tended to do while thinking of a memory. "Um, I took a bite out of the corner. It kind of tasted funny."

"Oh dear—I must have confused her by shouting out doubles of the required measurement. Or triples. Or multiple servings!"

"Great, Lill. That pie was a gift to welcome our new neighbor!"

"Oh darn!" Lilly said with a giggle.

***

10

Lilly—1934

"Lilly, you ruined my pie! It tastes too sweet!" Lilly's mother Sarah said as she stood by her kitchen counter with her hands on her hips.

"Is it my fault that you listened to me rather than your cookbook?" Lilly said as she placed her books in her satchel and whipped it on her shoulder. "Look, I must leave for school. Big math test today and I don't want to be late."

"Yes, we all know about that math test," Sarah said as she remembered Lilly announcing the test to the family when she was told about it at school and counting down the days until it was time to write it. "I want you in the store right after school, young lady!" Sarah instructed Lilly as she followed her out the door.

"Don't worry, I'll be there," Lilly said as she was halfway out the door, excited to get to school to show what she could do. A straight A student since the first grade, Lilly adored school because she had a real thirst for knowledge. It made her feel powerful.

"Mother, are you ready to go and meet our new neighbors before we head to the store?" Anna asked as she peeped her head into the living room doorway. Sarah turned around and nodded, while she walked back to the kitchen to collect the pie she made. "So . . . it's a little on the sweet side . . . does it really matter?" Anna asked as Sarah laughed.

Sarah and Anna walked across the street, with the sugar-loaded pie, and rang the doorbell to the home of their new neighbor. A gentleman in a three-piece suit answered the door.

"Yes?" he asked.

"Welcome to the neighborhood!" Anna and Sarah sang together.

"I heard about you people. What are you doing in Outremont? Get out of here and go to Palestine, where you belong!" he yelled and slammed the door in their faces.

Anna and Sarah's head flung back as though they have been hit but quickly composed themselves as this was not the first time they have heard a reaction to their existence like that. "Well, we saved him from eating the pie," Anna said.

"Let's leave the pie for him to eat and hope that he will choke on it—and get a cavity too," Sarah snickered.

* * *

"I did very well on my test today!" Lilly said in a sing-songy voice as she entered her mother's store after school and reached into her bag to present her victory. "Feast your eyes on this beauty!"

"Wow—good for you, sweetheart!" Sarah said as she glanced at the bold letter A, which was written in red at the top of her test, while caressing her daughter's cheek. Anna looked on and winked at her sister. Lilly felt a few inches taller, as there was nothing better than pleasing her mother and making her feel proud.

"Put your stuff away and come open up the boxes of canned green beans," Sarah instructed, and Lilly conquered the request, even though she wanted to be somewhere else—like at her friend Marie Ste. Claire's house, where she had a huge backyard with an old tire that hung from a tree and there was an endless supply of lemonade to drink. On occasion, Lilly was excused from working at the store after school and went to Marie's house to play. After they played outside for a while, the girls came inside to get a snack. Lilly stopped in her tracks, as there was a dark cherry breakfront cabinet that displayed the prettiest plates, teacups and saucers, and wine glasses that had an etched design detail.

"Not too close, dear," Marie's mother warned as Lilly was inches away from the antiques, as she was just itching to pick them up with her hands to study them closer. "That's my grandmother's china, that has been in our family for five generations. Do you have any heirlooms in your home?"

"No, we had to escape from Russia, so there was no room to pack any fancy plates or glasses."

"I beg your pardon?"

"Yeah—we had to flee—as my mother told me. I wasn't born yet."

"Flee? Why did you have to flee?"

This was a question that Lilly knew was coming, but didn't want to answer. As she bit her lip, and scanned the space that she was standing in, she tried to find the words to describe the Pogroms, but didn't know how. The only way to answer Marie's mother was to tell her what she knew for sure.

"Nobody liked us in Russia."

"Why?"

"Because we're Jewish."

Vivian: War Just Sucks—1942

It was 1942, and Vivian had turned seventeen. School had finished, and she had nine weeks of freedom. Most of her friends were hanging out at their parents' country homes. Some were even going to a summer camp to be counselors. There was only one place that Vivian wanted to be, and that was at Sunderland's—the most glamorous, coveted department store in Downtown Montreal—and she wanted to be surrounded by beautiful clothes and cosmetics, all day, every day.

Even sitting in the department store lunch counter and watching all the buzz from the salespeople and customers moving about gave Vivian such a thrill. She wanted to jump right in and be a part of it all as soon as possible.

And jump she did, beginning with her job interview, which took place at the lunch counter of Sunderland's. Mr. Sand, a senior sales associate, sat across from the tenacious Vivian, who was as eager as a student who studied for weeks waiting to write an exam that she would score perfectly. The opposite of what she was able to score in school, as her academic achievements remained the same since those early days. However, she didn't get whipped on her hands anymore,

Vivian: War Just Sucks—1942

as she was able to run out of the classroom the moment her teacher had that look in her eye.

"What do they need to know?" Mr. Sand asked as he crossed his arms and tilted his head to get a closer feel for his potential employee.

"What to wear. There are so many people that are full of indecisions when choosing a simple pair of trousers. They have no idea how to get dressed in the morning!"

"I beg your pardon?" Mr. Sand's eyes widened.

"Doesn't anyone read *Vogue*?" Vivian shrieked.

"Keep your voice down, young lady, and I'm afraid not. These days, the newspaper and radio are where all the news is shared, and good morning to you—we are in the middle of a war!"

Vivian quickly shrunk down into her chair from fright, afraid of what she just said and how she acted. The world didn't revolve around blouses and skirts, even though it was all Vivian wanted to learn and talk about. As for her analysis of fashion, her mother kept warning her to soften the blow when it came to criticism or, what Vivian liked to call it, constructive feedback on wardrobe choices.

"Oh, I'm sorry. I get so excited sometimes."

Mr. Sand smiled. "Vivian, there is a way to show a woman how to dress. A gentler way.

One that's less intimidating."

"I know. I need more patience—that's what my mother tells me."

"I agree with your mother. Anyhow, I have seen you here. A lot."

"I am a fan of the store. I like to come and do my research."

"Yes, I've noticed," Mr. Sand paused and gave some thought. "Alright, discreetly study the woman to my right who is wearing a red purse. Tell me what you think of her outfit."

Vivian beamed and thought that this was her lucky day—that was an easy one. She could answer that while whistling with peanut-buttered crackers in her mouth. Vivian took a deep breath, smiled, and began.

"Surely. The skirt is too long and should be hemmed at least two inches. Tuck in the blouse and add a belt from Elsa Schiaparelli. Change the pearls to a simple gold chain to match the earrings. Or you could even forgo the necklace all together, say the powers that be. As it's either one or the other. Never both. I disagree with that decision, as it depends on the woman. In this case, she can carry both. Finally, the shade of her stockings is far too dark for her skin tone. I would go with a lighter shade." Vivian smiled as she gazed at her fingernails, which were polished cherry red. She didn't dare flip her hands over to reveal the marks on her palms still lingering from her beatings so many years ago.

Mr. Sand stood up straight, gazed ahead, and raised his eyebrows. "You are quite young."

Vivian looked straight at him, smiling.

"And well, being in the middle of the war and all, we do need extra women on our floors. And you certainly know your stuff—so you're hired."

Vivian giggled at the thought of spending the entire day surrounded by beautiful clothes that she could make even more beautiful by putting them together on customers. Belts to frame blouses. Shoes with kitten heels. Silky pencil skirts! Her joy was written all over her face as she smiled from ear to ear.

"I'm first placing you at the Revlon counter; then we will see where you will go next. And we need you as soon as possible. Tomorrow!" Mr. Sand said as his new employee felt like a hot potato was tossed into her hands that she really wanted to dig in and eat with butter. While Vivian looked straight ahead, she tried to picture herself working with makeup, as she knew her way around a cosmetic counter but not as well as the clothing racks. However, she just got the green light to work at the most amazing department

Vivian: War Just Sucks—1942

store the very next day! So she was one happy girl, no matter where she was placed.

"I'll be here tomorrow!" Vivian said cheerfully.

With a firm handshake, she thanked Mr. Sand for the opportunity and skipped all the way home to put together her wardrobe for the next day.

Upon arriving home, Vivian dumped her purse on the hall room floor, right next to her beloved emerald-green rug, and flew up the stairs to her room. She opened her closet with full force and hummed "A String of Pearls" by Glenn Miller while she chose her outfit for the following day—her best cream chiffon blouse and a navy-blue cotton skirt, purchased from babysitting and birthday money.

As she held each piece on their hangers, she wondered if she would be eligible for a discount at Sunderland's since she was officially an employee.

As she draped the outfit on her bed, she gazed at the collection of *Vogue* magazines neatly stacked on her bedside table. They were her everything. Every word and every picture had been taken very seriously since she could remember.

It was obvious that Vivian wanted to pursue a career in fashion, and Miriam and Henry saw this fascination and wanted to enrich it further when she was in high school.

"Why don't you study art at McGill?" her mother innocently asked, as the expectation of getting married and having children popped up as natural as wearing a dress to a party. As she gazed at her daughter, waiting for her to answer, she secretly hoped she would run into a nice Jewish boy in the school library, and of course, the same wish went for her sister Marsha. Miriam and Henry were forward-thinking modern parents of perusing education and a career—but they also wanted marriage and children for them too.

"I don't need school!" Vivian shot back, with a wave of her arms as if she was shooing away an unwanted stray dog, knowing very well that stepping into any classroom brought back a storm full of memories that made her feel suffocated. She pushed away those painful memories deep into her soul so that she didn't have to face them.

Her parents were both born in Poland who had come to Canada for a better life. And it was a good thing they did. But so far, her grandparents were still safe in Poland, according to her mother. Relatively, her mother would say above a whisper.

As Mr. Sand reminded Vivian, it was 1942, and World War II was in full swing. Like the rest of the world, Vivian read the newspaper, listened to the news, and, of course, practiced good old-fashioned eavesdropping while planting her ear to the wall.

Hardly a peep was shared with the world about what was going on with the Jews in Europe. Even though mail was being banned, some information was leaked, but it was scarce. And occasionally, if the Steiner family was lucky, a letter from Poland reached their home.

During dinner that evening, a lucky moment occurred, and her mother, Miriam, brought a letter to the table and swung it around like a medal.

"Oh, that handwriting I can spot it anywhere," Vivian said gleefully.

"You are correct! It's from Bubbe and Zaida!" Miriam announced with a bright smile as she raised the letter up high over her head.

Vivian had never met her grandparents, but her house was filled with photographs of them. Writing letters, along with her parents, to them was a weekly ritual for as long as she could remember. Her letters, which had begun as a scribble, were now several paragraphs long with lots of details. How she longed to give them a hug and touch their faces.

Vivian: War Just Sucks—1942

Her mother read the letter out loud, and Vivian couldn't believe what she heard. All Jews must wear a gold fabric star on their coats, have strict curfews, can only shop at Jewish stores, and their children must only go to Jewish schools. Two weeks prior to the writing of this letter, Vivian's grandparents had to move into a ghetto where they had to share an apartment with another family, and all their beautiful silver candlesticks, jewelry, and family heirlooms were taken away. Vivian's heart sank; she wished they could come to Canada so that they can be safe.

Miriam put the letter down, and as her cheery mood splattered into tiny pieces on the kitchen floor, she stared straight ahead as her lower lip began to quiver. The forced smile was a far cry from the look on her face that Vivian saw before her that screamed pure horror and fright. Her father, Harry, put his hand on Miriam's and took a deep breath in silence.

"What are we going to do?" Vivian said in panic.

"What can we do?" Henry asked.

"I don't know. . . . Can't you do something? Bring them here?"

"How?" Miriam said between tears.

"It's too complicated," Henry said under his breath.

Vivian felt so frustrated; she just wanted to burn the letter so she wouldn't have to witness the pain her grandparents were going through. Unable to cope, Vivian left the kitchen, away from the sadness, uncertainty, and fear. She felt that the only way to escape this mess was to dive into her new job.

* * *

Since Vivian was to begin her job the following day, the outfit was set, along with the perfect lipstick and face powder that was laid on her dresser. She contemplated taking a hot bath with baking soda, followed by a manicure with a bright red nail color to raise her spirits.

Yes, that would be a great plan, she decided as she suddenly felt a piercing pain in her arms. Her fingernails were the culprit, digging themselves into her soft flesh. So much for the distraction. The reality of her grandparents' situation didn't want to leave her subconscious. As she stared at the steaming hot water that fell into her bath, she felt guilty to be able to enjoy such a luxury.

The following morning, with great enthusiasm, Vivian awoke at six, right before her alarm clock rang, as her hot bath with baking soda did her a world of good, calming her nerves, but she was still thinking of her grandparents. Nevertheless, she was ready to face the day.

After a generous stretch, she sat up in her bed and took out the homemade cloth curlers from her hair, feeling quite pleased with herself as she saw the results in her vanity mirror. Old rags make the best hair curlers, she thought as the last strip of cloth released the perfect ringlet.

Vivian swung her legs onto the floor, slipped her feet into her slippers, and walked to her bedroom mirror to begin brushing her creation into a smart but sophisticated hairstyle. She finished the look with a gold-plated hair clip, which was a gift from her grandmother. As she fastened it in her hair, the tears began to form, but she quickly wiped them away.

"No. not now. Not on my first day," she whispered to herself.

After a quick trip to the bathroom, she got dressed in the outfit she carefully chose the evening before and walked downstairs to the kitchen, where she greeted her mother.

"Vivian, where's your lipstick?" Miriam asked as she was tying an apron around her waist.

"Going to put it on after breakfast. Plus, some face cream—my skin has been so dry lately."

"Good idea. Use mine on my dresser."

"Mm-mmm," Vivian nodded while she drank her Ovaltine.

As the last sip was devoured, she put down her glass and squealed, "I am so excited!"

"Of course, you are! This is your debut! Oh, they will just adore you. Wait until you begin to put outfits together—they won't know what hit them!" Miriam said while Vivian looked down at the floor.

"Why the long face?" Miriam asked.

"I forgot to tell you. I was placed at the Revlon counter." Vivian looked like she swallowed a sour lemon.

"Oh, don't you fret, young lady—you are still working at Sunderland's. It doesn't matter where you start, you just must start. Do your best, and they will see what a star you are. Then they will put you where you belong—in the clothing department."

"Really?" Vivian asked.

"Really. Mommy always knows," her mother said, "if anyone can handle this, it's you."

Vivian smiled, then dashed upstairs to put on her mother's face cream.

A bouquet of Chanel No. 5 welcomed her into her parents' bedroom. Her father was already at work, and their bed was made. Everything was in its place, as her mother had a habit of making her bed as soon as she awoke—a ritual that made the rest of her day productive, so she said.

Vivian did the same, as her mind could not think clearly if her bedroom looked like a tornado hit it. Every clothing item in her closet had its place. Pants hung with pants, skirts hung with skirts, and so on. Sweaters were folded in drawers, blouses were hung, and shoes lined up like little soldiers. Vivian was tidy and organized as long as she could remember; if you took care of your clothes, they would not only look great but would last longer too. Clothes belonged on your body, not on the floor and needed to be placed away properly.

The face cream was on her mother's dresser and still in the box. As she began to open it, a framed picture of her grandparents that stood on her dresser caught her eye. The tear that was already in the works when she put in her hair clip not long ago was now fully developed into a full droplet of fluid and made its way down her cheek.

"Damn," Vivian said under her breath, smiling as she thought about the novel *The Postman Always Rings Twice*. It was the second trigger that opened the gate of unwelcomed emotions.

She paused from opening the box, took a deep breath, and looked away from the picture to resume what she came upstairs to do, to apply the face cream, which made her skin glow as if there was a lightbulb underneath her chin.

"Not bad," she announced with approval. Vivian was thankful that one of her favorite shades of lipstick was from Revlon. It was called Fire and Ice, and it was the perfect red, making her teeth as white as the first snowfall of the season, before the buses, trucks, and dog pee polluted it. After painting her lips with her trademark shade, she smiled and nodded at her reflection, then went downstairs.

Miriam was waiting in the hallway, holding the front door open. "You look wonderful!"

"Thank you," Vivian said as she knew that all this happiness and cheerfulness felt tampered while her grandparents were trapped in Poland. Last night's question about her grandparents escaping to Canada was not answered with what Vivian wanted to hear. And of course, she very well knew that there wasn't enough time to ask the question again as one foot was out the front door. As she stood there, the topic was screaming inside her head so loudly she couldn't stand it. Maybe she would receive a different response if she asked again? Her parents had at least twelve hours since last night's conversation to come up with a plan. New identities with fake passports or even tickets to Switzerland. Something. Anything. "Mother, why can't bubbe and zaida come to Canada?" Vivian asked.

Vivian: War Just Sucks—1942

Miriam's face suddenly aged twenty years. "I don't think they can. I don't know how they could."

The weight in Vivian's chest returned, and she could tell that her mother felt the very same weight that was infused with the word *why*.

Why did she have to even think of an illegal plan with fake passports and escaping to Switzerland? Why couldn't they just board a train? A boat or even a plane and come to Canada? Who was stopping them? Why couldn't they just go? And the most crucial question that Vivian wanted to shout on her rooftop and scream was why were they forced into a ghetto with all their possessions taken away? What did they do to deserve this? Why wasn't *anyone* doing something about it?

These questions remained unanswered, and the feelings of uncertainty and horror were never shared out loud, and it drove Vivian mad.

"Stop clenching your teeth, dear," Vivian's mother said as she touched her daughter's cheek.

They both stood in the doorway and looked outside. The sun was shining, and there was a slight breeze for a June morning. With a nod and a kiss on the cheek from her mother, Vivian went on her way and finally unclenched her jaw by the time she arrived at her bus stop.

* * *

As Vivian pushed the heavy hunter-green doors to Sunderland's open, it was 8:15 a.m. Her shift didn't start until 9:00, so she had some time, which was a good thing because her day hadn't even begun, and she was in agonizing pain. Her feet were on fire.

"You're bleeding," said an older lady standing at the scarf counter, who was filing her nails.

"I'm not surprised," Vivian answered. She looked up at the woman and tried to smile through the pain.

Vivian stood in the middle of the department store aisle like a lost deer in a forest. People were buzzing around, getting ready for their shifts, while she just stood there, each of her heels felt as if they had their own personal knife slicing away at her skin. Vivian took deep breaths to plow through the pain, just as she did when she tweezed the hair off her upper lip.

"I can't believe these shoes are giving me trouble. It's not as if I haven't worn them before!"

"But have you walked from home to the bus stop and then to the department store in them before?"

"Only to parties."

"Completely different worlds. Treat your shoes accordingly." The woman snapped her fingers and pointed to her shoes. Vivian slumped in defeat.

"What have we got here?" Mr. Sand, the man who interviewed Vivian, came into the scene. "Ahhh! Hello, my dear!"

"Mr. Sand! Pleased to see you again," Vivian said enthusiastically, trying not to make a big deal out of her blistering feet and her punctured ego.

"Your first day isn't going so smoothly. Here." Mr. Sand reached into his pocket and pulled out some tissues and a bandage. "I see you are not wearing hose—mistake number one. Alright, take the tissue, blot, and then bandage."

Vivian nodded as she diligently mended her feet while standing on one leg at a time. Those ballet classes she took as a child were finally paying off.

"Good luck. See you soon!" Mr. Sand said as he scurried off into another department.

Vivian was just finishing cleaning up her ankles when she said, "Oy vey! I can't put my shoes on now!"

The woman walked over to Vivian. "Excuse me . . . are you the new girl who is starting today?"

"Yes, I am!"

"Oh, right . . . then never wear high-heeled shoes to work. Wear them at work. Got it?"

"Yes, madame."

"Never say that 'oy vey.' Nobody wants to hear that."

"Oh, okay." A lump in Vivian's throat appeared as she swallowed hard. Facing an anti-Semitic moment but too distraught to process.

"Got a name?"

"Vivian."

"Elaine."

"Pleased to meet you, Elaine."

"Likewise," she handed Vivian a pair of fuzzy slippers.

"You want me to wear these? Here? Now?" Vivian asked in shock as she couldn't believe she was asked to put on bedroom slippers right then and there, in the middle of a department store! It was a good thing there were no customers around to see this parade of awkwardness.

"Oh, yes. Not to worry."

"What will my boss say?"

"Honey, I am your boss."

Vivian's eyes widened in shock while Elaine smiled without showing her teeth. Vivian's eyes darted around as she wondered if Sunderland's gave out prizes to their employees who felt the most humiliation on their first day. She would win one for sure, and it would probably be a year supply of bandages.

"As you know, you will start at the Revlon counter, but due to the state of your feet, you are in no condition to deal with the customers, so you will begin with inventory. Follow me."

Elaine straightened her dress and walked along the shiny linoleum department store floor while Vivian pitter-pattered behind in her borrowed slippers. As expected, Vivian scanned what Elaine was wearing from head to toe as she always did to any human being who stood before her. All of her pieces of clothing were recently advertised in the newspaper the other day—it was a Pierre Balmain dress in the color red, accessorized with a pair of black heels that she would bet were Christian Dior, along with a string of pearls that hung just below her collar bone. Elaine's platinum-blonde hair was tied up in a chignon. Her whole ensemble framed the dress beautifully as she smoothed the sides of her hair as she walked the aisles of the department store, casually swinging her hips as she passed by each display, studying them to make sure they were just so.

Vivian watched in amazement and declared to herself that she had officially arrived at a world she wanted to be a part of so badly, for so long.

The rest of Sunderland's staff stood by their counters arranging what they were selling that day in neat piles and proper order. Ties were fanned out. Creams and lotions were faced in the display cabinets making sure not to have any empty spaces that would reveal that there was a missing product. Most importantly, everything was spotless. The cabinets gleamed, and the staff that stood behind the counter were standing tall, without a hair out of place, nor any trace of lipstick smudges on their teeth.

The fuzzy bedroom slippers that Vivian was wearing made her feel juvenile, as if she was following her babysitter to bed early because she was a bad girl. Funny enough, the employees didn't seem that shocked with the situation. They walked past the Revlon counter as well as the perfume collections, which showcased a generous bottle of Chanel No. 5, which Vivian decided she would love to buy for her mother one day.

At the end of the aisle, both facing a door, Elaine turned around to look at Vivian.

Vivian: War Just Sucks—1942

In her peripheral vision, Vivian noticed a man fixing a hat display while raising one of his eyebrows as he watched. Concerned, she looked around to see if her slip was showing or if a button on her blouse was undone. All was tucked in and buttoned.

Elaine beckoned with her index finger, and Vivian followed her down a case of wooden stairs into a basement that was cold and damp, which made her reconsider the outfit she had chosen to wear that day.

Right in front of her was another woman surrounded by shoeboxes. She was dressed in dungarees and a work shirt that was tied at her waist.

"Oh, hi! Just making pairs out of misplaced shoes!"

"Oh, that's nice," Vivian replied.

"No, it's actually not that nice," the woman said with a straight face. Vivian got the sense that she didn't want to be there, and to be honest, neither did she.

"That's not for you, dear. Follow me," Elaine said.

Vivian sighed in relief as she followed Elaine around the corner. She soon faced two huge metal shelves that held hundreds and hundreds of different colored nail polishes from a selection of brands. Vivian scanned the humongous collection with wide eyes.

"I've never seen so many nail polishes in my life!"

"That's what they all say," Elaine replied as she reached down into a drawer and pulled out a huge spiral-bound notebook that had the Revlon logo on the front cover and presented it to Vivian with a pencil.

"This is the Revlon inventory list. Go through each color and mark down how many we have. You may find other brands here, and if you do, put them to the side in a separate box and mention what they are and how many we have of them."

"I'll be counting nail polishes?"

"Counting *and* cleaning."

Vivian looked confused.

"We can't have dirty nail polish bottles on our floors! Look at this!" Elaine took her finger, swiped the top shelf, and placed her finger that was covered in black soot in front of Vivian's nose. "See? The dust from the shelves falls onto our nail polishes, and then we have dust-covered nail polish bottles. How could we sell these, and most importantly, who would want to bring dirty nail polishes into their home?" Elaine said as Vivian slowly scanned her eyes up and down the nail polish rack.

"At the end of your day, come see me so you can fill out your employment papers."

Vivian nodded, thinking how official this was becoming. Working at the department store of her dreams had finally come true, but she did not sign up for this! Putting her clothes properly away and making her bed is one thing. But cleaning? In a cold secluded basement? Where were the beautiful clothes and all the pretty shiny things?

"*Feh!*" she said as Elaine walked up the stairs to the department store.

Lilly's Doctor—1942

Seventeen-year-old Lilly was waiting in line at the drugstore to pick up a prescription for her mother. While she glanced at the sleeves of her blouse, the corner of her lips pulled down as she wasn't pleased at what she saw. The material was faded and worn, and there were a few oil stains that couldn't come out in the laundry. She wondered how her blouse looked originally when bought from the store, as it was a hand-me-down from her cousin. As she closed her eyes and inhaled a deep breath, Lilly wondered what it would be like to purchase a brand-new blouse right off the rack. She decided that it would feel empowering, just like the scores she received on her report cards. Lilly still loved going to school, ingesting every subject like a sponge and hoped to continue onto university after graduation. However, her mother's grocery store needed help, and just like Anna, she was expected to be dutiful. She wondered what it would be like to sit in a real university classroom, until a man walked up to join Lilly in line, which completely interrupted her daydream and brought her down to an attractive reality.

* * *

The author interrupts this vignette, to clarify an issue that may confuse the reader. The male character in the chapter of Lilly's Doctor has been named He and/or Him, for reasons that the writer felt was necessary for what you will read below.

* * *

He was dressed in a three-piece suit, with hair that was well groomed and smelled like fresh pine. He had the lightest blue eyes she had ever seen. They were almost white, which accentuated his pupils that grew larger as he smiled.

Small talk sprouted like warm spring raindrops, as he waited patiently for Lilly to pay for the prescription, and then they found themselves outside of the drugstore, and beside his car. As He opened the car door for Lilly to climb inside, feeling hypnotized, she got in, and their first date officially began.

He insisted on replacing the blouse that made her feel sad, and she was game.

Off to a nearby boutique they went, where Lilly became the owner of a Hattie Carnegie blouse in a delicate pink shade that tinted her cheeks in the same color, while she was told that there would be more.

Another date turned into two, and then three. She felt safe with him. Taken care of.

He was a doctor by profession, and celebratory thoughts burst into Lilly's mind like fireworks. Ooh, this is what my mother wants, and maybe if I married Him, I would be able to go to school and not have to work in the store!

"Oh, my goodness! He's a DOCTOR!" Sarah squealed.

"Calm down, mother. They have just been dating a week or so," Anna added, who was in her early thirties and had a family of her own. She was visiting her mother that day and, as usual, had the voice of reason.

Lilly's Doctor—1942

"I don't care—he's a *doctor!*"

Lilly was thrilled that her mother and sister were pleased with Him. Heck, more than pleased. They were *kvelling*—not only was he a doctor but a *Jewish* doctor. He was a graduate of McGill University, beating the odds of admittance as they only admitted one or two Jewish men per year. Twenty-four years old and already at the top of his game at The Jewish General Hospital, wrote the head of the psychiatry department on a recent performance review.

The Jewish General Hospital was bursting at the seams with only 150 beds. And they needed doctors like Him on staff as this was a place where Jewish patients were welcomed.

But something happened with one of His patients that was not recorded on his file, as it probably didn't happen. Or maybe it did. No one knew for sure, and with that doubt, it was forgotten, as any negative scandal regarding a Jewish doctor could not be afforded by the Jewish community of Montreal. Eight years prior, in 1934, *The Days of Shame* occurred, where the doctors on staff at Notre Dame Hospital went on strike all because a new Jewish intern was hired. What would explode from a scandal like this would be astronomical, as it would align with the anti-Semitism that was rampant in Montreal, mirroring the propaganda that had already been initialized in Europe that made its way to Canadian soil, continuing to fuel the racism. If word got out about what this intern did, every newspaper and radio station would be bursting with this news like fireworks, negatively exploiting the Jews even more than the world was already doing.

Mistakes are a part of being human, but God forbid a Jew could make one, as he was prejudged before he could even begin to apologize. And so, the file was destroyed, along with all witnesses who washed their hands of it, forbidding it to leave the walls of the hospital.

"You must be brilliant!" Sarah said over the Shabbat table. That Friday night, the whole family was there so they could meet Him. Lilly reached out to hold his hand, while looking at her mother to exchange a joyous gaze. It was official. As far as everyone was concerned, Lilly won the grand prize of the year with this new beau. It was if she brought home another straight A report card. He was handsome, polite, and a doctor! Her whole family, extended aunts and uncles and cousins, applauded in unison with their smiles.

"I won't be needing your blouses anymore," Lilly proudly announced to her cousin.

"Tell me, what's it like to work in the hospital? It must be so sad," Sarah asked.

"Mother . . . don't be rude!" Lilly said.

"It's Ok, really," He said, while he smirked. Sarah felt relieved as she sat on the edge of her chair hanging on to every word He said. "You folks want to hear a great story?" He asked, while everyone at the table waited in anticipation, like a herd of dogs wagging their tales, waiting for their supper. How unfortunate what was gifted to him academically didn't leave much room for much emotional intelligence.

"The other day, as I walked into my gynecology rotation, I had to close my lab coat—if you know what I mean!" He announced with triumph as He slapped his knee and enjoyed a hearty laugh. As the story left his lips and collapsed unto the dining room table, all felt the debris explode. Lilly and her family inhaled the dust of obscenity, and Sarah fell silent. Cousins nervously giggled, while Lilly was appalled and embarrassed. That poor female patient who was lying on the gurney table, that Lilly, Sarah, and Anna have laid upon countless times as well, was teased behind her back. Questions stormed through Lilly's mind, thinking what if her doctor looked at her sexually while she was being examined. Or worse—looked at her mother sexually! Eeeewww! Lilly's face puckered as if she had eaten a moldy strawberry as she looked up at the dining room window, hoping that she could break through the glass and fly away. No such luck.

Feeling completely humiliated and ashamed, she slowly raised her hands to her head so that she could massage her temples, telling herself that what she heard was probably just a joke and that all will blow over and will be alright. He was a doctor, and His word was gold. The rest of the family composed themselves and probably thought the same thing. Lilly was privately begging for someone to change the subject as she metamorphically lifted the carpet for someone to sweep that God-awful story under.

"How about those Habs?" said her beloved uncle, who took the broom and granted Lilly's wish.

While the men began to talk about hockey, she played with the chicken on her plate and tolerated the sweat that gathered at the back of her neck. She thought about asking why he would share such a story at the dinner table. How he would react if she asked. Would he get upset? Break up with her? Afraid of the repercussions but determined to get some answers, Lilly decided that a quick, yet productive, conversation needed to be had in private. But that conversation backfired.

The next evening, when everyone was asleep, she crept into the living room to call Him. Slowly lifting the receiver and dialing his number as her heart pounded, she waited for Him to pick up while her sweaty hand twirled the telephone wire. This was the first time she ever encountered such a situation, as she had no prior experience on how to confront a man who said something that bothered her, as her father had been gone for such a long time.

Lilly wanted to get to the bottom of this, and the only way she knew how was to march straight through, so she stood on her mark and was ready to run.

"I can't believe you said what you said at the Shabbat Table," Lilly nervously said at lightning speed. Waiting for a response, there was nothing but silence.

"Hello? Hello?" Lilly asked in a panic. *Say something!* She screamed in her mind, as she knew He was there because He was breathing heavily. Panic enveloped her, as she thought that maybe this was all a huge mistake. She shouldn't have called Him so late at night, as he probably had to get up early for work. Why did she do such a stupid thing? Why disturb Him with her nonsense? Why ask such a silly question in an abrupt tone rather than a sweet and patient one that would have been more appropriate?

But there was no answer, except an eventual dialing tone. Lilly slowly hung up the phone, thinking that she ruined everything and thought that her life was officially over, including her dream for university.

The next morning, refraining from sharing the details of her bombardment of accusations, Lilly walked into the kitchen and met her mother sitting at the table.

"Don't worry about it. He didn't mean it. Be kind, and all will be well." And it was repeated yet again, "He's a doctor."

These were the phrases that her mother kept repeating to her, which Lilly obeyed as that was what she was used to. Throughout her life, her mother always knew best. Even though the heaviness she felt in her chest was telling her that something wasn't right, she wasn't ready to face that realization, just yet.

Once again, her mother was right. She didn't need to worry about it. The story He shared was a harmless joke. Maybe there was an underlying meaning that she didn't get? The next time the two young hopefuls saw each other, all was more than well. Lilly put on the brightest and happiest face she could muster and was as kind as ever. The phone call was long forgotten, as was the story that went with it, and two weeks later, He proposed!

Even though she completely heard what he asked and was elated, it was her head and her heart that began to have an argument that didn't allow her to answer right away.

The evening before, she had a dream that she couldn't speak. As she stood in her living room, with her entire family around her, she grasped at her throat, trying to talk but couldn't. She stomped her feet and tried to yell and scream, but nothing but air came out of her mouth. Feeling frustrated, she fell to her knees as her mother comforted her and spoke for her.

"No! That's not what I want to say! You're getting it all wrong!" She yelled as her voice finally worked, but only toward her mother. Not for Him.

Lilly wanted the world. To continue her education. Be a doctor's wife and get married to a man who was not only smart but also handsome, someone like herself, an equal. To be able to have a family. To own a house and a garden, so she could grow her own vegetables. To have money in the bank, so she could continue to buy new shoes. And not have to work in her mother's grocery store. This was a tall order, and it was so exciting that it made her body shake.

"I mean it. Let's get married," He said.

"But I'm only seventeen!"

"Oh, come on—you know it's right."

"But I'm not finished high school yet!"

"Graduate first, and then we will get married," He said, the magic words. It was all she needed to hear, so Lilly decided to listen to the doctor, as He was smart, and He was right. She wrapped her arms around His shoulders and said, "Let's do it!"

* * *

After high school graduation and being married for several weeks, a welcome routine evolved. The doctor would go to work, while Lilly would clean the house, iron His shirts, and shop for food. With her keen mathematical skills, her monthly allowance could manage to a new dress, fresh stockings, or shoes. Occasionally, a gift would accompany Him when he got home from work.

"Oh, you shouldn't have," Lilly said one evening as she greeted Him at the front door.

"I should have—I want you to be happy," He would say.

As Lilly opened the bottle and spritzed the perfume into the air, she let out a happy sigh. "Ahh . . . 4711 cologne. It reminds me of freshly picked lemons and oranges from the trees."

"Yeah, I would put that under your armpits, too, as your deodorant is clearly not working," He said as he took off his coat and hung it in the closet. Lilly couldn't believe what she just heard. He couldn't have meant it, she thought to herself as she stuck her nose in her blouse to see if she had body odor. Maybe just a little bit. But did he have to say it that way?

And then, several weeks later, it happened again. Not a story that would make Lilly's skin crawl, but a simple question that could be presented in many ways that chose to go south that evening at dinner as he stared at his Salisbury steak.

He asked why the ketchup wasn't on the table.

His light blue eyes expanded to their full capacity, showing the full circumference of his eyeballs. His pupils stood out like bullseye targets while his eyebrows remained raised, causing deep creases on his forehead. His body remained still as he stared straight ahead, only to slightly tilt his head, waiting for a response. Lilly couldn't stop staring at the very angry man who sat before her. She was speechless and filled with worry and panic, as she had never heard of someone getting so mad over a condiment.

"Lilly, I need the ketchup," He said.

"I'll get it. It's in the fridge," Lilly said, thinking that she could easily fix the problem with a simple trip that was just a few steps away. As she got up, she noticed that her knees were shaking while she pushed her chair backwards on the linoleum floor, which caused it to make a rattling noise.

"Will you be careful of our kitchen floor? Do you think kitchen floors grow on trees?" His eyes were still bulging, and now his face was flushed.

"Sorry," Lilly said, as that was all she could think of saying. This whole scene was becoming more awful by the moment, and all Lilly wanted to do was shake her husband and ask what the problem was. Why was he getting so upset over ketchup?

The walk to the refrigerator gave her a few moments to breathe and think of why he could be acting that way. Maybe he was stressed from work? Perhaps a patient got him upset? Maybe someone died in his arms? Lilly shuddered at the thought, thinking that could drive anyone insane. Yes, that was it. Being a doctor is hard work and can make someone very stressed and angry. As she reached for the ketchup bottle, she decided that she was going to make everything right. All she needed was a plan. As she thought of what she was going to do after she wrapped her arms around Him, she was interrupted by a bark as loud as a rottweiler's growl.

"WHERE IS THE KETCHUP, YOU IMBECILE?"

A shudder of weight fell upon Lilly's chest, which burned. With the fridge still open, she closed her eyes, inhaled a deep breath, and then forcefully exhaled. After closing the refrigerator door, she walked toward Him, tightly gripping the ketchup bottle with both hands, and slammed it on the table so hard that it made the plates and cutlery jump. Lilly then left the kitchen and ran to her bedroom to fall on her bed and cry. Thankfully, He left his wife alone for a while.

After Lilly washed her face and got into bed, she brought the blanket up to her chin and stared at her bedroom window for what seemed like an eternity. Repeated thoughts spun around Lilly's head like a hamster running on its wheel. Where was he? What was he doing? What was he thinking? Did she overreact? Finally, a knock at the door was heard.

"Come in," Lilly softly said, hoping it was Him. And it was. She turned her body around and sat up in her bed to see that he was holding a bouquet of white lilies and another bottle of 4711.

"You got me a bottle a few weeks ago, I haven't even skimmed the top!"

"I want you to have more of what you love!" He said, while resting his hands upon Lilly's, and she felt relieved that everything was going to be okay. Husbands and wives are supposed to fight, but they must make up like this! With not one but two bottles of cologne, she thought to herself as she inhaled the flowers. But as soon as she unwrapped the box of cologne, it didn't smell as good as she remembered. The clean, fresh scent had turned to the aroma of rotten pines. Something wasn't right, and she wanted to get to the bottom of it. She also wanted to talk to him about taking a few courses, as she missed that part of her life.

To make sure that she wasn't overreacting, the next morning, while He was at work, she called a friend and asked if her husband gets stressed and angry after work.

"Are you kidding? Is my husband stressed? Very! Yelling and swearing while he opens the bills.... Telling whoever will listen about what his boss said that day. Even to the kids! But I know how to handle it—I am ready, by the front door with his favorite drink. A whiskey on the rocks with a splash of ginger ale. Works every time!" the friend reassured. But when Lilly reenacted the ketchup scenario, making sure to add the imbecile part, the friend didn't answer for a few moments, which felt like hours on the receiving line. Waiting for the diagnosis from her friend was pure torture.

"I'm sure it's only a phase," she finally said, which made Lilly feel relieved for a while. Several nights later, at dinner, Lilly brought up the idea of taking a few courses.

"Correspondence will work. Why bother yourself with going into the classroom. Such a schlep," Lilly agreed, as it was a pain in the ass to get downtown as they didn't have a car. And waiting for the bus in the brutal weather amongst the winter ice and slush was not very enticing. But it would be so worth it, Lilly thought, as there was nothing better than being in the classroom. The exchange of ideas. The questions you could ask. How she missed that time in her life. Maybe she could ask again, soon.

* * *

But then she became pregnant with their first child, and life moved forward as it had, and Lilly was no closer to taking courses. That summer, they went camping. Lilly had never gone before, but she was a good sport and was game to try anything new. He gave her a list of things to buy for the trip, and Lilly returned with everything, all packed in a suitcase. As they drove to the countryside and found a camping site, they parked the car, unloaded the equipment, and He asked for the matches.

"Matches?" Lilly asked.

"Yes, matches."

"Matches weren't on the list."

"EVERYONE KNOWS TO PACK MATCHES WHEN YOU GO CAMPING!"

There was that voice roaring again, along with the frozen expression, bulging eyes, and the lines on his forehead that made an indent in his skin. Of course, Lilly's body knew exactly what to do from past yelling scenarios like these. Shake. Sweat and question. Why was this man getting so upset? Once again, she thought that if she found what he was looking for, she would be able to fix the problem. As she shook her head and bit her lower lip, she began to search for the matches in the bags that they had packed. As she went through the third bag, a silver lining appeared, and she was so delighted to announce it!

"I have the ketchup!" Lilly proudly said. But unfortunately, He didn't share that proud moment with his wife. Bile rose to the top of Lilly's chest as her eyes filled with tears that held on tight to the edge of her eyelids. She wasn't going to let Him see her cry. Not today.

Geronimo! The tears dropped, and the crying didn't stop. Scenes like this became more frequent. Even after more apologies and bouquets of flowers, nothing seemed to stop it, except a newborn baby.

From the moment He laid eyes on their first child, it was as if someone had given Him a "calm-down pill" that lowered his rage dramatically. He was kinder. Yelled less. And patient. What would normally make him scream with rage was replaced with serenity. Lilly was amazed and quite relieved. It was obvious that the more children they could have, the better He would be.

And so two more children were born, and unfortunately, the anger reappeared. Lilly was astonished, as her theory proved wrong and was as confused as ever. What was going on? She thought.

Oh. My. God. She said out loud one evening, as she was going through his trousers and found a written prescription for Chloral Hydrate, which was a sedative and am anti anxiety medication that her aunt was also taking, as her mother said over the phone one evening while Lilly was eavesdropping. This was why he was so calm! Lilly thought. She had to get to the bottom of this—the only way she knew how. Praying that he wouldn't blow his top, she approached the bench.

"I found this prescription in your pants. Did you want me to fill it at the drugstore?" she asked, acting helpful and feeling hopeful.

"Oh, that? Years ago, my doctor said that it would help me to deal with my patients. All of the whining and complaining. I took them for a while. Meh—I don't think I need them. And they made me too tired."

Oh yes, you do! *Oh, yes, you do!* Lilly's mind screamed in her head as she walked away, unable to defend herself for now.

When Lilly heard the house keys rattle at the front door at the end of the day, a pang in her chest immediately appeared as she prayed that the family dinner meal would be able to get through without any yelling. While en route to get groceries, she would find herself fantasizing about swerving the car around in another direction to drive away and never come back. Even though Lilly grew up without a father, she knew in her gut that these feelings were not normal in a marriage, and so she consulted with a friend once again, at a nearby drugstore lunch counter, while the children were at school.

"Don't get. . . . You know. . . ," her friend whispered, under her breath, while looking around.

"Get . . . what?" Lilly asked, feeling completely confused. She had no idea what her friend was talking about. Lilly leaned in closer and cupped her hand around her ear to amplify her hearing.

"You know . . . divorced!" her friend said it in a whisper, as if *that* course of action were of the utmost taboo, which it was at the time. Lilly sat with that word for a few moments to think about what that meant for her.

The notion of leaving her husband filled Lilly up with hope as her shoulders finally dropped a few inches, even though she didn't even think *that* was an option, as she didn't know anyone who got divorced. Ever.

"What would people think?" Her friend gasped as Lilly imagined, feeling almost giddy, what it would be like if she was finally free from all the yelling. She imagined how peaceful her home would be.

"You don't want to do that to the children. And to your mother!" She added as Lilly's shoulders rose up once again, fearing how her children would cope. Would they hate her? Would they lose their friends? Would her mother's store be banned?

Thanking her friend for the advice, Lilly went home and called a lawyer.

Filing for divorce in the late 1940s was an anomaly, and every human being who lived within a three-mile radius of Lilly and her children let her know it.

But they didn't let it get to them. Because they had a mother who took care of that.

Lilly gathered her children each night after dinner, held their hands, and repeatedly told them how much she loved them and that they needed to stick together like a team. And they did, and with time, the power of resiliency took over.

* * *

Several years later, Lilly came home from her mother's store to find a brand-new shiny red bicycle decorated with a blue satin bow on its handlebars in the driveway.

"Who's this?"

"Corrine's," Lilly's son said.

"How did she get it?"

"We bought it for her," Lilly's son said as he motioned to his other brother.

"Why? How?"

"I made it happen—let's leave it at that," Lilly's son said as she shook her head in disbelief. She couldn't believe that her eight-year-old son had arranged a brand-new bike for his little sister and prayed the transaction was legal, as she was not prepared for any form of juvenile detention. It almost seemed impossible, but she thought about Mozart and how he was able to read music at five and began to compose at six. As Lilly opened the front door of her house, she thought about how this adversity was building such strength for her children and how proud she was that her sons were a couple of negotiating prodigies.

Vivian: Does Anyone Have a Bonbon? 1942

Vivian went to work. It was not easy, and it was not fun. To pass the time, Vivian reassured herself with the healthy, solid advice that her parents had given her after gently and lovingly calming her down from the good old-fashioned temper tantrum she had when she got home on her first day.

> *This is just your first week.*
> *Everyone starts somewhere.*
> *No job is beneath you.*

That nail polish rack in the department store basement took a full week to clean from top to bottom. When it was done, Vivian stepped back, brushed the hair out of her face with the back of her hands, and admired the gleaming shelves and colorful little glass bottles that now had a shine to them. As she collected the cleaning supplies and danced a celebratory jitterbug dance in the basement washroom, she realized three very important facts about herself, despite her parents' advice:

She did not like cleaning.
She did not like cleaning.
She did not like cleaning.

Regardless, what she wanted very much, more than anything, was to work at Sunderland's, and after some reflection, her parents were right. She was willing to do whatever it took to be there and stay there, and if cleaning an entire rack of nail polish was her official initiation, so be it.

"Very nice," Elaine said as she placed her reading glasses on her nose to inspect the nail polish rack. Vivian waited by her side, her arms behind her back, tapping her foot on the cold stone floor. Elaine stopped inspecting and followed the sound of Vivian's foot tapping, then slowly looked up to meet her eyes, which put a complete stop to her fidgeting.

"Come with me," Elaine instructed.

Vivian felt relieved and joyfully followed Elaine upstairs to the main floor of the department store, where shoppers scattered the floors of Sunderland's with shopping parcels in their hands and vigor in their step. It was if Vivian was a child who stood at the front gates of an amusement park.

The bright lights shone on the countertops that held the merchandise that Vivian wanted nothing more than to pick up and play with. An eye pencil that she saw in a recent magazine that she wanted to see up close and draw on the inside of her wrist so she could study the color and feel the texture of the crayon, as Vivian knew better than to test it on her eyes. A sure way to pick up any eye infection—said a recent article.

Vivian's eyes melted as she saw an array of skirts of various lengths, patterns, and material that she so desperately wanted to hold up to her waist to see how they looked on her. Directly in front of her stood a middle-aged woman who was eyeing a rose-colored mid-length pleated number. Oh, how she desperately wanted to yell out, "Put that pleated skirt down and reach for the pencil skirt! The pencil skiiiiirrrrt!" She knew it would suit her better as it would elongate her legs. But she didn't, and she bit her lip instead. It was amazing how all this stimulation wouldn't make her trip on her own two feet, but walking and critically analyzing all that was in front of Vivian was second nature. Studying who was wearing what, where, and how was like breathing, but now it seemed as if Sunderland's was administering extra oxygen, giving more life to Vivian's purpose.

"Are you all right?" Elaine asked, as she noticed that her brand-new employee's eyes looked as if they were going to pop right out of her eye sockets.

"Swell!" Vivian gleefully said.

The two women walked to the Revlon counter to greet another lady with blonde hair, which was pulled back into a Gibson roll at the nape of her head.

As usual, Vivian quickly analyzed the outfit that was presented in front of her. First, she decided that this woman was her mother's age and was smartly dressed. She wore a pink chiffon dress that had built-in shoulder pads. Very Joan Crawford, Vivian thought to herself. However, a button on her blouse was missing; she reserved this observation and restrained herself with all her might from commenting on this fact. Her parents would have been pleased, she thought to herself.

"Vivian, this is Madame Tremblay. She is the manager at the Revlon counter."

"Pleased to meet you, Mme. Tremblay."

"*Enchanté*, Vivian," Mme. Tremblay said with a warm smile. "Although I should also say pleased to meet you, too," Mme. Tremblay added, because English was often the preferred language in Montreal during that time.

"Elaine?" Vivian asked.

"Yes?"

"Is there any chance I could one day move to the women's clothing department?"

Elaine stood at arm's length from Vivian, where she was able to witness her lightning speed transformation. Her pleasant disposition flipped to a furious rage that she desperately tried to tamper with. It looked as if she had become a pot of boiling water that was ready to spill over its rim. Vivian sensed what was coming wasn't going to be good as Elaine fluttered her eyelids, breathed deeply, and placed her hand on the base of her neck, which gave the impression that her question shouldn't have been asked, but it was too late.

"Even though you seem to know fashion, there are a lot of women twice your age who have worked here for a very long time. These women have earned their position, and right now, times are tough. We need you here at this counter. Please cooperate and do your best."

It was as if Vivian landed on Mars, with aliens who were not in the least bit friendly to their visitor. What was this place? Why was she getting into trouble? Why were people looking at her like she had a run in her stocking? What did she have to do to receive praise? From the minute Vivian walked into Sunderland's Department Store, there was no doubt in her mind that she was paying attention, and in no way was she misbehaving.

Vivian's stomach twisted and turned. So many questions without answers. Life was growing more confusing by the minute, which was driving her as mad as the conversation that she had with her mother that morning. She knew one thing. She didn't get fired, and that was a relief. "Yes, madame," was all Vivian managed to reply to Elaine.

"Oh, and please refrain from saying any of those . . . I don't know . . . those things your people say."

"Excuse me?" Vivian asked.

"You know . . . words like 'oy.'"

"You already mentioned that last week, on my first day. Remember?" Vivian's eyes widened as this conversation clearly stated that she was officially having her second anti-Semitic moment. *What kind of harm would it cause to say oy?* The only reaction she could manage at that moment was sheer panic and fear. Would she be fired for being Jewish? How could Mr. Sand not mention anything during their interview? All this was way too much for Vivian's sixteen-year-old mind to handle. Keeping quiet was the only way she knew how to handle the situation, and Vivian did just that.

"Oh, yes, right. Well, it's just a reminder that I wouldn't advertise who you are," Elaine said quietly.

"Alright," Vivian said again, as her heart made its way up to her throat as one thing was clear. Most people don't like Jews.

"I'll leave you two to get acquainted," Elaine left, and Mme. Tremblay's warm face quickly turned sour like an old milk bottle as she slowly waltzed up to her new opponent.

"Listen to me, young lady. I don't know how old you are, but I'm in charge here. This is my Revlon counter. Understand?"

"I-I want to do my best," Vivian stuttered.

"Ah . . ," Mme. Tremblay said with her finger up in the air.

Vivian took a few steps back and leaned against the back counter that stored the department store bags.

"I've been here for twenty years, and I'll be damned if some little young thing like you takes over my place."

Vivian bit her lip, then wondered if she just ruined the perfect pout she created moments before Elaine came downstairs to inspect the nail polish shelves.

"See these lipsticks *ici*?" Mme. Tremblay pointed to the sample tray full of used lipsticks. "I want you to clean this tray when you arrive each and every day."

Oh no, more cleaning, Vivian thought.

"Then, for the next two weeks, I don't want you to say a word. You must watch me work with the customers. Pay close attention to what I say. And don't stand too close. I need the space to use the arms," Mme. Tremblay said as if she were beginning a calisthenics class.

Vivian felt her stomach turn, again. *Can this day get any worse?*

* * *

The next two weeks were an eye-opener for Vivian.

The good news was that cleaning the sample lipstick tray in the middle of a bright, happy, and delightful department store like Sunderland's was a hundred times better than cleaning nail polish bottles in a dark, cold, and lonely basement. The department store was busy, with people coming and going, and it was fun to watch all the action and listen in on the conversations while she cleaned.

As she spritzed the cleaner on the tray and removed all the lipstick smears, dirt, and fingerprints, Vivian had a great time studying each color up close. She also wondered which lipstick shade would look best on certain skin tones, and which color would make an outfit look simply smashing. So many ideas were spinning around in Vivian's head; she began to write them down in a notebook. She also observed how Mme. Tremblay interacted with the customers.

There were a few times when Mme. Tremblay flat out lied to a customer, and Vivian found that to be odd and reacted accordingly.

"Beautiful blouse," Mme. Tremblay said to a woman looking at face powder.

"It was a gift from my husband. He gave it to me before he left for the war."

"It's gorgeous on you. Really brings out your eyes. God bless him," Mme. Tremblay said dearly.

"Excuse me? That blouse is dreadful. Two sizes too big and the color—awful," Vivian whispered to Mme. Tremblay, who quickly whipped her head to face Vivian.

She responded with clenched teeth and piercing eyes. "Don't. You. Dare."

"It's the truth!"

"I don't care if her blouse was the color of vomit. You must engage with the customers. Make them feel good so that they will buy something! We would not be standing here, taking home paychecks if it weren't for them. My God, her husband is fighting in the war. *Calisse,* I hope he makes it home."

"I didn't see it that way," Vivian said in a shameful tone, not realizing this possible backstory that the woman could have.

"It's time you do."

Although Mme. Tremblay could have softened the blow, she did teach Vivian a thing or two while making sure that her dues were properly paid.

"What are you writing down in there?" Mme. Tremblay asked one morning as she witnessed Vivian writing in her notebook.

"Ideas about pairing lipstick shades to wardrobe ensembles."

"I see," Mme. Tremblay nodded suspiciously and then added, "You missed a spot here."

Vivian took to the spot immediately and began to clean it.

* * *

One afternoon, a breathtaking fuchsia Christian Dior dress zoomed by on a rolling rack, and Vivian's eyes blew up like balloons.

"Calm down, Vivian. Only the elite salespeople get to handle that merchandise. Not someone like you," Mme. Tremblay said.

"What do you mean by that?"

"Oh, nothing."

"No, what do you mean? Who is someone like me?"

Madame Tremblay paused. "You are nothing but a spoiled young Jewish girl. In a few years, you're going to get married, have children, and be a housewife. You're going to sit on that sofa of yours, eat your Bonbons, and listen to the radio all day long while the hired help raises your children."

Vivian's mouth dropped open.

"Don't keep doing that, *chèrie*—it will ruin your complexion," Madame Tremblay said as she waved her hand around Vivian's face. "Right now, you're just working for pocket change so you can buy yourself a new dress, maybe get your hair done—which, by the way, I suggest you do as soon as possible as it looks like a rat's nest. Anyway, before you know it, this place will be nothing but a faint memory," Mme. Tremblay fiddled with her hair bun.

"That is so not true," she said with an annoyed tone, as she very well knew that contrary to what the rest of the young female population and what her parents wanted for her, a husband and babies were not on her radar. And what was wrong with her hair?

"Ah, *oui*, it is. I've been here a long time," Mme. Tremblay said matter-of-factly. "It's just how it is. Oh, and don't be surprised if people don't want your help here. They much prefer to work with an elegant Catholic madame like myself than a Jewish girl." Mme. Tremblay smiled as she reapplied her lipstick. "It's just how it is."

When she smiled, her two front teeth revealed a smear of lipstick. Vivian was dying to tell Mme. Tremblay about it, but held back, as she was too angry to make that kind gesture.

Vivian was completely distraught. She didn't want to jeopardize her job, yet she didn't want Mme. Tremblay to get away with her uncalled for and downright cruel lecture. Vivian stood in front of the gleaming lipstick sample tray, nostrils flared, each hand in a tight fist.

"I'm going to get a coffee. Be back soon," Mme. Tremblay said, and walked away.

Vivian felt relieved that she was gone, though she still stood in the department store floor as angry as ever but determined to not let her stop her from becoming the best salesgirl she wanted to be.

"Don't let her get to you," a familiar man's voice said. The rolling rack and the Christian Dior dress came by again. This time, it stopped right in front of Vivian, and a warm and friendly Mr. Sand popped his head out from behind the side of the dress.

"Hello again! I had to check on you to see how you were doing. And I was right. Am I terrific or what? I hire with such great instincts! I knew you would be a winner," Mr. Sand said, as if he had picked a winning horse. Vivian smiled as best as she could while she was filled to the brim with a cup of freshly poured anger; the Dior dress was an outstanding distraction.

"She is a beauty," she said, while she admired the dress, allowing her foul mood to lift.

"And so are you," Mr. Sand said.

Vivian liked how he made her feel—appreciated and worthy, which was quite the opposite of the treatment she was receiving from Mme. Tremblay, who made her second guess her ability to do her job.

"But Mr. Sand, I'm not doing so well."

"Oh yes, yes you are."

"No, I'm not—I'm awful. All I did so far was clean rows and rows of nail polishes. And now I'm trying to sell cosmetics, but Mme. Tremblay has made it crystal clear that she does not want to share her territory."

"You did a fine job downstairs, and you will do a fine job right here on this department store floor. I just know it," Mr. Sand said as Vivian stared at the floor. "Don't let her get to you. Hey, I'm talking to you, Ms. Fashionista."

Vivian looked up into Mr. Sand's warm hazel green eyes, which reminded her of the green meadows in the Laurentians. He really believed in her, and that was all she needed to hear.

Mr. Sand looked around before he spoke. "You keep going on your own path. Get your goal. Ignore all that interfere."

Mr. Sand zoomed away with the Christian Dior dress.

Vivian stopped for a moment to think, just as Mme. Tremblay returned from her coffee break.

It was then that Vivian had a great idea.

"Mme. Tremblay, would you mind if I walked around the floor and studied the rest of the cosmetic lines? I want to learn all about what we sell here at Sunderland's."

"That's fine," Mme. Tremblay replied, not understanding the purpose, but it didn't matter.

Vivian discovered a twofold solution to help her get through the rest of the day: to get away from Mme. Tremblay and to educate herself.

The Need for Mrs. G

"You're lazy."

Six-year-old Vivian sat at her desk at school, shattered. Not knowing what to say to her teacher, who was scolding her for daydreaming again. She slowly opened her mouth to try to say something, but no words came out. All she could manage was to place her hands on her hips.

"What? You want to say something? What? What is it, Ms. Vivian? What's on your mind?

Actually, WHAT mind, right, children?" her teacher said as she spun around the front of the classroom.

A roar of laughter came from all the desks around Vivian, which felt like lion scratches all over her body. She could feel her eyes beginning to fill. The teacher swirled around her ruler, tossed it into the air, caught it, and gazed her eyes wide at Vivian while the children watched in anticipation. "Give them to me," the teacher instructed.

Vivian swallowed hard, closed her eyes, and laid out her hands on her desk. The teacher lifted the ruler and slapped her palms five times.

"That will keep your mind on my lesson and not in dreamland!"

The stinging of her hands made Vivian wince with pain, and her mouth filled with warm saliva that trickled down the corners of her lips. Vivian closed her eyes and cried; her teacher's final words, which were yelled at her, hurt even more than the physical abuse: "You will never amount to anything."

When she came home that day, with her hands squeezing the fabric from her dress to numb the pain, Miriam was there waiting for her. She saw her daughter's hands and her face fell.

"You've got to start to pay attention. I can't have you come home every day like this."

"But it's so boring, Mama," Vivian admitted while crying.

Miriam held her daughter and tended to the scabs on her hands.

This charade became a constant pattern for the next three years, despite the teacher changes and the many meetings that her parents had with her school.

"Why must you embarrass her like that?" Miriam held her purse tightly on her lap and propositioned her daughter's teacher with clenched teeth.

"Embarrass her? What about me? What about the lessons that I am teaching?"

Henry shook his head as the two women fought neck to neck.

"Why can't you just let her be?" he asked.

Vivian clearly had no interest in paying attention while her teachers lectured the class. Her mind was elsewhere, and she routinely got punished for it. The beatings became so typical: Vivian began to lay out her hands before they even asked her to do so, which was becoming nothing short of ridiculous. Thankfully, they eventually stopped because the physical abuse of slapping her hands wasn't helping her pay attention, and the sight of her hands was just plain awful. The teachers would wince at them and say, "Never mind."

Nevertheless, the verbal abuse didn't stop. And it wasn't only from the teachers.

"Stupid," classmate Scott Sheraton would say to Vivian on their way home from school. Vivian would squint her eyes and run away from him as fast as she could.

Then came the 5th grade, when Vivian had a teacher named Mrs. G, who had noticed her student looking out the window and twirling her hair whenever she taught. Many comments were shared from her colleagues about this child, such as "She's got her head in the clouds."

"That girl does not belong in the classroom."

And the one comment that made Mrs. G perk up her head like a Dobermann Pinscher when something suspicious was nearby.

"Why won't she listen to me?"

Ah ha! Mrs. G squealed with delight to herself. How she loved figuring out our missing pieces with a student like this. The question was *why* the student wasn't listening. Mrs. G. was an educator who was ahead of her time—careful not to be the victim while pointing her finger at the culprit. Yes, most of the classroom was on board with the material being taught, but that's not to say that everyone absorbs information the same way, and why should the student get punished for it? Did any teacher think that maybe they were the problem?

Mrs. G. entered her new classroom that fall with an open mind, as she did every year. After ten minutes of teaching, she saw what her colleagues were talking about. It was as clear as day that Vivian's head was somewhere else when Mrs. G was teaching.

Right in the middle of her lecture, she walked up to Vivian and gave a piece of paper to her.

"Write what you're thinking," she whispered.

Vivian's eyes widened, and her face glowed like a lantern. She sighed happily as if she had been given a new toy as she took the paper from her new teacher's hands and started to fill it up with her thoughts.

After class, Mrs. G handed her a booklet and privately said to the young girl, "If you're not going to pay attention in my class, I need you to pay attention on your own time."

Vivian gazed at the booklet, which was filled with math problems, and nodded her head, as she was eager to try this new regime. As she took the booklet with both hands, she looked up at Mrs. G and screamed with her eyes: *thank you—you get me! Can you be my teacher forever, and can I come and live with you?*

The next day, Vivian handed in her homework booklet and continued to write her thoughts on the blank piece of paper that she received every day while her teacher taught her lessons. All was well received by her parents and Mrs. G. Praise, and, most of all, acceptance was bestowed upon her, and Vivian relished in the moment.

"Why didn't we think of this before?" Henry asked one night at dinner.

"Not all teachers are like Mrs. G," Miriam said.

"Thank you," Vivian said to Mrs. G. on the last day of fifth grade.

"You've got a lot going on in there," Mrs. G said as she pointed to her head. "Sometimes you need someone to see the other side of the coin."

Mrs. G was a one-hit wonder, and sadly, there were no further pioneering educators like herself to come across Vivian's classrooms. Alas, the wicked and impatient teachers took center stage and pushed all hope for any academic potential to the ground.

If it wasn't for Mrs. G, along with the honor of her family members turning to her for all things fashion, Vivian would not have been able to get up and dust herself off after each challenge Sunderland's brought her.

Mrs. G's influence and the Fashion Police title weren't strong enough for Vivian to venture to college after high school and to battle the demons that screamed *lazy and stupid.*

It's amazing how such negative influences can shadow our potential.

Fun with Blinders with Vivian

"Keep going on your own path; get your goal; ignore all that interfere." These were the words that Mr. Sand said to Vivian, which were repeated over and over like a mantra as the morning shift began.

Sometimes, Mme. Tremblay arrived late, and on those days, her hair was not in a Gibson bun at the nape of her neck but in a sloppy ponytail. The button that was missing from her dress when the two first met now had a friend. In place of her trademark Revlon Pango Peach lipstick, she had chapped lips and very bad breath. Vivian sometimes wondered if she brushed her teeth in the morning and couldn't figure out why she would present herself this way—while working at Sunderland's of all places!

On the days when Mme. Tremblay seemed out of sorts and in a foul mood, Vivian busied herself before she had a chance to bark her orders for the day. Of course, even when the lipstick tray was as clean as a surgeon's tools, Mme. Tremblay would still make a negative remark.

"If you keep cleaning like that, you'll be mistaken for a *femme de ménage*."

Vivian couldn't win, but maybe she wasn't supposed to.

***

"A full house of kids. Husband took off years ago. She's alone," Mr. Sand shared this one day after closing as he was walking Vivian to her streetcar.

"I had no idea," Vivian said softly.

"If I could tell you one thing today, it would be that everything is not what it seems. Everyone has a story that you don't know about, so when someone doesn't treat you as you think you should be treated, or vice versa, give them the benefit of the doubt. Don't be so quick to judge. It's just good measure," Mr. Sand said matter-of-factly.

Vivian nodded her head, feeling badly for judging Mme. Trembley when she was frustrated with her. She looked directly into Mr. Sand's eyes to make sure that he understood. She heard every word loud and clear, as she was so appreciative of his kindness, which she knew was genuine.

"Thank you for telling me," Vivian said softly, not realizing that this piece of advice carried so much weight in her life. No one knew what Vivian had been through when she was a little girl at school except her immediate family, and the trauma that she experienced lived through her daily, even if she didn't notice it.

For the rest of the summer, Vivian kept the advice that Mr. Sand had told her close to her heart. After much thought, during her nightly bath, Vivian came up with an idea of imaginary blinders. Miniature blinds on the side of her face that resembled a pair of glasses, but instead of the lens being in front, they would be on the side, so that no one could distract her from what she wanted to do: to be the best darn sales lady she could be at Sunderland's and maybe even get promoted to manager one day. And even though Mme. Trembley came to work still carrying the stress that she endured at home, dumping her frustrations on Vivian wasn't fair, and it was mean. She could have been such a role model for Vivian—someone to look up to and learn from, but Vivian needed to protect herself with the blinders she thought of.

Each morning, Vivian got creative with these blinders, as they were not clear, like the lens of glasses, but happened to blend perfectly with what she was wearing. With a chuckle, she would say to herself something like, "Are these the brown coral pattern blinders? Perhaps I should pull out the ones with the red roses on them? Nah, the bright yellow ones will look just darling with this ensemble today." It was all about the details as she closed her eyes and really thought about the blinders she was wearing, which would make them work in her favor.

Mr. Sand was often found working in the women's clothing department, where Vivian would visit as often as she was able and was quickly taking on the role of a mentor. Those few words that he shared with Vivian never left her mind, and she was grateful for that.

Vivian decided that no one was going to stand in her way, especially Mme. Tremblay, and decided that she was going to really make her mark at Sunderland's and, most importantly, to help women feel beautiful, regardless of where she was working in the store. She quickly learned that clothing wasn't the be-all and end-all, even though she was still a huge fan of that world.

One evening, as she left the department store after her shift, she paused for a few moments as she stood outside the hunter green double brass doors and thought about her original dream: *Vogue* in New York. Although that was a fun and exciting goal when she was a child, there was something about interacting with customers that made her want to stay at Sunderland's. Where this was going, she had no idea, but that was part of the fun, as Vivian found it fascinating that the swipe of a lipstick, a bit of rouge, and nail polish could completely transform a woman, more than she ever realized.

An observation that Vivian quickly made and appreciated was that there was so much preparation behind the final sale of a product. Cleanliness was the first on her list. Besides polishing every inch of the counter around her every morning, she was sure to brush her teeth and rinse with mouthwash and to carry the strongest mints in her pocket to refresh every few hours, especially after drinking coffee.

Research on the latest trends and the care of Revlon's products was also crucial. Besides reading the latest advertisements in magazines and receiving product information from management, Vivian took it upon herself to ask her customers what they were looking for, what they wanted to learn, and what disappointed them in the line. She wanted to be known as the girl who found the perfect cosmetic product for them, and she stopped at nothing to earn this status.

There was a small catch, though. The war was in full swing, and everyone was on a shoestring budget. Yes, there was a niche of women who had a generous budget to enjoy themselves at Sunderland's, but most customers needed to put food on the table before they could purchase a face powder.

There were several occasions where a woman would stop by the Revlon counter and just linger—longingly gazing at the lipsticks or perfume bottles as if they were lost past lovers, admiring what was on display for the week, picking up a sample powder compact and trying it on in front of the mirror. Vivian would think it was a prime opportunity to sell something, but this type of customer was not interested. And in a matter of moments, Vivian understood.

"May I help you?" Vivian asked a woman who came by the counter.

A shocked and mute response was given, as this woman would stop applying the sample powder that was displayed for customers to sample and gaze up at Vivian, allowing her face to fall as if she had been caught. The sample powder that she held in her hands slipped away from her and fell onto the floor. Aghast, she ran away.

At first, Vivian was in total shock from this behavior, as she hollered across the department store aisle, "Wait—come back—wait until I show you a few more colors!"

"Let her go...," Mme. Tremblay said. She waved her hand in the air as if she were swapping away an annoying fly and then walked around the counter to retrieve the powder compact from the floor to place it back where it belonged on the display.

"But why would she just try it on and run away?" Vivian would innocently ask.

"Oh, my goodness—do you ever have a lot of learning to do," Mme. Trembley replied with a deep sigh, as Vivian obviously lived in a privileged bubble and had absolutely no clue what went on behind closed doors in people's homes that influenced their actions, despite Mr. Sand's explanation of Mme. Tremblay's world. Being well-groomed and able to converse under pressure wasn't at the top of the to-do list for those who were struggling.

"Well, teach me!" Vivian bravely replied as Mme. Trembley shook her head with brows that slanted south.

"Isn't it obvious? She can't afford it! Where have you been?" Madame Trembley said.

"But it's only $1.10!" Vivian stated.

"Only? If it's between lipstick and a loaf of bread, what would you choose?" Mme. Trembley shot back, while her eyes glared like daggers. "*Merde!*" She said, shaking her head.

Vivian's face fell lower than that of the woman who ran away. And her heart, too. She didn't know anyone in that situation, and the idea of not being able to buy one measly lipstick was something that she wasn't used to.

"May I help you?" Vivian would ask another woman who was holding a lipstick she was sampling. Not shy in the least bit as she boldly told Vivian that she used to wear this color all the time before the war and now couldn't afford it. "My dirt-cheap husband can't spare the measly $1.10 for me, but of course, he could spare it for his God-damn beer every night after work, that son-of-a-bitch."

Vivian nodded with wide eyes.

"There he goes, day after day. Can't enlist because of his back—he fell off a ladder when he was a kid. Damn luck, I tell you; he so could have gone! Lazy son-of-a-bitch . . . all he does is go to work, come home and go out for beers with his buddies. Yeah, what about me? I'm cooking. Cleaning. Buying the groceries. It just doesn't stop. Where's my fun? Where's my lipstick?" Vivian remained nodding with even wider eyes, making marriage and children a stronger deterrent than ever before.

"Please take care of this order," Mme. Trembley would come and interrupt the monologue, allowing for a quick getaway, even though the idea of getting away didn't cross Vivian's mind, as this kind gesture of listening to someone vent didn't bother her at all.

"Oh, boo-hoo! Those ladies waste my time. I don't want to hear it. Don't want to hear one peep of their sad stories," Mme. Trembley would say, as Vivian now knew that she not only witnessed the exact same conversation but also took part in it as well, in her very own living room, which now made sense of her impatient tone. Thankfully, Mme. Trembley could afford a new lipstick, thanks to samples and her discount, but other things like a new winter coat or a fur stole were out of the question, as she was constantly reminded.

Vivian felt awful for these ladies and didn't mind listening to their sad stories because that's all they really wanted. For someone to listen, not necessarily to fix the problem. If they were heard by somebody, they walked away from the counter feeling a little lighter than before, including Vivian herself. And that was a part of her job that she was beginning to like.

But there was still a great deal of work to be done regarding Vivian's habit of sharing whatever that was on her mind.

"The mademoiselle said you look gorgeous, not enormous," Mme. Tremblay apologetically said once to a customer, followed by a stern look at Vivian, who rolled her eyes again for being scolded for her authenticity.

"You keep comments like these up, and you will be kicked out of here so fast, I will choke on your dust," Mme. Tremblay said while wagging her finger inches away from Vivian's nose.

Vivian shook her head because she knew Madame Tremblay was right. "I'm really sorry."

"*Think* before you speak!" Madame Tremblay said while shaking her head.

Thankfully, she learned over time what to share with the customers, remembering they had the final word in all that she was working for.

* * *

Another roadblock that was encountered was the fact that Mme. Tremblay also wanted to sell Revlon cosmetics. How was she going to compete with a twenty-year department store veteran, even with her sloppy appearance and her territorial attitude?

"With patience. Kindness. And more patience."

Vivian looked up at her mentor, Mr. Sand, and smiled.

"Just be the lovely, adorable, oh-so-knowledgeable, *Vogue*-addicted sixteen-year-old lady that you are. Nobody can compete with that." Then he paused, looked around, and said, "Don't let her . . ."

". . . get to you," Vivian answered.

Vivian smiled and thought how similar Mr. Sand was to her Uncle Irving, who never married and always brought a male friend to family functions. She loved how he always agreed and chuckled while she openly gave her feedback on what her family members thought was a stylish thing to wear.

"Oh, my goodness, those words did not leave your lips!" Mr. Sand would say.

"Oh, yes they did!" Vivian shared and laughed.

"Serves her right for wearing *that*!"

Although no one talked about it, she knew that Uncle Irving was homosexual. She guessed that Mr. Sand was too, which took the pressure off any threat that he would one day pinch her behind or, worse, make her do things that she had not the faintest desire to do with him. It was a stress-free mentorship, which Vivian was grateful for.

Mr. Sand hummed as he dressed a mannequin in a pink silk pencil skirt; "I don't know how the average woman will wear this. So not forgiving. At all."

"The appropriate undergarment will make it more flattering," Vivian said.

"There are a thousand and one ways to ask for a glass of water, and you got it, my dear!" Mr. Sand replied proudly.

Vivian looked confused.

"Darling, we've had this conversation already. I don't need to repeat myself."

Vivian looked down at the floor, and discreetly looked up, while she waited for a response.

"Relax—you're improving."

Vivian never felt prouder, although it did take her a while to get to this point.

***

After hours of observing Sunderland's staff, their customers, and listening to the tips from Mme. Tremblay, one day, it all just clicked. At the corner of Vivian's eye, she could see a woman looking at her. Vivian slowly turned her head to greet her. This time, before she spoke, she reminded herself to choose her words carefully, as if she were at a brunch buffet, looking for the good stuff to put on her plate. *I'll have a scoop of kindness, a double serving of patience, and no negative remarks, please—as I have eliminated that behavior from my Superior Saleswoman Diet.*

"Hello there," Vivian said.

"Hi," the woman responded.

Vivian quickly scanned her appearance and knew in her gut that this woman did not fit into the category of typical war-affected women, but she was taught not to assume anything. One thing was for sure, she was wearing a scarf that made her skin crawl. Vivian wondered who in their right mind would choose such a color and pattern. Nevertheless, Vivian carried on with her duties, which included knowing that her taste for the scarf did not need to be shared with this potential customer. With all her might, she erased the snot-colored scarf that made her look seasick from her vision and focused on one positive characteristic that lay before her, and retaining focus on that was the best lesson she learned to date.

"My, I do admire your trousers!" Vivian warmly said.

"Oh, you think so? My husband doesn't like me wearing pants outside the house."

"Well, he has good taste. But I must admit, I love the new look of pants on a woman."

"Me too!" the woman giggled. "It's so liberating."

"I know," Vivian said while she waved her hands and smiled.

"You're young to be working! How old are you?"

"I'll be seventeen next month."

"Age, shmage—she is a whiz when it comes to fashion!" Mr. Sand interrupted.

"Oh, Mr. Sand, please," Vivian giggled.

"I love your lipstick!" the woman remarked.

"Oh, thank you, it's so moisturizing on my lips. It feels wonderful! You know what? Why don't you come with me, and I will show you the collection I'm representing."

The two women went off to the Revlon counter, where Vivian not only sold the woman a lipstick but also taught her how to apply it and take care of it, and showed her tricks to make the tube last as long as possible. The two of them had a grand ole time, laughing about makeup and life itself, while customers nearby stopped what they were doing to eavesdrop.

Of course, when it was time to pay for the lipstick, the woman also bought a pressed powder, a moisturizer, and a mascara.

"You must set the lipstick before you apply! It will last much longer, and you will end up saving money as you will use less," Vivian advised, feeling giddy with pride as the interaction with the woman was going so well. Rewarding for the fine work, she reached into her wallet to pay for her purchase.

After the customer left, with a bag that was filled to the brim, Mme. Tremblay and Mr. Sand came over to congratulate their protégé.

"You have arrived," Mr. Sand announced, and Mme. Tremblay nodded with agreement as she put her arm around her and gave a gentle squeeze, while Vivian breathed a sigh of relief, feeling proud, but exhausted. "Sales work is hard stuff!" she announced, as the three of them laughed together.

Scenarios like these were repeated every day between 11:00 and 2:00 p.m., the lunch hour window, with different women from all around Montreal, and the sales were coming in like wildfire—in the middle of a war!

Pretty soon, word got around, and the Revlon counter became so crowded that Mr. Charles Revson, the company president of Revlon, called Sunderland's from New York to speak to Vivian herself to congratulate her. Mme. Tremblay couldn't believe it. Neither could the management team at Sunderland's. Or Elaine.

"Don't let her go," Mr. Sand observed and whispered to the owner of Sunderland's.

Just before school began on the following Monday in September, Elaine asked her to stay on part time while she finished her final year of high school.

And she agreed.

Vivian worked all day on Saturdays and on Tuesdays and Thursdays after school and during school breaks. After graduation, in the summer of 1943, Vivian became a full-time employee at Sunderland's.

"What about *Vogue*?" Vivian's father mentioned one evening at the dinner table.

"I want more than that," Vivian said triumphantly.

"What about McGill?" Her mother chirped in, for the umpteenth time that month.

"Please stop reminding me about McGill. I don't need McGill. Everything I need to know is at the store. It's called the school of hard knocks, and I'm learning as I go," Vivian said as if she were zipping the bag that contained all her painful memories as a child in school. Making them stay in there for good.

"Does that mean you will want to settle down one day, marry, and have a family?" Miriam asked.

"Don't push it, Mother."

Vivian: Dressing the Part—1945

Since her first day back in 1942, Vivian's alarm clock would ring at the ghastly hour of 6 a.m. five days a week. Her eyes would open quite easily, thanks to her mandatory eight-hour-a-night sleep schedule.

"Sleep is part of my beauty regime!" she would say to any beau who dared to take her out on the eve of a workday. "I must be in bed, asleep by ten."

After she stretched, yawned, and pulled on her cotton strip hair curlers, she swung her legs over her bed and placed her pedicured feet into her bedroom slippers, which were purposely placed inches away from her bed each night. On her way to the bathroom, she picked up her basket of skincare to take with her, as she wouldn't dare leave her coveted products for her mother and sister to get their hands on. What she put on her face every day was pure gold and was to be enjoyed with her hard-earned work. But how could she afford such luxury, on her salary?

Oh, the power of schmoozing. Each month, sales representatives from the cosmetic companies that Sunderland's worked with would visit the store to train the sales staff and find out what the customers were saying. And every so often, Vivian would sit down with each representative on her lunch time and present an accurate analysis, along with direct quotes from customers. Of course, a plate of cookies from the department store lunch counter would always be on the table, which sweetened the meeting.

"Oooh—these cookies—they are delicious! So light and buttery—my how they melt in your mouth! And they give me such a happy feeling...," the sales representatives would say.

"Yes, they are special—and pair so well with the coffee," Vivian would say, as she bit into her little piece of heaven. Schmoozing over coffee and cookies, along with my detailed reports, was a sure win, Vivian would think to herself. Working at Sunderland's was a dream come true, but she wanted more. Even though she wasn't sure what "more" was, she knew in her heart that it had to be big and exciting. "Now on to what this lady said about the Elizabeth Arden face cream."

And after the final report, more feedback for the following month's visit was offered by Vivian, and without hesitation, the sales representatives nodded their head and said, "Yes, please!" And then Vivian added, "If I could test them out myself, I would give even more accurate reports."

Like clockwork, a complimentary supply of skin care, perfume, and cosmetics were shipped in a separate box, addressed for Vivian, one week after the visit.

One month, a Marcelle skin care regime was on the menu, along with a special treat from the very famous Elizabeth Arden.

The moment Vivian arrived home after work, she couldn't wait until bedtime to test the products. As she dumped her purse on the floor, she ran to her bathroom, placed the brand new bottles and jars on the edge of her sink, and admired the pretty packaging. "Hello you, Elizabeth Arden Eight-Hour cream," she serenaded. After she read the instructions with an eagle eye, she pulled her hair back with a soft headband and began to administer the contents of each, respectively, onto her face. To say that this activity sparked joy would be an understatement.

Afterward, Vivian admired the glow from her skin in the bathroom mirror, of course with a knock at the door from her mother. "What the heck are you doing in there?"

* * *

Of course, wardrobe complications arose during the winter months.

How would you be able to put on a winter coat over a bulky sweater? Is there a matching scarf? How will the hair be wrapped in a hat so as not to ruin the curls? What about winter boots? Are they elegant enough to wear in the store by bringing an old dish towel to clean the salt and slush off them, or does a separate pair of shoes need to be brought with them? All these questions needed to be solved before Vivian lay down to sleep each night. And they were.

Next came the makeup. After the face cream du jour dissolved into Vivian's face, she carefully put on her stockings—a task that didn't seem difficult but actually was. In order not to create a tear, fingernails needed to be kept far away from the nylon as possible—even though they were millimeters away from the pads of the fingers themselves. Yes, it took Vivian a few weeks to figure that all out, but after the third week of her job, she finally got the hang of it and could pull on her stockings in a flash. Then, a light powder was pressed all around her face, followed by at least three minutes of focused concentration to fill in her brows that had been plucked religiously since her teens so that she could follow the eyebrow trends of the day. Next, a little rouge was smudged onto her cheeks for some color and then, the icing on the cake, the lipstick.

In the 1940s, it was known around the world, due to the war effort, that every face cream and pantyhose was a pure luxury that only the wealthy could afford. Petroleum jelly was quite popular to

Vivian: Dressing the Part—1945

soothe a woman's dry skin as well as painting their legs with gravy extras and drawing a line up the back of the leg to look like real stockings. Vivian was grateful that she didn't have to resort to those choices.

But lipstick was saved up for by many women as it could make one's whole appearance turn 180 degrees, no matter what kind of day they were having.

Vivian had a picture of Bette Davis taped to her bedroom mirror, as she believed that she was the ultimate glamorous movie star. Her lips were the perfect example of the Hunter's Bow. After studying the shape of Ms. Davis's lips from the picture, she brought her attention to her own lips, where she corrected her discrepancy with the magic of her lip liner pencil. Then she would take her lipstick and fill in the gap; that would be as easy as drawing with crayons when she was a little girl. But way more fun, as far as she was concerned.

As soon as the last button was fastened on her blouse or sweater, Vivian would grab her large satchel and greet the rest of her family, who were beginning to have breakfast. As she opened her bag, she would place the sandwich that was prepared the evening before by her mother, a piece of fruit and a blueberry muffin, a hairbrush, and a coin for coffee. Vivian couldn't wait for that cup of coffee before her shift began each morning. It cost about 5 cents, which added up throughout the week, but to her, it was the ultimate treat, as there was something about sitting quietly and peacefully at the Sunderland's coffee shop before the customers arrived.

Shopgirl life became a welcome routine that Vivian embraced. She loved showing up for work each day—spending eight hours in a beautiful store, surrounded by beautiful things. Now, that was Vivian's idea of a swinging good time.

Most importantly, helping customers find what they were looking for gave Vivian such a rush of excitement. Helping them find what they didn't know they needed felt like a ride on a roller coaster. When this happened, a faint "eeek" would escape from her lips. Yes, almost the same amount of joy as putting on that Elizabeth Arden Face Cream.

"I beg your pardon, ma'am," a customer would ask after the "eeeek."

"Oh, not to worry, that's just my excitement of helping you find that Max Factor pancake shade—that looks just darling on you. Hey, did you know that this powder was originally for Hollywood movie stars in the 1930s?"

"No!" the customer responded with wide eyes.

"Oh yes . . . until all the movie stars began stealing it from the makeup trailer to take home with them. Can't look good enough for those Hollywood parties, journalists and photographers, right?" Vivian said as a matter-of-factly, as if she was best friends with the Hollywood producers.

Back stories on all the juicy gossip that lived behind the products always lured the customers into her grasp, even the difficult ones, which at times led to an extra ring a ding ding on the cash register. "Hey, do you think you have a lipstick that would pair—like Grace Kelly wears?" the customer would ask, and that would make Vivian almost faint from excitement.

Vivian: Parents No Longer

However, not all days were as happy and as joyful as these.

One evening, Vivian was out with a new beau and lost track of time. Again. This caused her to only sleep for a few hours before she had to rise for work. "Damn, passionate drive-in movies take me off my game!" Vivian would mutter to herself as she wiggled out of her skirt while getting ready for bed. "Ah . . . but it was worth it," she would whisper to herself.

"Did he propose?" her mother yelled from her bedroom.

"No, mother—it was just a date," Vivian cringed as she answered.

"Shmuck."

"Mother—it is not my be-all end-all to get married!" Vivian yelled back.

Silence. This meant that her parents were silently praying that she would change her mind.

* * *

"Storing bean bags in your eyes for the winter, Ms. Vivian?" Mr. Sand would tease.

"Oh, shut up," Vivian would tease back and say, referring to that late rendezvous that ended a little too late, "It was worth every minute!"

"I'll bet!" Mme. Tremblay would add. "And by the way, where are the cold creams?" Mme. Tremblay would ask Vivian, as she would respond by staring blankly into her eyes, which meant she had no idea.

"I asked you to bring up the shipment from the basement yesterday," Mme. Tremblay responded looking like a kettle about to blow it's top.

"I-I was with a c-customer," Vivian stuttered.

"Sure, you were," Mme. Tremblay paused as she stared at Vivian, deciding what to do with her. Not the basement. Not the basement. Please not the basement, Vivian would silently pray.

"Go and bring the creams up from the basement."

Vivian breathed a sigh of relief that all she had to do was go down to the basement and get the cold cream. She thought that she would have to stay there and clean the nail polishes again.

Yet, cleaning the nail polishes was very much welcomed when those types of customers came in. At least in the basement, it was free from those that brought all the baggage that was filled with rudeness and rage from home, from work, or wherever they have been.

"I need that face cream, at once!" someone would bark. Vivian sprang to her feet, raced to the customer, reached out to her hands, and drew her closer so that she could get a good look at her face.

"Don't touch me! Just get me that cream. I know the kind!"

"All I was doing was looking at your skin! You don't want the wrong type of cream, do you?" Vivian responded in a soft, warm tone that her mother used to use when she couldn't find *her* favorite face cream, which worked every time. She remembered how her rage would somehow disintegrate.

"What would someone like you know? How old are you?"

"Twenty."

"You're just a baby! What do you know?"

"I know a lot—as I've been here for a few years," Vivian said as she pushed back her shoulders.

"And why aren't you married, for crying out loud?"

Vivian winced at the comment, as she was a walking contradiction, but at that point, she gave up as she wasn't going to win, and who cared anyway. She simply wanted to satisfy the customer so that she could get the heck out of the store. It wasn't worth her time to help her if she wasn't willing to accept Vivian's kindness. With a hand on her forehead that she hoped would postpone a headache, brought on by stress, she gave in. "Um, I'll just get you that cream you wanted."

"Good girl," the customer replied, as she put her hands on her hips to wait. Vivian felt as if she were being patted on the head like a schoolgirl as she fetched the cream and handed it to the customer with the best smile she could fake. And that was okay, as Mr. Sand came by as he heard all the ruckus, placed his gentle hand on Vivian's, and smiled.

"It's alright."

But it wasn't alright.

As Vivian thought that her day couldn't get any worse, she came home to the most dreadful news she could imagine. As she opened her front door, she found her parents in the middle of the hallway, on her favorite carpet, crying and holding a telegram from Germany. Vivian's chest felt heavy as she sank to the floor to meet her parents and hold them. They needed her now, as they no longer had parents any longer.

1950: This is Only a Pinch

Twenty-five-year-old Lilly was alone. Well, not completely alone. She had her three kids with her, and that's all that mattered. Oh, and a house with a mortgage and three mouths to feed. And with feet that didn't stop growing, which needed new shoes. Alimony only went so far. Lilly needed to make money, and her mother's store was the low-hanging fruit that she needed, but first she needed to get groceries.

As she stood by the dairy aisle, she felt the eyes all around her. Everyone was staring. As Lilly was inspecting an egg carton for any damaged eggs, faint whispers were heard, almost like an annoying fly that was circling around her. Without moving her head, Lilly skillfully raised her eyes like a detective from the egg carton to locate the whispers, which she did, just steps away from her. It was Marie Ste-Claire from elementary school and her friend, who had their heads together, looking at Lilly, who closed the egg carton and placed it in her basket.

"Marie! It's been ages! How are you?" Lilly asked as she put on the most positive facade she could master while she rolled her shopping basket to meet the two ladies, who did not smile back.

1950: This is Only a Pinch

"Fine, Lilly. Just fine," Marie said. Lilly nodded, wishing she could say the same thing, but couldn't.

"And you?" Marie asked.

"Well . . . I don't know if you've heard."

"Oh, we've heard!" Marie's friend said, as Lilly's heart shriveled up like crumbled paper.

"Well, that saves me some explaining!" Lilly joked.

"What are you going to do, Lill?" Marie asked as Lilly stood there, gripping the handle of her shopping cart tighter and tighter as the sweat of her palms slowly began to slide around the handle. What she really wanted to do was reach into her shopping cart and grab her egg carton and throw each egg—all twelve of them—directly onto Marie and her silly friend's face. But fighting back was not her forte, and tossing eggs wasn't the lady-like thing to do. Besides, the store would probably make her pay for the eggs, and she needed them to feed her family, so they stayed in their cardboard carton, nestled between the loaf of bread and bottle of milk. Marie and her friend tilted their heads in unison, waiting for Lilly's response. What was she going to do?

"I'm going to live my life," Lilly said proudly as she turned her cart around to head to the fruit section of the store, leaving the whisperers behind in her dust.

Could this day get any better? Lilly sarcastically thought as she walked home with her groceries.

* * *

"Oh, good you're here!" Sarah said as soon as she saw her daughter walk into the store the following day, as she placed her purse behind the counter, where she also shoved her feelings from the grocery store there too. There was no sense in bringing them along for her afternoon shift.

"I'm here. What do you want me to do?"

"There's a shipment of green peas coming in. Go get them in the receiving room," Sarah said as Lilly nodded her head and went on her way to the back of the store, where she saw a man outside his truck standing next to a stack of boxes.

"Green peas?" Lilly asked.

"Yes, young lady—green peas!" the man said, as Lilly walked over to the stack and wrapped her arms around the stack of boxes, quickly realizing that it was too heavy to carry all at once.

"I need to carry one box at a time," Lilly announced.

"How about this—you take one, and I take two," the man offered, as Lilly felt relieved and welcomed this act of kindness. Finally, she thought—a decent human being who does not know her story. As she wrapped her arms around the box, she turned around to walk, and felt a pinch on her buttocks. Lilly felt the blood rush to her face as she stopped in her tracks and whipped her body around.

"What are you doing?" she asked.

"It's only a pinch."

"Only?"

"I heard you're a divorcé! Sexy."

How did this delivery man find out? Did her mother tell him? And how could getting a divorce be sexy? Leaving Him was the most difficult and humiliating thing she had ever done in her life. How she wished she could wrestle him to the floor and punch the lights out of him. The feeling of her fists smacking against his cheeks, making his face swing while leaving a mark as red as a rare steak would be so gratifying. Perhaps she would also pinch his ear as hard as she could. Unable to gather the strength to physically beat him up, she fought back with what she could.

"Sexy? Pinch this!" Lilly shrieked as she threw the box of peas onto the man's legs as he stumbled to the ground. Lilly ran back into the store and grabbed her mother by her shoulders and cried.

1950: This is Only a Pinch

"Lilly, what's wrong?"

"The man. Peas. Pinched me."

"Pinched you where?" Sarah asked as she held her crying daughter, but she didn't need an answer.

Vivian and Mrs. Linton

Women from all over Montreal flocked to Sunderland's to meet the famous cosmetician. The lineup would be at least twenty people long that were waiting to witness Vivian's expertise and a chance to be under her care. The crowds kept getting larger and larger. It was amazing what she could do and what could arise from with one little three-inch tube that could fit in your palm, trouser pocket, or evening bag.

It was the 1950s, and people's spirits were lifted as if a grand weight was removed from their shoulders. Canada was in a healthier economic position, which meant more sales opportunities for the Sunderland's employees.

"Ladies, we need you to sell, sell, sell! Show how the creams work magic by taking some out of the sample jar and gently placing it on the top of their hands so they could feel the texture. Spritz on some perfume on customers' wrists and let them experience how a scent can lift their spirits and change their mood. And don't forget to wear nail polish! You ladies are a walking billboard! We want to see a different shade each week on those nails!" Elaine and Mme. Tremblay announced minutes before Sunderland's opened, just as a football coach prepared its players. And Vivian was more than game to score a touchdown.

"Watch Vivian! She knows what she's doing," Mme. Trembley said, with a waggle of her index finger. Vivian thought that she misheard, as Mme. Tremblay had never uttered a kind word regarding Vivian's work, except for the time that she agreed with Mr. Sand's decision that Vivian had officially arrived. But that was 3 years ago, and she hadn't uttered any words of encouragement since. This made her feel dreadfully confused, as she distorted her face in deep thought.

"Watch your facial expressions. Premature lines," Mme. Tremblay softly said.

"But you never . . . Uh.. ever..?" Vivian stuttered.

"Don't let it get to your head. I pushed you because you could do it. I hate to say it, but you proved me wrong," she said as she placed her hands on Vivian's shoulders and gave her an endearing maternal smile. It was if someone placed a light bulb underneath Vivian's chin. Despite the endless negative remarks, Vivian wanted the approval of the Sunderland veteran. The positive accolade from Mme. Tremblay was welcomed and monumental—as earning a blue ribbon—not only from Mme. Tremblay, but from everyone else.

"Being with Vivian is better than reading how to apply it in magazines," said one woman to another, while standing in line to await their turn.

"This way I can ask her questions in person!"

"And she's nice and not snooty!"

"She's better than any cosmetician I know."

Once Vivian had a customer in her care, there were several times that a whole laundry list of products was bought. Pressed powder, rouge—in several colors! Don't forget the night cream and day cream. "It's a complete look that you deserve!" Vivian would gush, and the customer would eat every word up, like a homemade cake. As for the icing, Mr. Sand would casually waltz over to the Revlon counter to join in on all the excitement and lure the women to his section of the store to look at the line of the moment—a nifty domino effect that worked beautifully.

This success fed Vivian's ego as a mother fed her baby. And in this case, the baby grew and grew and felt that she could do anything. The demons that screamed spoiled, lazy, stupid brat be gone!

At about 5:00 p.m. one evening, Vivian was putting away some face powders in the glass cabinets. Her shift was almost done, and she was looking forward to going home, kicking off her shoes, and taking her ritual long, baking soda bath. However, little did she know that her shift was not done and neither was her job description.

Mrs. Linton was on her way to Sunderland's, from her nine-bedroom, three-bathroom Westmount mansion, which was situated at the top of the city, with magnificent views. Residences from Westmount were grand, exquisite, stately, and obviously equipped with the proper staff to keep them that way.

The wife of Henry Linton II, who was a part of the Linton fortune who manufactured freezers for every grocery store all over the country and according to Mr. Sand, who got the inside scoop from Mrs. Linton's third cousin, once removed, the freezers were expanding into the US. Their product was a successful one, backed by outstanding customer service and quality.

Even though the Linton family had been around for only two generations, they have been invited to all the society galas and gave to The Red Cross, just like a proper wealthy family would do.

"Third cousin, once removed, come on!" Vivian whined.

"It's a trusted source!" Mr. Sand sang, with his hands on his hips.

"Nouveau Riche?" Vivian asked.

"You could look at them that way," Mr. Sand replied, as this was not the first conversation that was had regarding a wealthy customer.

"My dear—we need to celebrate!" Mr. Linton announced to his dear wife one evening. And rightly so, why shouldn't they celebrate every rack of T-bone steaks to bags of peas that could be stored for months on end in grocery stores? A country home was bought in Vermont, along with seasonal trips across the pond and the freedom to enjoy all of the lovely treasures from Sunderland's.

The driver stopped at the curb, as to not make a scene. Mrs. Linton didn't like drawing attention to herself. Not really. Well, maybe to just a few, like those awful girls she used to play with in the schoolyard that teased her to no end. Let them see her now, she thought as she reached into her purse to pull out a compact to reapply her lipstick. With a quick swipe of her finger to remove a bit of mascara that smudged on her cheek, she stepped out of her 1946 light blue Bentley in her Ferragamo tan heels. It was August, and Mrs. Linton was wearing a light pink blouse and cotton skirt that flowed as she walked and waved to her driver, as she knew her errand wouldn't take long.

A few steps and a forceful tug at the generous hunter green doors, Mrs. Linton was inside Sunderland's, her favorite place to go shopping and spend time with her favorite "Lipstick Girl" Vivian.

"Mrs. Linton!" It's so lovely to see you here again! Vivian beamed as she saw one of her favorite customers walk in her direction.

"Hi dear, I feel so silly, as I was just here last week!"

"Silly Shmilley—does it really matter? Tell me, what can I do for you?" Vivian asked, even though she was exhausted. For the past eight hours, she was on her feet while she served her customers, organized merchandise and rearranged a hairbrush display on a counter that was just all wrong. Her last coffee break was hours ago. She was starving, had to pee, while she declared, in a giggly overtired manner, to whoever was in a two-arm's length of her, that she officially couldn't feel her toes.

However, once she saw Mrs. Linton come waltzing her way, all of what ailed her poofed into thin air. As far as she was concerned, she would do anything for that lovely woman. It was not about how much she would spend, because obviously that was a perk, but it was the way Mrs. Linton treated Vivian that made her feel appreciated.

"You're right—what the heck! There is absolutely nothing wrong with a couple of visits with my favorite cosmetician!"

"You got that right!" Vivian said while nodding her head. "What can I do for you, m'lady?"

"I just found out that I'm going away next week to Vermont. It's so quiet there, during the off season," She said.

"Oooh—fun!" Vivian added.

". . . I would like a new face powder and lipstick, please," Mrs. Linton said as she unbuttoned the top button on her blouse to reveal a diamond the size of an olive that rested at the bottom of her neck. Vivian tried not to stare at the stone that took her breath away, as it wasn't polite.

"Well, I just sold you a new face powder and lipstick a few days ago," Vivian asked as she closed one of the glass cabinets.

"Oh, they're perfect, but I want new ones. Special designated trip makeup."

"Special for your trip?"

"Yes, that's correct. For my trip."

The instructions were loud and clear, but Vivian tried to process the situation because the idea was so foreign to her. "Pardon me, but why would you want to purchase a whole new face powder and lipstick when you have perfectly good ones right now. Are the colors I sold you not right?" Vivian asked, knowing very well that she was repeating herself; nevertheless, she was still trying to understand what Mrs. Linton wanted.

"I told you they were perfect. The colors are wonderful—I love them both. It's just that I would like to have special, or shall I say separate ones for travel."

Vivian still didn't get it but agreed anyway. Why should she argue for another sale?

After a shrug and a smile, she fetched the exact same products the woman had bought the other day and placed them on the counter:

a face powder in the shade Fatal Apple and a Raven Red lipstick. After paying for her purchase, Vivian slipped a perfume sample in her bag. "A little something extra for your trip!" She winked and smiled at Mrs. Linton while she handed over a shiny black Sunderland's bag and watched her walk down the department store aisle and push the large hunter green doors open into the busy Montreal streets.

"You okay? Mr. Sand asked Vivian who looked like she saw a ghost.

"Oh, I'm fine. I think."

"Did Mrs. Linton do well?"

"Yes," Vivian answered, but her mind was spinning into another world.

All was quiet at the dinner table, which worried Miriam and Henry. Marsha was out that evening with her boyfriend.

"Penny for your thoughts. . ," Miriam asked that startled Vivian from her trance.

"What's going on?" Henry asked.

"Oh, nothing." Vivian did not like to lie to her parents, but really, there was nothing going on, not yet.

The next morning, Vivian woke up before her alarm clock. The bright morning sun beamed into her bedroom, lighting it up with a burst of energy.

Today is going to be a great day." Vivian sprang out of bed to get dressed. She thought of Mrs. Linton and how lovely she looked when she was in the store that day, which inspired her. As she went through her closet in her bathrobe, she eyed a new outfit that was bought just last week but wanted to save it for a special occasion. As Mrs. Linton said, *What the heck,* Vivian did too, and reached for the outfit that still had the price tag on it. "Why not?" Vivian said out loud as she reached for it and put on a pair of bright green shoes to go with it.

Lobster, Growth, and Other Things

How does a lobster grow out of its shell?
Through a process called molting.
As a lobster grows, its rock-hard shell becomes very confining for its soft and durable flesh.
The lobster feels a tremendous amount of pressure and must go through an excruciating process.
So it can grow.
But it must be done, no matter how uncomfortable and painful it may be.
Growth is a painful process, for any living creature.
But is so much more bearable with a friend.
To reveal the strength that you didn't know you had.

xo,
SNA

1950 Lilly: Happiness Is a Great Pair of Shoes

"I honestly don't know what to do," Lilly said to Anna one morning in her kitchen.

The two of them sat face to face at the kitchen table over cups of coffee with cream. Lilly cradled the mug between her hands, appreciating the warmth it gave her. She looked up at her sister for advice and hope, as she was desperate for some direction.

"Do you have a skirt?"

Lilly looked straight ahead at her sister and nodded.

"A blouse?"

Lilly nodded again.

"You're ready. Go and look for a job."

Lilly looked around the kitchen, waited for a few moments to digest it all, then nodded in agreement. She had no choice but to move forward and take her sister's advice. Working at her mother's store worked for a while, but after the pinching of her behind scenario, and the full staff her mother already employed, it was decided that Lilly should find another job.

A pang of heaviness landed on her chest as she thought about her current household situation. Her husband had left the premises just six months ago, and the money he had left her was quickly beginning to run out. With three mouths to feed, it was now up to her to put food on the table.

"This was not how I envisioned my life at twenty-eight," Lilly said while exhaling a deep breath.

"Angry?"

"I was. Now, I'm okay. It was time for him to go."

Her sister smiled and said, "You can do this. I'll help whenever I can."

"Hey, can I borrow your shoes?" Lilly asked her sister.

"Of course. Thank heavens we are the same size. You can take my new red ones. They will look great on you."

Lilly smiled and began to feel excited about this new adventure yet hesitant as she was about to swim in unknown waters. Would there be sharks?

The next morning, as her last child left for school, Lilly left her home and walked to the bus that would take her downtown. The sun was shining, and she was looking forward to being outside as she put on her sister's shoes to begin her job hunt.

However, once she arrived at the bus stop, her feet were throbbing with pain, especially the right one, toward the back. She pursed her lips and closed her eyes as a shot of pain tore through her foot. To ease the discomfort, Lilly balanced her weight on the other foot. After waiting about ten minutes, the bus finally arrived. Each step was more painful than the next. She inhaled a deep breath as she took out her change, paid her fare, searched for a seat, and sat down with a deep exhale.

"I think you're bleeding," an older man said to her and pointed to her right foot.

"Oh, dear," Lilly exclaimed as she saw blood around her ankle that matched her sister's red shoes. She reached for a tissue to blot it, although it didn't do much good, as she was wearing stockings.

1950 Lilly: Happiness Is a Great Pair of Shoes

Lilly began to panic. How was she supposed to find a job with a bleeding foot?

She closed her eyes and took a deep breath. When it was time to get off, she gathered all her strength and stood up, clutched the pole before her and hobbled off onto the streets. She looked up and gleefully smiled at what was in front of her. A fire hydrant! A beaming Lilly hobbled up to it and hunched over it to rest just for a little while. She filled her cheeks up with air and blew it out, then looked down at her foot. She shook her head and thought, what am I going to do now?

A pair of bright green shoes—the color of a perfectly manicured summer lawn—entered her view, along with a sweet voice.

"You all right?" the voice asked.

"Not really. I've had better days," Lilly chuckled as she pointed to her foot.

The woman with the green shoes noticed the blood running around her ankle and down the front of her foot in a straight line.

"Oh, I know that song!" the woman said with a giggle.

"Excuse me?" Lilly asked in disbelief.

"What I mean is, I've seen that before, I can't believe that this exact same scenario happened to me years ago. I know exactly how it can be fixed. Follow me."

With an intuition of trust, Lilly stood up as straight as she could and followed her new friend, who seemed to be just a few years younger than herself. No more than twenty-five for sure, she thought. While hobbling and wincing at the piercing pain from her foot, Lilly noticed that this woman was impeccably dressed. It was if she walked out of a magazine shoot. Her hair was elegantly styled in a chignon, while her face was framed with a rose-colored scarf that perfectly matched her lips. She wore a beautiful three-quarter-length canary-yellow cotton pleated skirt and matching blouse, with its collar standing up to frame her face. The rose color on her lips looked so bright and cheery next to the yellow. Lilly couldn't help but stare at the picture perfect young vision that stood before her.

Completely amazed, Lilly wondered if she did that on purpose and was impressed with this young lady's attention to detail and care for her appearance.

As they walked across the street, Lilly looked up to try and see the name of the building they were headed toward, but the sun shined right into her eyes, preventing her.

"Mmmph!" her new friend said as she used both arms to push open two hunter-green double doors that were framed in brass.

"Ah, here we are!" the young woman proudly said as she quickly walked to her counter, while Lilly followed her and quickly realized that they were in a department store.

"Your shoes look so great with what you're wearing!" Lilly called it like she saw it—as it truly did.

"Oh, thank you. I do love a pretty yellow. It reminds me of a flower. And my shoes are like the stems," she said. The girl placed her foot in front of her body like a ballerina and twisted her heel with pride to show off the vibrant green shade. "Living in Montreal, our warm days are few and far between—we must take advantage of them while we can." She kicked up her heel and laughed. "Funny, I was saving this outfit for a special occasion, but I decided to wear it this morning."

It was like looking at a ray of sunshine. This girl was oozing with enthusiasm, and it was magnetic. As she began to look around, she realized that they were in the cosmetics department; it was so glamorous and smelled wonderful, with the bright lights, shiny countertops, and pretty things everywhere. Lilly watched the salespeople and customers spritz on perfume and try on lipstick. For a while, she almost forgot about the bulging, bloody blister on her foot and realized where she was.

"Is this Sunderland's?" she asked.

1950 Lilly: Happiness Is a Great Pair of Shoes

"You bet it is!" the young woman answered as she placed her hands on her hips and smiled as if she built the department store herself and was damn proud.

"Oh my, what have we got here?" A man in a dark suit came over to the two women. He wore a name tag that read Mr. Sand.

"Morning, Mr. Sand, this is . . . I'm sorry, I didn't catch your name," the young woman said.

"Lilly."

"Pleased to meet you, Lilly. I'm Vivian."

"Lilly, you stay here. I see that we have a little issue with your foot. I'm going to get you a bandage," Mr. Sand said then added "Deja Vu, Ms. Vivian! What a lovely coincidence this is." Lilly made a confused face, while Vivian laughed.

"I told you that the exact same scenario happened to me—well, it happened on my very first day! Isn't that a riot?"

"That is crazy!"

"I know!" The two women smiled at each other, as a bond between them was beginning to immerse.

"I could really use a drink," Lilly blurted out.

"Oh, but it's only 9:30 in the morning," Vivian laughed as she checked her appearance in a nearby mirror. "Can you at least wait a little while?"

"Do I have a choice?" Lilly responded.

Vivian walked up to Lilly, held her hands, and said, "We've all had bad days. Take a deep breath and know that Mr. Sand knows what he's doing. Trust me. I've been there." Vivian looked to the right at the store clock. "Geez, I got to make like a tree and leave! My shift starts in ten minutes, and I haven't had my coffee yet."

"Your shift?"

"Yes, why?"

"I'd like a shift."

"Are you looking for a job?"

"You can say that."

"Got any experience?"

"I worked in my mother's grocery store since I was nine!"

"We might have something here."

"There's something else," Lilly said hesitantly, as Vivian waited in anticipation and lowered her chin so she could see right into Lilly's warm, caramel eyes that would just pop with the new eye shadow they received last week. Ah, she digressed. Back to what this lovely and sincere young lady was going to say. "I kicked my husband out. I have three kids. I really need a job."

"Holy Moses. Give me your number."

Lilly reached into her purse and tore off a piece of the paper that enveloped her cigarettes. She then dug deep into her purse, praying that she would have a pen, found one, and happily wrote down her number before handing the paper to Vivian and thanking her. Vivian gave her a warm smile, squeezed her shoulder and waved goodbye as she went on her way. "Joe . . . I'm coming for yooouuu!" Vivian sang as she went on her way to the department store lunch counter.

Lilly hobbled to a quiet corner of the store where a bench was, took off her shoe, and said, "Ahhh," A tremendous weight of relief left her shoulders and her mind as the pain subsided from her foot and was replaced with a feeling of hope that she might just get a job in this beautiful palace.

Mr. Sand soon arrived with some cloth, a bandage, and a new pair of stockings, along with an agenda for Lilly to follow. He bent down to Lilly's height and spoke in a soft tone, as it was a confidential matter of course.

"Go to the ladies' room around the corner and make yourself comfortable on the couch near the mirror. Remove your old stockings and place them in your purse. When you get home, soak them in one part vinegar and two parts water for twenty minutes before

1950 Lilly: Happiness Is a Great Pair of Shoes

hand washing them. As for what you can do now with your poor foot, blot the blister, and place the bandage on top. Then, put on these new stockings!"

Mr. Sand presented the package of stockings to Lilly as if he was offering her an hors d'oeuvre. Lilly hung onto every word that left Mr. Sand's lips like Godspell and then took a few moments to make sure she understood, which she did, but wasn't sure about one thing that seemed too good to be true.

"You're going to give me a pair of stockings . . . for free?" Lilly asked.

"We like to take care of our customers."

Now Lilly understood how her kids felt when they found the Cracker Jack prize.

"Finally, after all is completed, have a cigarette!" Mr. Sand said as he giggled, and so did Lilly, who couldn't believe her luck.

Now this is what I call job hunting! She thought.

Now more than ever, Lilly wanted to work at Sunderland's, and could anyone blame her? From the moment Lilly walked through those hunter-green doors, she felt comfortable, cared for, and respected. Lilly didn't want to leave. She wanted more and wanted to reciprocate those feelings right back to Mr. Sand, Vivian, and anyone who entered the department store.

"Take off those shoes!" Vivian hollered as she saw Lilly hobble down the department store aisle on her way to the ladies' room.

"What?" Lilly looked around, as she tried to find where that voice was coming from.

"It's me, Vivian . . . just trust me. Take them off," Vivian said thinking to herself how strange it was that she not only had the exact same problem but also the same solution when she began at Sunderland's years ago—minus the fuzzy slippers.

Lilly threw her hands up in the air and took off her shoes, then made her way to the ladies' room in her blood-stained stockings, where a great long dusty rose couch greeted her so she could follow Mr. Sand's superbly specific instructions. "I really need to work here," Lilly said to herself.

As soon as the cigarette was finished and Mr. Sand's directions followed, she got up, walked down the department store aisle with more ease, and thanked Vivian and Mr. Sand before she left Sunderland's to walk to her bus stop.

On the bus ride home, Lilly quietly prayed that a job would open for her and promised to wear proper walking shoes and carry a purse full of bandages.

***

Back at the department store, Mr. Sand turned to Vivian, who was creating a display of face creams on a nearby table.

"First of all, you look absolutely stunning today, my dear . . . do spin around and let me see the whole ensemble!" Vivian giggled and put down the product line she was rearranging to twirl in a circle like a ballerina.

"Ta da!" Vivian sang as she bowed, and Mr. Sand applauded. "Blame it on Mrs. Linton, she sure inspired me this morning."

"She should come around more often."

"That's not all she inspired. . ." Vivian walked back to the table, while Mr. Sand tilted his head to zone in on what was no longer his young protégé but a colleague who looked so happy that morning. Beaming with enthusiasm, practically flying like an eagle on her feet. "Something is brewing, and it isn't the coffee down the hall," Vivian said as she moved a box of cream to the left.

"Think about it. Give it time. It will come," Mr. Sand said as he patted her on the back.

***

1950 Lilly: Happiness Is a Great Pair of Shoes

Later that night, after the last dish was washed and put away, Lilly sat in her living room with her feet propped up on a pillow.

The phone rang. It was Vivian.

"Do you know anything about shoes?" she asked without even saying hello first.

"Not really. As you can see from my poor choice today!"

"You're about to now. There's an opening in the women's shoe department, effective immediately. Do you want it?"

"What time do I need to be there tomorrow?"

"I would show up for nine thirty. Your boss, Mr. Fine, needs you there for nine fifty."

"Goodness—yes! I'll take it! Thank you!"

Lillian hung up the phone and sighed in relief as she smiled from ear to ear, giggled out of pure glee, and yelled, "Happiness!" Then she turned on the television and watched an episode of *What's My Line*.

Happiness was the word she used to describe anything that brought her joy. Jam and toast, a funny TV program, a great book to read, a walk in the park with her children— "Happiness," Lilly would say, and her three kids even got into the act on their own.

"Happiness, Mom! I won at marbles!"

"Happiness—I love hot dogs!"

"Happiness—I punched Larry's lights out."

Most of the time, her kids understood the real meaning of happiness. As far as the divorce between their parents, they became quiet whenever Lilly asked about how they were doing. Except for her middle child who said, "There's no more noise in the house. I like that."

The other two had their moments, but Lilly made sure to check in with them every so often. To remind them how much she loved them and how strong they were capable of being. She also made sure they felt safe and enjoyed their time with their father every other weekend and during some holidays. Her mother Sara, and siblings were also around, a lot, which helped tremendously. It wasn't easy, but Lilly's children were her world and she would do anything for them, and they felt that.

The next morning, at dawn, Lilly sat upright from her bed and looked around. Today is the day, she thought, to make a new start, even make some new friends. She gave a generous stretch and a yawn and reached to the side of the bed where he used to sleep. She glanced at the empty space and frowned, then shook her head and looked at her foot to inspect the blister from yesterday. Still red and inflamed. Lilly reached for a cigarette and lit it.

"Mom!" was heard outside her door.

"In a minute!" she yelled back, staring outside of the window. The sun was blaring in, and it felt warm on her face. Two hours later, Lilly was on the bus downtown, this time wearing a pair of comfortable shoes. Walking in them was as close to wearing slippers, and Lilly began to relax a little and to think about what had happened just thirty minutes earlier.

Perhaps Lilly rushed the kids a little too much this morning. Did any of them brush their teeth? She didn't want to be late and disappoint Vivian, who got her the job.

As Lilly waited for her bus, she took inventory. *I am going to be great. Anna's skirt and blouse, mom's pearls, and my new "Cherries in the Snow" lipstick.* Her eyes popped out of their sockets when she saw a model wearing it in the latest *Chatelaine* magazine just the other week. She had to have that color; lipstick was a luxury she could afford occasionally.

Once the bus stopped in front of the building, Lilly marched off that bus as if she was saving her country. Passersby frowned at her aggressiveness, especially those that were in her way and got shoved to the side by her shoulder.

"*Excusez moi, mademoiselle!*" a man in a brown hat shouted to Lilly while rubbing his shoulder as she walked past him.

1950 Lilly: Happiness Is a Great Pair of Shoes

"Oh, sorry . . . but you were in my way," Lilly politely responded.

The man shook his head and whispered, "*Merde*! Go home to your kitchen!"

Lilly thought she heard what she heard but decided to keep on walking. She had somewhere to be. It was 9:20 a.m., and she had some time to spare before she met her new boss.

Once again, Lilly was faced with the monstrous department store doors and made a *hmph* sound, just like Vivian did the other day, as she pushed them open. Once she was inside, a man in a suit greeted her.

"We're not open until ten, madame."

"Today is my first day! I work here. In the women's shoe department."

"Right. You will have to fill out a few forms. Walk down the hall. Take the elevator to the third floor."

Lilly stood at the front entrance of the store to stare at what was before her. The elegance headquarters. Every square foot was dripped with shiny and enticing I-just-want-to-pick-up-and-touch all-of-these bottles, jars, accessories, and clothing. As she was just at the store yesterday, but that day it looked different. It was awfully quiet as there were no customers around, except for a few employees who were getting started on their shifts. Her eyes scanned the entire main floor from top to bottom as she widened her eyes and thought to herself how she lucky she was to work there, but suddenly became enveloped in panic as she had no idea how she was going to do this job! What did she know about selling shoes?

Besides housework, and the time she worked at her mother's grocery store, she didn't know what to expect while working in a fancy department store like Sunderland's. Her older sister Anna reassured her the evening before: "Just be the warm, and genuine lady that you are, and the customers will adore you. Everything will fall into place."

"You make it sound so easy," Lilly said.

"And don't forget—you were an incredible student! Remember those grades you brought home? You're a smart girl. Remember that."

Anna's advice was what Lilly needed to hear so she could begin her journey at Sunderland's on the right foot, and for that she was grateful. But Lilly's youngest son's five magical words gave her the ammunition to go out there and conquer any doubts she had about herself. On his way to school, he spun around with his books and lunch bag in hand to say "You're gonna be great, mom!" This made her giddy with joy, purpose, and strength. It was exactly what she needed to hear as she left her house. Children don't lie, especially the ones she was raising.

The aroma of coffee reached her nose as she reached the elevator. She promised herself a cup during her break.

Lilly: Just Do What He Says

Lilly reached the third floor of Sunderland's and saw a sign for the administration offices as soon as the elevator doors opened and followed it. As she walked down the hallway, she passed a secluded area. As she slowly creeped inside, Lilly looked around and thought that she was standing in someone's personal bedroom closet. But not just someone. Someone who was the First Lady of Canada. Someone who was a movie star and someone who wore "Everyday Diamonds."

There was a large three-way mirror in the center of the room that had a wooden platform in front of it to stand on. Several dining-room-type chairs with arm rests, embroidered with silk fabric, sat in a half circle around the mirror, and a small table was set near the chairs equipped with a coffee and creamer set and a plate of cookies.

Lilly's mouth watered and wondered if anyone would notice if she took just one little cookie. While looking around she slowly walked over to the table and stretched out her hand and picked one up. The buttery, sweet aroma quickly made their way to her nostrils as Lilly brought the cookie to her mouth to take a small bite. "Wow—that's good!" she caught herself saying out loud, and as unladylike as ever, she popped the rest of the cookie into her mouth and devoured it, while letting out a slight moan as she received a rush of euphoria. "That's some cookie."

Lilly looked around and declared the fact that she had landed in a super fancy area and decided to take advantage of her surroundings. As she was wearing a raincoat that day, she took it off to inspect the outfit that she was wearing in front of the three long mirrors that stood side by side of one another. As she stepped on the wooden platform step stool placed in the center, her reflection revealed every angle of her physique. "Oh my . . . oh no. . .," Lilly said as her reflection revealed the truth. Her sister's skirt was much too short to wear. Could she help it if she was 4 inches taller than her? Why didn't she notice this when she left the house that morning?

"Excuse me, may I help you?" a woman asked, wearing a measuring tape around her neck, while holding a dress on a hanger.

"Oh, I'm sorry—I'm just looking for the administration and I got sidetracked. What is this place?"

"The dressmakers. Administration offices are down the hall and to your left." The woman replied, while looking Lilly up and down with her wide eyes that burned right through her clothes. Her reaction to Lilly was so obvious, it was almost embarrassing, as Lilly had never experienced anything like that before.

"Is something wrong?" Lilly asked boldly, hoping that the woman wouldn't notice.

"Oh, no, not at all," the woman said softly as she looked away and walked to the coffee set by the chairs, not showing Lilly how high her eyebrows were raised. Lilly stood in front of the dressing area and once again looked at her reflection, hoping that it wouldn't be as bad as what she saw just minutes ago, but she was sadly disappointed. The reflection in the mirror confirmed the truth. Her skirt was much too short, as it was more than 3 inches above the knee and not appropriate to wear to work. She thought of putting her raincoat back on, but it was the summer she didn't want to welcome any further perspiration. With a quick shrug, she turned on her heels and continued on her way as she had no other choice.

Ah, this must be the place! Lilly thought to herself as she came across the glass door that read Administration in bold black letters. At the front desk, sat a woman who lowered her reading lasses to her nose, to get a focused view on Lilly who stood before her. Her lips parted while her whole face froze. *Oh, no . . . she's noticing too.* Lilly thought, hoping this madness would stop, but it couldn't unless she got rid of her skirt all together—but that would leave her in her underwear and stockings and the reaction for that would not only be raised eyebrows and a frozen face, but escorted out of Sunderland's and on to the streets.

"Hello. . ," Lilly said.

"Hi. . .," the lady said while she kept her expression as icy enough to be plopped into a glass of scotch.

"It's my first day, I believe I have some papers to fill out."

"Oh yes," the woman said as she kept her eyes on Lilly while she reached into her desk to fetch a stack of papers. "You can fill them at the empty desk around the corner."

Lilly thanked the woman as she took the papers with her head slightly lower than usual as one by one, she was being treated like she was a lady of the night.

After she scribbled her name and address, she immediately wrote her ex-husband's name in "next of kin."

"Damn. Habit," Lilly said out loud as she heard the click clack of heels enter the office and a familiar voice speaking to the receptionist.

"Do you know where . . . ah! Thank you" Vivian's voice said, followed by "Good morning, dear!" Vivian announced as she walked toward Lilly.

"Vivian," Lilly looked up from her papers and smiled. She was the perfect distraction to her mistake on her employment papers, but her supposedly too-short skirt was still the star of the show of her first-day jitters. "I've got to fill out those employment forms today before I start," Lilly said as she got up to fix her skirt that was riding up her thighs.

"Oh—Oh!" Vivian said in shock as she laid eyes on her new friend.

"I know. I know. It's my sister's skirt! I didn't realize it was this short!"

"Ah—this can be fixed. Fill out the papers and come see me at my counter."

"Ok, but what are you going to do?" Lilly said as she looked down.

"Don't worry your pretty little head over it, this is as easy as pie to fix—even though I don't bake pies. Ever."

After Lilly finished her paperwork, she decided to risk the added perspiration and put on her coat. Three sets of glaring eyes that burned through her soul a day was her official limit. As soon as Lilly approached the main floor, there was Mr. Sand, with a skirt, in Lilly's size already on a hanger for her.

"It happens to the best of us," Mr. Sand said.

"How did you. . . ?" Lilly asked.

"We all work together."

Lilly took the skirt and walked to the ladies' bathroom to change. As she held it up in front of her and placed it at her waist to see if it was the right length, Vivian popped her head into the washroom.

"Hi—listen, I've got the best idea. You finish up here, and I'll stand in line at the coffee shop. There is still a little bit of time before the store opens. What do you take in your coffee?"

"Do they have those cookies there, too?" Lilly said as she stepped into the skirt and zipped it up while studying her reflection in the bathroom mirror. "Oh, my goodness—How did you know my size?" Lilly asked in shock.

"We all have our talents," Vivian responded while Lilly stood there, with her hands on her hips. "How do I . . . how can I . . ."

"We will work it out later. Consider it loan. Now about that coffee?"

"With a cookie—ah, make it strong!" Lilly said, as she needed that douse of happiness.

"You got it!" Vivian disappeared and zoomed to the coffee shop.

Lilly looked at her reflection in the mirror once again and decided that Mr. Sand and Vivian were her two new favorite people in the world because they just saved her ass. Yes, pun intended.

As Lilly left the ladies room, a fascinating sensation came over her, and she began to feel a few inches taller. Her shoulders were no longer hunched over from the morning's rendezvous from the seamstress and receptionist, but pulled back and she couldn't help but smile. What was the reason for this sudden triumph feeling? Was it because of this brand-new skirt that was on trend? That it was the right size for her? The fact that all the salespeople were stopping to smile at her. While nodding as if they appreciated the way she looked. Well, hold on just a moment there. It very well could be, Lilly thought to herself. Imagine what she could do with the right pair of shoes? For herself? For her customers? All because of a brand-new skirt that not only fitted her perfectly but made her look and feel like a million bucks.

Just before the coffee shop, stood one of the perfume counters. As there were several, scattered throughout the main floor.

How convenient, she thought. The perfect place to test my willpower as the perfume bottles looked so enticing. Lilly just adored perfume, especially the expensive kind, and her old bottle of 4711 that He gave her years ago was left unopened on her dresser. And besides, she didn't want that scent anymore. She stopped to stare at one bottle.

"Want to try it?" a saleswoman asked.

"Oh, no, I can't. I work here."

"All the better! You should really use your perks!"

Lilly looked confused.

"It's a sample."

Lilly still looked confused.

The saleswoman was losing her patience.

"Look, take a spritz whenever you want. I do."

"Whenever I want?"

"Yes!"

"But how?"

"Like this!" The saleswoman took a bottle and sprayed it on her wrist, then smelled the aroma. Her eyes looked up at the ceiling as she smiled.

"You mean, I can sample any one of these just like that?" Lilly felt like she had just won the lottery.

"Oh, my goodness. Yes!" the saleslady said impatiently.

Lilly picked up the Chanel No. 5 and spritzed a little on her wrist. "Thank you."

Lilly headed to the coffee shop. I'm going to like it here, she thought to herself. New skirt. Free perfume. Could it get any better?

At the coffee shop, there were five people in line that morning, and Lilly felt a pang in her chest. Her shift was starting, and even with the pep talk from her sister, and son, the beautiful skirt and the sophisticated scent of Chanel that she wore, she still didn't know what to do. Self-doubt reared its ugly head. How the heck was she going to do this job? She thought.

"Lilly! Over here!" Vivian waved her hand. Lilly walked over to the table and noticed two coffees and two cookies waiting to be devoured.

"Your papers are all filed, and you are ready to go, *Miss Cherries in the Snow*! Oooh, I see you tried on the *Chanel*! Delish, right?" Vivian said in a sing-song voice.

Lilly laughed and took in the warmth and enthusiasm that Vivian carried as she bit into a cookie.

"Which department do you work in, Vivian?"

"Cosmetics. The Revlon counter."

That explained Vivian's knowledge of the Revlon shade of Lilly's lipstick.

"But I won't be there much longer! Just wait, Lilly—wait until you see what I have been up to!" Vivian said with a twinkle in her eye, then glanced at her watch "Geez, will you look at the time? It's almost ten! I got to hustle. And so do you. I'll see you soon."

"Ok," Lilly said as she sipped her coffee. "Jeepers, I'm really going to like it here," she said to herself again. Lilly felt like a queen, enjoying every sip and bite and wondered what Vivian had up her sleeve.

* * *

It was 10:20 a.m. and Lilly reapplied her lipstick, smoothed out her hair and stood up to look at herself in a nearby mirror to see that all was in good form—and it was. She felt relaxed and ready to show everyone what she could do—just like she used to feel before she dove into her math tests at school. As she walked down the aisle, she passed by the perfume counter once again, and waved at the saleswoman who was busy with a customer but took a moment to look up and winked at Lilly, who welcomed the warm gesture to send her on her way to begin her new career.

The shoe department was on the second floor, so Lilly took the escalator. As she reached the floor, she saw a balding man in a three-piece dark brown suit whose face was as purple as a freshly picked beet from her grandmother's farm. He stood by the children's saddle shoes, waiting for her. His fists were clenched by his sides, and his shoulders were at the same level as his ears.

"Ms. Krovchick!" the man shouted in a loud whisper.

Early morning shoppers who were at an earshot began to stare.

"Yes?" Lilly said in fright.

"Come with me," the man said firmly and motioned for her to follow him. They quietly walked together. Lilly could hear her heart beating violently underneath her blouse; she knew that her Odorono deodorant was beginning to fail.

"I'm Mr. Fine, your boss," Mr. Fine said as he took a seat at a small desk in the corner of a cramped office filled with shoe boxes.

"Oh, it's so nice to meet you," Lilly said as she thought that it was a bit odd that she didn't meet her boss before she got hired; however, the word at Sunderland's was to listen to Vivian. Every employee that she brought to Sunderland's was honest, hardworking, and kind. She could read people like a fortuneteller, which translated to an excellent ability in recruiting outstanding employees. She just had great instinct.

Comments such as these were on repeat:
"How did you know that he would work so well here?"
"I just had a hunch."
"How did you find her?"
"I met her at a party, and she really knew her stuff!"

Management threw their hands up in the air and gave in to whatever Vivian suggested, as she proved her point countless times over as she was an expert at reading people—most of the time.

Vivian's word was all fine and dandy, but so far the instinct situation was not going according to plan, and Lilly wondered if she really belonged there. Trying to smile to keep it together, her fear took over and her mind zoomed to the worst—she was going to be fired right then and there. That's it—it was over. Sayonara shoe saleswoman career! Goodbye coffee and euphoric cookies! Au revoir Vivian, Mr. Sand, free stockings, and skirts that fit like gloves. And the worst thought—how was she going to support her children?

"I don't know who you think you are, but no employee of mine comes waltzing in here at 10:23 a.m. on their first day. Customers come in at 10, and I need you to be here at 9:50 a.m. at the latest!"

"But I was filling—"

"Do. Not. Talk back to me, young lady. You know, we don't normally hire Jews."

Lilly's mouth sealed shut as tight as she could, while she felt her face begin to tremble while she fought to keep her tears inside her tear ducts, where they belonged. Lilly closed her eyes and inhaled as if she was taking a drag of her cigarette. Did she ever need one of those now, she thought.

"Mr. Fine. It's my fault. I was with her at the lunch counter."

Mr. Fine's head quickly turned to the entrance way of the office, where Vivian stood, looking straight ahead, like a bear protecting it's young, which was Lilly.

"Oh. I see," Mr. Fine said as he nodded his head.

Lilly began to unclench her mouth and took a deep breath as she realized that she dodged a bullet.

"I will arrive here at 9:45 a.m. from now on and will save the trip to the coffee shop for break time," she said obediently.

"You better. I expect more from you people." Mr. Fine scooped up a handful of shoe boxes that were sitting on a nearby desk and took them away with him as he left.

Lilly looked to the left and furrowed her brows while she thought about the two phrases that stung like hornet stinger, "you people" and the "we don't normally hire Jews." She also thought about the man in the brown hat who told her to go home to her kitchen. Vivian walked up to Lilly and put her hand on her shoulder. "Just do what he says," she said as she scurried off to her post, leaving Lilly, standing there, in the office shoe department with a handful of questions that were not going to be answered anytime soon.

Vivian: Let the Sunshine in

On a bus ride home a few days after Ms. Linton's visit, Vivian thought about what Mr. Sand suggested and took his advice. To let the hypnotizing sales experience simmer in her mind and see what becomes of it. To be honest, she could not stop thinking how silly the whole situation was. Why would someone want to purchase a whole new face powder and lipstick just for a weekend away? Especially when they already had a brand new one that probably did not even have a dent in it yet.

"Hi, how was your day?" Miriam greeted Vivian at the front door.

"Oh, I forgot to tell you, we hired a new girl, about my age. She seems nice," Vivian said nonchalantly completely distracted by her other thoughts.

"That's terrific! It's always great to work with other girls your age, so you can go on double dates together!" Miriam excitingly said, still hoping that Vivian would meet someone one day.

"Yes, that would be fun," Vivian agreed, even though she didn't care. At that point, there was no sense in arguing with her mother as she was not going to win, and her mother would just get upset. Besides, she had larger fish to fry.

Vivian walked right past her mother and threw her purse on the coat rack, only for it to fall on the floor.

"VIVIAN! Really. The butler quit, pick it up."

Vivian ignored her and continued to walk to her bathroom in a trance. Lipstick and powder.

Lipstick and powder. Travel. She repeatedly said as she took off her work clothes, got into her bathrobe and slippers and walked to the bathroom.

"What has gotten into you?" Miriam asked and the story with Mrs. Linton was retold as Vivian sprinkled baking soda into her bath, stepped into it, and sunk her body up to her chin, while ending her tale with "And now I can't stop thinking about it."

Miriam looked straight at Vivian and crinkled up her nose to ingest the scenario. "Interesting."

"Don't do that, mother; it will ruin your complexion," Vivian responded.

***

The next day, Vivian awoke extra early as she spent the night tossing and turning. So much was on her mind that when the clock read 5:15, she decided to get out of bed. After she dressed in a hurry, grabbed an apple from the fridge, and shoved it in her purse, she quickly wrote a note to let her parents know that she had extra inventory to do.

Arriving at Sunderland's too early for the doors to be opened, Vivian walked to a nearby diner to get a cup of coffee, but it was a huge disappointment after the first few sips as it tasted as if the pot had been sitting on the burner for weeks. A couple of doses of sugar and cream did the trick, and off she went to walk the empty streets, inhaling the Montreal summer morning weather. Not too warm, with a hint of a cool breeze. As she closed her eyes to push away her thoughts, she relished in the moment that all she had to think about was herself. No one was asking her to count inventory or do the dishes at home. *All I have to do right now is just be. Why don't I do this more often*, she thought to herself.

As soon as her wristwatch turned to 8, she thought she would take the chance and see if anyone was at the store. With a lighter feeling in her head, she walked briskly as her stomach began to growl. It was time for a cup of real coffee and a breakfast Danish from the lunch counter.

As Vivian reached the front doors, she leaned against the glass to hunt for a familiar face. "Ah—goodie!" she happily whispered to herself as she saw Mr. Sand standing by the hat display. Vivian knocked on the glass door and caught his attention.

Mr. Sand gave Vivian a look that read *What brings you here so early* as he fiddled with the locks to open the door for her.

"Couldn't sleep. Too much on my mind."

"The lunch counter will open momentarily—shall we?" Mr. Sand said, which made Vivian stand on her tippy toes to hug him. Startled at first, Mr. Sand did not reciprocate, but then slowly put his arms around Vivian, as he knew what he was offering was just what she needed. And together, in an empty department store, sat Mr. Sand listening to everything that was on Vivian's mind.

The floodgate of tears that released delicious laughter came quickly, which lifted Vivian's spirits to no end, as her head became clearer, and she felt calmer. She knew Mr. Sand wanted to tell her something as he was fidgeting in his seat, looking as if he was about to burst. "You've got to find out a way to make this work! If Mrs. Linton wants a separate makeup collection for travel, hundreds.... I mean thousands of other women would want this too."

"But how?" Vivian asked, looking like a lost deer in the forest.

"Darling, I have no idea, but why not do a little research," Mr. Sand instructed, knowing very well that Vivian was no stranger to this task. Years of reading *Vogue* magazine, taking correspondence courses and visiting Sunderland's often enough that Mr. Sand recognized her snooping around before her official job interview just a few years ago. Vivian began to nod and take it all in.

"Yeah, I could research," she said with certainty.

"Of course, you can," he assured her.

And with a half hour to spare before she had to begin to clean the counter where she stood for eight hours, she walked the aisles of Sunderland's to get a closer look to what they were selling and what they were missing. And on her way home, she would take the long way and walk past drugstores, walk in and study the packaging of creams, lotions and cosmetics. Then she would walk to another department store and see what and how they were selling their merchandise.

As soon as Vivian placed her key to unlock the front door of her home, and placed one step into her foyer, her mother said, "You're late! I was worried!"

"Sorry, research," Vivian replied, hesitating because she very well knew that those two words would not be enough for her mother, as more details were wanted. Already rolling her eyes as her mother began to speak as the interrogation was on its way.

"Research for what?" her mother asked, not skipping a beat.

"A new line the store is thinking of buying," she proudly said, which was half true.

After dinner, Vivian would study the pages of her fashion magazines. Not only *Vogue*, but *Chatelaine*, *Good Housekeeping* and *Life* and get lost in the many advertisements and editorials. Putting her social life on hold as she had to get to the bottom of this.

"What kind of life are you having, with no time for fun?" Miriam asked.

"I need to create something—I can't be distracted!" Vivian replied as she carefully read the pages of her magazine on her favorite spot in the house. In the middle of the hallway, on the very same rug she laid on when she was a little girl.

"Make what?"

"A travel set—a collection of cosmetics for travel," Vivian said.

"Is that because of that one fancy customer you told me about last week?"

"Yes—Mrs. Linton started the fire."

"But why make such a thing? And how are you going to do it? You're just a young girl who works in a department store," Miriam asked while Vivian shrunk slowly into the fibers of the carpet she lay on. These series of questions, along with the final disintegrating comment that expressed her mother's vision of her daughter felt as if a kettle of boiling water was poured on top of her head. For the first time, Vivian was speechless as she stared straight ahead into space.

"Well, you are very dedicated," her father noted, as he knew that he had to say something after his wife's commentary.

"It's not like she's joining a biker gang," Marsha commented while her mother nodded in agreement.

"Ooh—that would be fun," Vivian joked, as she sat up from reading her magazine, hugging her shoulders, as to self soothe herself from her mother's comments that still burned.

"Don't encourage her!" Miriam said to everyone while Henry raised an eyebrow. "Miriam, what's the problem?"

"The problem?" Miriam shrieked as Vivian decided to go back to her magazine on the carpet, where she felt safe and happy.

"We're waiting, mother," Vivian announced, from the floor, flipping the pages of her magazine and losing patience.

"What happened to meeting men and dating?"

"Yeah—I've been on a few dates. Meh—to tell you the truth, they bore me," Vivian sighed, which made Miriam turn several shades redder than normal.

"Bore you? What are you expecting, fireworks? I've got news for you—that doesn't happen in real life. Henry—tell your daughter she's out of her mind!"

"I am not out of my mind. I am focused!" Vivian announced.

"The problem is that our daughter is a hermit!" Miriam exclaimed, which made Vivian whip her head away from her reading to glare at her mother with piercing eyes.

"Henry, do something before our daughter becomes an old maid!"

"I. Am. Not. A. Hermit," Vivian slowly said, with clenched teeth. "And I am not an old maid. That's for sure," Vivian said as she flipped her hair off her face to continue reading, but she really couldn't read anymore because she lost her focus and began to bite her lower lip, which of course, ruined her lipstick. This fiasco was driving her up the wall and more importantly, was interrupting her research time. As Miriam's voice kept going on and on, Vivian tuned out by staring at a Coty advertisement for face powder, admiring the beautiful container, and the pretty model that held it. When will she shut up? Vivian thought to herself. When she finally did, Vivian held her head in her hands and breathed deeply.

Why couldn't she understand how important this project was for her? How she was going to change thousands of women's lives by making traveling with their makeup easier for them. How rich she was going to get. To be known all around her community—her country or even the world that Vivian Stein invented *this*. Why couldn't her mother see how amazing that would be? But what really upset Vivian the most was the fact that she felt that her mother did not approve of what she was doing and did not believe that she could invent something like this. That hurt the most.

"Miriam, you are overreacting," Henry reassured his wife as he placed his hands on his waist. Marsha sat down next to her sister, as she began to feel sorry for her as she knew that it was no fun to witness their mother lose it, and she was really losing it.

That was it. Vivian had to drop the bomb and say what was on her mind, as it was the only way.

"If I was a boy, you would be singing a different song."

"But you're not a boy. You are supposed *to meet* a boy! Get married. Have children. What are you doing?"

"What makes me happy. Look, I don't want to get married!"

"But why not?" her mother yelled.

"Why do I have to?"

"Because you do! That's what people do!"

"So why do I have to do what people do?"

"That's a great question," Marsha pointed out. Henry shrugged and Miriam left the hallway and walked into the kitchen to pour herself a Sherry.

***

Several weeks later, with gusto and extra makeup underneath her eyelids to hide the dark circles, Vivian walked into the department store promptly at eight-thirty a.m. Bursting with excitement, as she had big plans to share her idea with Mr. Sand. Her research was finally complete.

She motioned for him to come to her counter to talk to her as she polished the sample tray and countertops before the customers began to arrive.

"What? What's the bee in your bonnet?" Mr. Sand asked.

Vivian explained her creation as Mr. Sand listened and beamed with pride.

"Oh my! This is fantastic! How are you going to create this?"

"I have some ideas. Come with me to tell Elaine!"

Lilly: A New Year's Risky Request—1951

Life at the department store became a welcoming routine for Lilly. Her boss, Mr. Fine needed staff during the weekday while Lilly's kids were at school, which worked perfectly.

On Sundays, Sunderland's was closed, which was a huge bonus for everyone, especially those who attended church, which was not the case for Lilly.

It was September of 1951, and the Jewish New Year, Rosh Hashanah, was coming up in a few weeks. That year, it was celebrated on the evening of Sunday, September 30th, and ended on Tuesday, October 2. Lilly needed to go to synagogue on Monday and Tuesday, so she decided to wait as long as possible to ask for those two days off because she was too scared to ask. She had just begun her job, and already made Mr. Fine turn beet red on her first day. What was next? Making him turn purple like an eggplant?

For the first week of working in the shoe department, Lilly was instructed to watch other salespeople so that she could learn the name brands and get familiar with the storeroom where there were hundreds of shoe boxes neatly organized. Lilly wanted to learn the best way to go about finding each pair.

Hardly any contact with the customers was required, as Mr. Fine didn't trust her yet and she didn't mind. What she was doing was easy and fun, as she learned fast and got along very well with the other employees.

"So far so good!" Lilly reported back to her sister on the phone one evening after work. "They don't want to kill me, yet!"

"Did you ask to get Rosh Hashanah off?"

"Are you kidding?" Lilly joked.

"Do it, Lilly! It's your right."

"I know, I know. . ." Lilly sighed.

On the first day of the second week, Lilly was hoping to begin selling shoes to the customers, but that was not what Mr. Fine had in mind. Instead, she was given a job that didn't involve selling shoes at all.

"Come with me," Mr. Fine said to Lilly as she put away her purse and packed lunch in the employee locker room. They both walked through the hallway and passed the women's and men's shoe department. Other salespeople watched Mr. Fine and Lilly as they walked past them, nodding, and smiling, as if they knew where she was going.

Lilly heard footsteps behind her. It was Vivian.

"Take a break when your arms get tired," she said, as she knew that Lilly was going to have a similar initiation as she had—and she was correct.

Lilly looked at her and furrowed her eyebrows in confusion.

"Get back to your post, Vivian. She'll be all right," Mr. Fine said. Lilly wondered where she was going. Her stomach turned the way it used to feel before a test at school she didn't study for. Which only happened once in her life—but she never forgot that feeling, even though she ended up with the highest score in her class.

Mr. Fine opened a door that led them to a staircase, and his feet quickly tickled the stairs as if he was flying over them. Lilly tried her best to catch up with him.

"Ah, here we are!"

Lilly looked around her. She was in some sort of basement. It was damp and dark, compared to the bright lights of the department store. However, it was nice and cool in the basement, which was a welcome retreat from the summer heat.

"It is nice and cool down here, you may want to pack a sweater. Well, you can bring one with you tomorrow, I suppose," Mr. Fine said.

Lilly looked confused.

"A sweater you wouldn't mind getting a little dirty."

Lilly's eyebrows raised as she tried to guess the task, she would be doing in this cold basement. Alone and unsupervised.

"See all this?" Mr. Fine pointed to a wall of shoe boxes.

"Yes," Lilly answered.

"You are going to take each shoe box off the shelf, dust the box, clean the shelf, and then make sure that each box has the right pair. Same size, style, and name brand. *Capisce*?"

Lilly nodded and smiled as she sadly came to terms with what was just explained and expected. Not the most glamorous job, but an initiation, she supposed, that probably Vivian had to go through as well when she first began—hence the advice she gave her of resting her arms.

While standing on her tippy toes, Lilly scanned the top shelf to the bottom and thought about how long the job would take her. She decided that she would finish by lunch time, at the most.

"And then when you are finished with this area of shelves, you will proceed to the next area and so on, and so on," Mr. Fine said as he walked to another part of the basement.

Lilly's eyes widened as she followed Mr. Fine around the corner. Her heart dropped to the floor as there were at least ten separate shelves full of shoe boxes.

"Yes, there are quite a number of boxes here, with very dusty shelves!" Mr. Fine looked around and smiled. "It's been a while since we had a new girl with us to do this sort of, um, I guess you could call, initiation?" Mr. Fine said with a chuckle.

Lilly smiled politely.

Her eyes continued to scan the shoeboxes as her jaw slightly opened from shock. She decided that she had no idea when she was going to finish this job.

"The cleaning supplies are under the sink over there," Mr. Fine said as he pointed to the corner bathroom.

Lilly closed her mouth and nodded.

"You can use the bathroom, of course. And have your twenty-minute lunch break."

Lilly nodded again.

"See you later," Mr. Fine said, and walked away, leaving her alone in the basement.

"Bye," Lilly softly said as Mr. Fine's footsteps quietly vanished.

Lilly brought her hands to her head to push her hair away from her face and looked around. There was a rectangular window just above the first bookshelf that let in the morning light. She gazed at the window, wishing she was on the other side, in the park with her kids. She took a deep breath, remembering the scent of each one of her children as she kissed them goodbye that morning. Tears formed in her eyes that blinked away and trickled down her cheek.

Housework. Lilly thought. She was used to it, as it was part of being a mother and housewife for the past ten years. Every Sunday was cleaning day in her home. The outfit? The ugliest most unflattering pair of slacks she could find in her closet paired with an old shirt that had old sweat stains that couldn't come out in the wash. Lilly rolled up the sleeves and pant cuffs, as she exposed her bare feet and ankles. Next, she tied her hair up in a handkerchief and swiped some Vaseline on her lips, as they got dry from the physical labour. There was no point in wasting good lipstick on cleaning day.

As soon as her handkerchief was fastened on her head, downstairs to her basement she'd go to fetch her bucket of soap and water, old towels, bleach, and sponges so that she could scrub the house from top to bottom. Of course, cleaning day could not be completed without music, and Lilly had all the latest records, and if she didn't have them, she would make sure to borrow some from her sister the evening before. "It's cleaning day—I need some great songs to scrub with," she would announce on the telephone, and her sister was more than happy to lend them to her like a borrowed casserole dish.

As for the kids? They knew to get out of the house as fast as they could on Sunday morning, to avoid being assigned a cleaning job. This worked most of the time, but once the music was playing, they didn't mind sticking around the house to fold towels, especially if she played some Tony Bennett on the record player.

A thump was heard from the ceiling that brought her back to where she was, and what she needed to do. Lilly touched her hair and looked around for a handkerchief of some kind but was out of luck. Luckily, she had an elastic on her wrist from the newspaper that morning, so she wrapped her hair into a bun with it, rolled up her sleeves, and went to collect the cleaning supplies.

As she placed the bucket at her feet and scanned the height of the bookshelf, a familiar voice entered her head encouraging her to come up with a plan.

"Dust falls from the top, so it's best to start cleaning from the top shelf." This advice came from her mother, who had told her this method when she would work at her store after school, as dust was not a welcome guest in a grocery store. "Nobody will buy these canned goods if they're dirty."

"Oh mother—your advice is ingrained in my mind!" Lilly caught herself saying out loud. She was relieved she was alone; while shaking her head in disbelief, she couldn't believe she had just responded to a voice inside her head. But the memory got the best of her, and she giggled and came to a realization. How appreciative she was toward her mother. The advice that entered her mind that morning was used every time she cleaned her own home, and now it would prove useful to her again at the job she had to get due to her current situation. *Shit, she knew her stuff.*

Lilly didn't have her record player with her, so she hummed instead. She then picked up that first shoe box and began her mission: to tackle one full shelf each day, starting at the top and making her way down. She needed to do whatever it took to finish the job properly, as there really was no rush.

Taking care of the basement shoe boxes soon became a pattern that created a sort of thrill, so to speak. Even though she only cleaned her home once a week, she never saw dust like this before. The amount that she collected on her cloth from the dust on the shelves was thick and dark. She made a sour face and whined "Eeeewww" as she dumped the debris into the wastebasket. After that job was done, she would open the shoe box and check the shoes. If not matched, just as Mr. Fine requested, she put the pair aside. The real thrill came when she found the matching shoe to the orphaned one.

"Yay, I found it!" she announced aloud while placing the pair together. "You found your partner," she would happily say to the shoes before placing the box back on the cleaned shelf.

Nobody heard her, so she didn't care.

She then she'd begin the next row. And the next. And the pattern went like this,

Lift

Spritz

Wipe

Eeeeewww

Plop

Check

Yay!

The pattern repeated over and over until her stomach growled as it was lunch time and she had completed half of the first unit of shelves. As she washed her hands in the bathroom sink, she felt accomplished, even though the task was as mundane as it was.

Once she opened the basement door to the shoe department, Vivian was waiting for her with her lunch bag.

"How did it go?" Vivian asked, looking concerned while playing with the pearls around her neck.

"You know, not that bad; I've got a system," Lilly said proudly.

Vivian smiled back like a proud parent and said, "We've all been there."

"I figured!"

"How did you pass the time?"

"My mother's cleaning advice, music from my head and the uncanny thrill of cleaning dust as thick as cream cheese," Lilly said proudly.

"Darling, you are a natural. Why don't we discuss this over lunch? Coffee's my treat." Vivian said as she put her arm around Lilly and the two of them enjoyed their lunch together for the full 20 minutes that were allocated.

For the next nine days, to the basement Lilly went to finish the job with her least favorite wool cardigan in tow. She didn't have a care in the world if it got dirty, as it had many holes that could not be sewn.

Mr. Fine came to inspect the shoe shelves from time to time. He didn't say much, except an *un huh* or an *okay*, which Vivian diagnosed as a good thing—and she was right.

The request to get two days off for Rosh Hashanah was quickly approaching. On the last day of the shoe box shelf-cleaning job, just before the last three rows needed to be done, as terrifying as it was, Lilly finally spoke to Mr. Fine.

Lilly bit her lip while she knocked on his office door.

The Most Amazing Department Store

"Yes? "Mr. Fine said through his closed door. Lilly opened it and gave the happiest smile she could muster to her boss, which was probably on the boarder of fake as the nervousness took away any sign of authenticity. "Are you done?"

"Almost."

"Then, what are you doing here? Go back downstairs and finish the job."

"Oh, I will, I just need to ask you something," Lilly bashfully said as Mr. Fine stared straight ahead, waiting impatiently, as he tapped his pen on his papers.

"If you will, Mr. Fine," Lilly began.

"Yes?" Mr. Fine responded, waiting Lilly to ask her question, but then frustratingly looked down at his accounting books, as this encounter was going nowhere, and Lilly was wasting his time.

"The Jewish New Year—Rosh Hashanah—is coming up next week. I was wondering if I could miss work so I could go to synagogue."

"Why can't you just go on a Sunday when the store is closed?" Mr. Fine responded but didn't look up from his papers.

"Because that's not when Rosh Hashana is."

"Well, why can't you just celebrate it on another day?"

Lilly stared straight ahead, not knowing what to say except, "That's like asking you to celebrate Christmas on the twenty-third of December!"

Mr. Fine's head sprang up from his books like a bobble-head toy to face Lilly. His eyes were piercing. "Excuse me?"

Lilly decided that she shouldn't have made a Christmas comparison. "I'm sorry, Mr. Fine. It's an important holiday."

Mr. Fine glared to the left. His lips were sealed so tightly that you could see a white rim around them. He then got up and walked away.

"Mr. Fine? Does that mean I can have it off?" Lilly asked, and wondered if she was just fired. She thought about it, and it didn't

Lilly: A New Year's Risky Request—1951

make sense to her. Why shouldn't she take off a Jewish holiday? She would totally work on Christmas. To her, that was just like any other day. She slumped on the wall and stared at the ceiling.

"Oh, my goodness," Vivian said behind her back.

Lilly turned her head to see her.

"I can't believe you asked to take days off for the high holidays."

Lilly raised her eyebrows.

"I have worked here for years, and I never asked for that."

"Why would you?"

"I'm Jewish too," Vivian whispered.

An immediate bond was felt by Lilly, which relaxed her shoulders, and made her eyes soften. A common background of rituals and spirituality was shared regardless of the degree of practice. At least that was what Lilly felt, as she wondered why Vivian didn't ask to attend synagogue during the holiest holiday of the year.

"Why don't you ask too?" Lilly prompt.

"I don't want to blow my cover, as I was told to keep quiet about it."

"Cover? Why are you hiding?"

"We shouldn't advertise it."

"Says who? Why do you have to hide from it."

"People don't like Jews period."

"But why?"

"You're new here—you have no idea."

Rosh Hashana and Yom Kippur arrived and miraculously, both girls were given the days off, but without pay. Mr. Fine may have had a narrow mind and a short temper, but he was fair. He ran out of his office that afternoon to speak to the administration, where he asked what the proper accommodations were for the situation.

And Vivian was right, as Lilly didn't know what it was like to be a Jewish woman in a department store in the early 1950s in Montreal as it was only her second week, but she learned quickly. Later that evening, Lilly's telephone rang.

"I need to continue what we were talking about. It wasn't fair that I dropped that comment on you about hiding who I am, without explaining," Vivian blurted out, without even saying hello first.

"Go on," Lilly encouraged, while the two ladies spoke through three cigarettes for Lilly and a whole row of brownies, eaten directly out of the pan for Vivian along with several nose honks into a tissue.

"How could you face Mme. Tremblay and Elaine after they said those things to you?"

"I don't know, I guess I just wanted to be at Sunderland's so badly, I just swallowed their comments and shat them out when I got home."

"Does anyone else go through stuff like this at work?"

"Hard to say, as I am the only one of my friends who works in retail. Although I do have a friend who is in pharmacy school that told me that his Christian classmates give him the missed notes whenever he takes off for the Jewish holidays. Without even asking. Just like that."

"Just like that, huh."

"Yeah. Just like that."

Breakfast at Beauty's

Saturday was the best day to work at Sunderland's. No deliveries were made to the store, not any inventory work or cleaning was expected, as that was the day of the week where it was all about the customer and how many times you could make that cash register ring. The department store got super busy on this day, and extra help was needed in every department. On those Saturdays that Lilly had custody of her children and needed to be in the store, the kids spent the day at their cousins'.

Each week, Lilly carefully saved up a part of her salary, along with her employee discount, and brought home a new toy for her kids. Either a new train set or a new doll. The hours she spent away from home was taking a toll on her conscience and hitting the red mark on the guilt meter, each day. Thankfully, family was nearby so their uncles and aunts would scoop them up from home to add them to their herd. In winter it was tobogganing and in the summer, they would turn on the sprinkler in their backyard. Lilly's middle son had a fascination with marbles, which kept him, his cousins, and the neighborhood kids busy for hours. *He really seems to have a knack for collecting a crowd*, she thought to herself one day as she wiped away his milk mustache, knowing a bunch of kids were outside their front door waiting for him to come out and play.

And then, a rare and enticing opportunity came up for Vivian, and she decided to take her new friend with her.

"What do you think of dining at Beauty's on the occasional Wednesday, sponsored by Sunderland's?" she asked Lilly as she was holding a stack of shoe boxes, which she dropped on the floor from shock.

"We would be observing what was out there," Vivian said as she crouched down to help her clean up the shoes from the floor while noticing the perfect black patent leather pump, wondering if it came in her size.

"Come again?" Lilly asked.

"We would go for brunch at Beauty's and study the clientele. You know, what they are wearing and stuff. Technically, we are still working, and we have to write a report for what we saw for the following day for the buyers."

Lilly's eyes exploded with enthusiasm, which meant yes, please! Having lunch at her favorite diner in the city was a welcome break from working eight hour shifts five days a week. Not rushing to the store meant that she could enjoy a "normal" morning while her kids got ready for school. And she could be there when they got home! And serve them milk and cookies, just like the rest of the moms of the world did! Getting to go to Beauty's for lunch—on Sunderland's tab? What will she order? Lilly's mouth began to water and wondered how much smoked salon she could cram on a bagel. Did she just die and get to heaven?

This time was a far cry from their usual routine of gobbling down their lunch and smoking a cigarette in the 20 minutes they were allocated for lunch each work day. Somebody else waited on them. Refilled their coffee cups. A delightful treat, indeed, and Lilly was more than game.

As soon the clock struck ten, one Wednesday morning, Vivian picked up Lilly in her mother's light pink Chevrolet, that everyone called The Powder Puff and off the two ladies went, dressed impeccably for brunch, just as if they were going to work, because they were, so to speak. The dates were a time to enjoy the food and the company, but also to conduct research and Lilly and Vivian thought that this little game was the most fun. Just as they got their food ordered, with a double order of smoked salmon for Lilly, and were sipping their coffees, they began to study the ladies who lunch.

And if they were lucky, which they were most of the time, a few prime prospects would enter the restaurant.

As nonchalant as they could manage, their eyes would dart back and forth, up and down to inspect what shoes, coat, blouse, sweater and shade of lipstick they were wearing. Did they like what they saw? Were the ladies wearing the garments properly and did it suit their figure and why did some women button their blouses to the top and others wore a pin? Most importantly, they wanted to know if they were wearing the fashions and cosmetics that Sunderland sold. If they weren't sure and they liked what they saw, one of them would walk up to their table and begin the interrogation. Most of the time, the investigation was well received, and the ladies would find out what the competition was selling and head straight to their buyer on Thursday morning to share the full report. But on other days, it went something like this.

"Viv, here comes a goodie!" Lilly said. Two women walked into the restaurant and sat down at the booth behind Vivian. "Oh, you go. I want to finish the pudding," Lilly joked as they were demolishing Beauty's famous rice pudding dessert, over their third cup of coffee. It was a slow day, and they didn't see anyone worth inspecting, until their pudding was served to them after Vivian enjoyed a lunch of half a tuna and half and salmon salad sandwich, while Lilly had her usual bagel and a smoked salmon tower, which was prepared by the owner's wife Freda.

"No, you go—*I* want the pudding," Vivian said, without turning around, as to not seem so obvious.

"Oh alright," Lilly said as she wiped her mouth with her napkin and then reached for her purse to fetch for her lipstick and a compact mirror. As she opened the compact, she paused and said, "Ok—the lady on the left is wearing a pair of shoes that I want myself. The heel is perfect."

"Oooh—I can't wait to see! Find out all the juicy details!" Vivian said in a loud whisper while Lilly swiped on a fresh coat of lipstick.

Vivian encouraged Lilly with a wink as she smoothed her hair with her hands and stood up to straighten her skirt. Click, clack, click went her heels as she walked over to the next booth where two ladies, who were dressed as if they were going to a dinner party sat having brunch, too.

Without a hair out of place and makeup tastefully applied, there was an aura of confidence at this table. Approaching these ladies didn't intimidate Lilly in the least bit, as she was used to the certain type of woman who walked into Sunderland's.

Vivian slowly turned around and immediately noticed that she had served one of the women before and helped her choose the rouge she was wearing. It looks great on her, she thought, felt proud and continued to watch Lilly interact with them.

By the time Lilly stood at the front of their table, both stopped sipping their coffees to gaze up at this stranger, yet an enticing one at that. Vivian looked on, as if she was watching her favorite TV show.

"Hello ladies. I am sorry for interrupting, and I hope you are all enjoying your lunch. I couldn't help but notice your shoes," Lilly said to one of the women.

"My shoes?" the woman asked.

"Yes. Where did you get them? I would love a pair, they are gorgeous!"

"Paris," the woman said, snootily.

"Paris! Oh my. I guess I won't be getting a pair then, as it's a little too far from here," Lilly giggled.

"No. No you won't. Especially with that nose."

"I beg your pardon?" Lilly questioned sternly.

"Nothing," the woman replied while Lilly stood there feeling distraught as she looked back at Vivian in shock. The message was read loud and clear, and Vivian got up to walk to the table for back up.

"Oh, I know you! You work at Sunderland's! You helped me find this fabulous rouge I'm wearing!" said the woman who sported the perfect hue on her cheeks, thanks to Vivian.

"I thought you looked familiar! So nice to see you again," Vivian gushed. At least that answered one of their missions, but they were far from done.

"I'm so glad you are enjoying it, as it looks beautiful on you. Really brings out your complexion. Brightens your whole face!" Vivian warmly said.

"Oh, thank you!" The woman replied smiling as though she was given a present she didn't like.

"Hey, don't be so friendly to them," the Paris shopper told her friend, which was followed by a silence so thick you couldn't cut it with a bagel knife.

"What's wrong with being friendly? Lilly asked.

"Nothing at all. To certain people."

"What do you mean, certain people?" Lilly asked with a raised voice.

The ladies at the booth each placed a hand under their chin and stared straight ahead at Vivian and Lilly and didn't crack a smile. Their silence spoke for them. Vivian and Lilly were distraught, and quietly walked away to pay for their bill at the cash register.

"Why didn't we say something better?" Lilly wined to Vivian on their way home in The Powder Puff.

"We'll get them next time."

"Why do they think all Jews have big noses? I do not have a big nose," Lilly said as she pulled down the passenger vanity mirror to inspect her face.

"No, you don't, it's a beautiful nose," Vivian said in a warm tone, reaching out to squeeze Lilly's arm.

"Yes, it is."

In silence, the two ladies drove to the top of Mount Royal Park. Got out of the car and enjoyed the breathtaking view that overlooked the city.

Vivian, The Kennedy's Don't Live in Canada.

Two weeks later, with a typed presentation and a large cardboard that was decorated with magazine pictures of women traveling in cars, trains, and even airplanes, Vivian and Mr. Sand were set to present the idea of the Travel Set in the department store office at 7:30 in the morning, so as to not disrupt Vivian's and Mr. Sand's shifts.

The presentation ensemble, if you please: One elegant crepe navy blue knee-length skirt and matching blazer and a silk white blouse, framed with a strand of pearls, simple solitaire pearl earrings, and the perfect shade of red lipstick, called Love That Red. Her hair was pulled away from her face, so as to not distract her or anyone else, and tied back in a bun, secured with a gold hairpin that was handed down from her grandmother.

"This should bring you good luck," her mother said to her as she twirled the pin in mid-air as Vivian was styling her hair that morning in her bedroom. "May I?" her mother asked, while Vivian's face lit up as if her own grandmother, whom she never met, was giving her the hairpin herself. As she bent down a few inches so her mother could reach her head to accommodate her mother's petite frame, to fasten the hairpin in place, Vivian backed away a few feet and raised her hands to her sides. "Voila!"

"You're going to be smashing!" her mother announced while clapping her hands together, while they both laughed.

"Thanks, mom," Vivian said, while a wave of happiness hugged her. She finally felt supported.

The Travel Set was a plastic transparent case, filled with five items: a cleanser, face cream, pressed powder, mascara, and a neutral shade of lipstick, one that was not too red and not too orange—a daunting task to find the right color, after Vivian tried on about fifty shades on her wrists. Of course, there was still room to add in a rouge and a nail polish if the customer so inclined. This Travel Set contained the standard basics that every woman needed while traveling.

One final trip to the Sunderland's ladies' room, to make sure not a hair was out of place, nor a smudge of lipstick was seen on a tooth. Vivian stared into the mirror and smiled at herself.

"Go," she said out loud and didn't care if anyone was in the stalls.

"Go where?" said a female voice from a bathroom stall. "Vivian, is that you?"

"It sure is," Vivian answered to one of the salesgirls from the floor as she exited the ladies room en route to the boardroom where she was going to change the world.

The room sat six balding men and Elaine around a large boardroom table. The men were smoking pipes and cigars while Elaine was smoking a cigarette. Coffee and cookies from Sunderland's coffee stand were placed in the middle of the table, that Vivian purchased from her own pocket, earlier that morning but was given a generous discount as the coffee shop manager knew what these refreshments were for. "Go, get 'em Viv!" She told her young and tenacious cosmetician as she walked away, profusely thanking the manager, and giggling with excitement.

Vivian, The Kennedy's Don't Live in Canada.

Vivian began her presentation by introducing herself in a shaky voice, but eventually relaxed when she began to repeat the story that was experienced at the Revlon counter with Mrs. Linton only a month ago. With a prepared typed script, research was shared that she found from visiting drugstores, other department stores and magazines while she pointed to the pictures that were posted on her cardboard. Although Vivian didn't need to read from her script, as she knew it by heart. And so did her parents, as they heard her rehearsing for days in her bedroom each evening until that very day. Mr. Sand piped in and shared a few thoughts on the clientele that entered the store and what they were buying.

After Mr. Sand finished talking, Vivian put her Bristol board down on a chair and waited. The presentation was over, and the room fell silent. Vivian's heart wouldn't stop pounding through her chest and her mouth felt as if she had a cotton ball in it as she waited for someone in the audience to speak. All that was heard was the puffing of cigars, the occasional cough, and Elaine tapping her fingernails on the desk. One man got up and helped himself to a cup of coffee and a cookie.

"My, these are so good. What do they put in them?" he asked with a mouthful.

"These types of women do come into the store!" Vivian blurted out, trying to make sure the topic wouldn't sway from her presentation to the cookies they sold at Sunderland's.

"The Kennedys don't live in Canada, Vivian," the cookie monster spoke while chewing, while helping himself to another.

All the men laughed.

Elaine gazed at Vivian and the men who sat beside her, and put her cigarette out in a nearby ashtray, crossed her arms, and didn't smile or frown. Vivian began to panic, as that comment wasn't funny at all. She knew that there were women out there, like Mrs. Linton, that needed a Travel Set exactly like the one she envisioned. She racked her brain to say something. "Women travel. To their country homes an hour from Montreal or across the border to Vermont to ski," Vivian bravely said, feeling pleased with her additional comment.

"Mmm-hmmm," one of the balding men smoking a pipe grunted, placing Vivian back in her spot, where she was jumping up and down inside yelling *someone believe me!*

"You're talking about 1 percent of the population here," another man said.

"Thank you, sweetheart, for taking the time to present to us today. You are very cute," said one man as he smiled at Vivian as if she was six years old.

"I'm cute?" Vivian questioned, feeling incredibly insulted.

"You are adorable. Everyone loves you around here. You come into work each morning, all bright-eyed and bushy tailed and ready to take on the world! The crowds of women that come in here to listen to what you have to say about makeup is quite impressive," one man said.

"To top it all off, you are in your early twenties! We really love that about you and want you to keep doing what you're doing," said another man.

"That's just it! I deal with these women all day and I know what they want!"

"Really? Did they all tell you that they wanted this particular Travel Set?" asked a man, which caught Vivian off guard, as he was right. Only Mrs. Linton asked for it, while the rest of the clientele wanted their regular order. A lipstick here. A face powder there. There was no mention of a Travel Set from any other woman. Vivian was at a loss of words.

"Vivian, did any other woman want a Travel Set?" The man said again.

"No, sir."

"Well, there you have it," the man said as he raised and lowered his hands.

Vivian whipped her head to her right to meet Mr. Sand's hazel eyes, hoping he would hand her a life preserver to keep from drowning, but there was nothing to hang on to, except for a warm smile while he shrugged his shoulders, which she took, as an empathetic gesture was desperately needed.

"Uh, ok," Vivian softly said, as she walked out of the boardroom, shaking, holding her Bristol board under her arm and the script in one of her hands. As she closed the door behind her, she walked a couple of feet away, and stopped once she got to a corner, not knowing where to go. Her Bristol board and script fell from her hands onto the floor, and she watched them lie there. Motionless, as if they had been shot with a gun.

Mr. Sand caught up with Vivian. "Where did you disappear to?" He picked up her wounded presentation materials.

"Oh, I just needed some air," Vivian responded, looking away, quickly wiping away a tear. This was partially true, as Vivian's disappointed and crushed thoughts needed somewhere to evaporate.

"You did great in there," Mr. Sand sweetly said, studying Vivian to make sure she was alright, and handed back her things. He knew she was not.

"Yeah," Vivian said while playing nervously with her pearl necklace, trying to force a smile, but couldn't. The click clack of heels were coming closer, and Vivian knew who it was, and she closed her eyes to breathe deeply to gather strength to face her, begging her tears to not move down her cheeks.

"Hey... you guys gave it your best shot. Really, they know their stuff there. It won't work. Look, if a woman comes in and wants another face powder or lipstick, or a face cream, sell it to her, no matter if you sold her the same one the day before," Elaine told Vivian, and Mr. Sand. Vivian felt as if Elaine was handing over a consolation prize that would be as welcome as a vacuum cleaner for Mother's Day.

"Okay, sure, right," Vivian whispered while still trying to smile, but her mouth wouldn't budge. A rejection like this was worse than she ever experienced. Sure, she struggled in school as a child, but it was well deserved because of boredom. Her first few months at Sunderland's was not a walk in the park as there were plenty of lessons to learn, but after a short while, she became a pro and skyrocketed quickly. But this! Weeks of research and rehearsing, giving it her all and working to the bone—down the drain. And she didn't like it. Not one bit.

The rest of the day was a complete blur. If you happened to be on the same bus ride home with Vivian that day, and ask her what she sold at Sunderland's, who she spoke to, and even what she had for lunch, she wouldn't remember.

"And. . . ?" Miriam shouted from the kitchen as she heard the front door open. Waiting for a response, she took off her apron and walked to greet her daughter and found her crouched down on the floor, with her coat and hat still on, crying. There was nothing Miriam could do but hug her.

"How am I going to go to work tomorrow?"

"With your feet," Miriam said, while Vivian looked at her mother as if she grew an extra head. "You may have lost this battle, but don't let them get all of you."

And after her favorite supper and a warm bath, Vivian went to bed and got up the next morning and let her feet lead the way, feeling grateful that her mother placed her meet-a-man-and-get-married-already wishes on the back burner so that she could properly comfort her.

***

For the rest of the week, Vivian dove right back into her work and shoved her feelings of rejection to the bottom of her boudoir and slammed the doors shut so she didn't have to face them. Downtime was spent buying stacks of fashion magazines and devouring them one after the other. Watching TV commercials, studying every female that she encountered—on the bus, at Sunderland's and on the streets. How did they put themselves together? What lipstick shade is that and where did you buy that blouse? These were questions that flew out of her mouth, as Vivian needed to be kept busy and help her not think about that morning in the boardroom where she felt like a rich spoiled princess whining about what she thought rich spoiled princesses needed. Just how Mme. Tremblay described her on the very first day she started. Maybe Mme. Tremblay was right all along, she thought, second guessing her true talent, but she still stood by the fact that there was nothing wrong with her hair.

"They just don't get it," Mr. Sand reassured Vivian over coffee one morning. They don't know a good idea if it hit them on the head," he added.

"Next time, finish your research," Elaine whispered to Vivian, in the stockroom on another day, while placing a gentle hand on her shoulder. She quickly looked around to see if anyone was standing by and leaned in a little closer to whisper "Between you and me, I think you really got something there. It takes a long time to produce a product. You need more data—that's all."

"I don't know what happened with your idea in the boardroom the other day, but whatever it was, I'm here to talk about it," Lilly said. A gesture that was appreciated, but declined as mentioned earlier, Vivian locked her boudoir, for now.

Comments like these lifted Vivian's spirits up and helped her go on and do her job that she loved. And to not give up.

On the Friday of that week, she stood up tall, looked around the department store, and said, "I'm not giving up."

"No giving up what, chèrie?" Mme. Tremblay asked.

At that point, in Vivian's eyes, due to the update from Mr. Sand, her relationship with Mme. Tremblay had changed. Yes, she was still hurt by her judgements, but she was just another sales lady that she worked with, and Vivian no longer felt threatened by her. As Vivian was about to explain her plan for her Travel Set to Mme. Tremblay, a customer came by, and Mme. Tremblay began to serve her. All the better, as Vivian would tell her another time. Perhaps when her plan worked out.

Vivian had work to do. Her blinders were needed again to focus on her job. She held on to her Bristol board and notes and placed them away in her bedroom closet as she knew that she would need them again, someday to present the Travel Set to somebody, but first, a need to play Frank Sinatra was requested.

Lilly and Vivian Play Frank Sinatra!

Sunderland's employees worked in separate departments, but when it came down to certain activities and situations, they had a secret code. A language that they used that only they understood.

A selective choice of words that described anything from a very much needed coffee break to a customer that made you want to rip their hair out from their scull. But the one code that was used for as long as Mme. Tremblay, Vivian and Mr. Sand could remember was to request to play a Frank Sinatra song, when a certain illegal deed occurred. A first for Lilly, in more ways than she ever expected.

The following day at Sunderland's, there was no snow on the ground, but there was a crisp and strong wind in the air. Winter coats—furs and wool, with complimentary hats, scarves, mittens, and gloves were all in full view on the racks and counter tops. Extra moisturizing creams were added to cosmetic lines to fight off the dry Canadian winter skin. Photographs of women modeling soft dewy skin, clothed in cozy warm sweaters were placed in front of the jars and bottles. The same went for the cooler shades for lipsticks and nail polishes. Of course, the classics were still flying off the shelves, as certain colors never went out of style.

The Christmas decorations were draped tastefully all over the store, thanks to the new company Sunderland hired for the task. Store employees complained on having to work the extra hours, as they were eager to return to their families after a long day of work.

Mr. Sand oversaw the whole Christmas decoration project that was installed on the evening of Halloween, and he loved every minute of it.

"It was like I had a blank page, and my job was to color it all in with crayons!" Mr. Sand boasted on the morning of November first as he sashayed around the center of the aisle. He looked as proud as a new father to be. Vivian wanted the chance to speak to Mr. Sand privately about the Travel Set. In particular, what her next move was going to be, but his head was in the Christmas spirit, so she decided to wait a little while longer.

The color scheme that year was silver and blue, Lilly's favorite. Vivian didn't care for it that much and preferred last years' colors.

"Oh well . . . as long as the customers like it, I suppose," Vivian said as she tapped a silver balloon.

"Sour grapes! It's because you don't celebrate it," Mr. Sand teased.

"So not true, Mr. Sand!"

"Oh yes, true my darling."

"Okay, maybe a little true. . . ," Vivian joked.

"Time to unload this new shipment," Lilly announced as she saw a delivery man with a stack of boxes. Mr. Sand's eyes widened as he clapped his hands in appreciation.

"Ah yes . . . the new gloves. I've been waiting for these. Viv—you are going to love these. Wait until you see these babies!"

Mr. Sand and Vivian were hovered over the box as one ripped it open with an exactor knife, and the other took out the tissue paper and raised a red suede glove in the air.

"Stuunnning!" Vivian gushed.

More oohing and ahhing over the new merchandise were shared, while Lilly looked on and took in the enthusiasm. She then gazed at her wristwatch as it was 9:45 AM and the store was going to be open shortly. Except for one or two occasions for not arriving on time due to illness or a dentist appointment, Lilly always arrived to work before the doors opened. Yes, of course to first savor the finest coffee in Montreal and yes, to also enjoy a cookie, but also because it was her job to arrive on time. Getting herself ready and her three kids out the door, alone each day was no small feat. Did Mr. Fine acknowledge this responsible behavior? No, but it made Lilly proud on her own.

At 9:55 AM, before the front doors were officially opened, Lilly walked away from Vivian's counter, en route to the shoe department, that officially opened at 10, but something stopped her in her tracks a few feet away from her. She saw a young woman slip a perfume bottle into her purse. A wave of nausea moved up Lilly's chest as she never saw this type of activity happen in real life. As she raised her hands to her mouth, she could feel her pulse quicken. Sure, she heard about people shoplift all the time on the radio dramas, and soap operas on TV, but in real life? In front of her own two eyes? What was she going to do? What was going to happen? Her instinct led the way as she whipped her body around and leaped back to the counter where her co-workers were ogling over the box of gloves.

"Girl. Bottle—purse," Lilly whispered like a gasp, and even though her words didn't make any sense whatsoever, Mr. Sand and Vivian fully understood and followed the protocol. What happened next, Lilly did not expect—especially of herself.

"Play Frank Sinatra!" Vivian yelped.

Mr. Sand froze, holding a glove in his hand. He let out a firm breath and put it down on the counter. "Frank Sinatra," he repeated loudly so that everyone within earshot could hear.

"Frank Sinatra," Vivian repeated while Lilly froze in her heels and was completely befuddled as she watched Mr. Sand and Vivian scurry about and each employee on the main floor began to mouth the words "Frank Sinatra" to each other, as that was the official code for a shoplifter on the premises of Sunderland's Department Store. A few of the employees left their posts one by one to join Vivian and Mr. Sand as backup and two security guards marched to the front doors and stood by.

"Come with me," Vivian said as she grasped the prospect's arm, who was also frozen in shock from all the hoopla.

"N-no, I won't," she wailed.

"I'm sorry ma'am, you have to."

"I didn't mean to take it."

"Yes, of course you didn't," Vivian gently reassured the woman and then motioned to Lilly to join her.

"Me? What do I have to do?" Lilly questioned.

"You saw the whole thing. I need you as a witness. Come on!"

Lilly panicked, as she had no clue on how she would be of help in this scenario, as she was certainly not qualified. What was she going to do, take laces from a pair of shoes and wrap her wrists with them? Or maybe take a shoe horn and smack her over the head with it?

"You better go, my dear," Mr. Sand said sternly, as Lilly followed Vivian with dread. "Want me to come with you, Viv?"

"I can handle this one."

"But I didn't do anything . . . it was just a little bottle! You guys aren't going to miss it!"

Feeling awful for the woman, Lilly continued to follow Vivian as they both held on to the shoplifter's arm, luring her down the department store aisle toward the basement door.

As Lilly opened the door and the three of them walked down the stairs to the basement, where Lilly and Vivian spent their first weeks, cleaning, organizing and paying their dues.

"Hey, it's company!" A new girl named Mildred happily announced as she was right in the middle of her initiation of cleaning the nail polish racks. She even began to clap.

Lilly and Vivian Play Frank Sinatra!

"Calm down, Mildred, it's not the company you want," Lilly said as Vivian and the shoplifter walked behind.

"Sit down," Vivian instructed the shoplifter. "How old are you?"

"Eighteen," the young woman said as she sat down on a bench, placed her hands on her knees and sighed, looking down at the floor.

"Hey, what did you do?" Mildred asked the shoplifter.

"None of your business—get back to work. . .," Vivian said.

"I was just asking!"

"Well, I don't need anyone asking me anything right now . . . I'm calling the police." Vivian reached for the basement phone, but before she could dial, the shoplifter got up and began to run up the stairs. Lilly gasped and ran right after her and planted her hands on her shoulders and squeezed them, almost to the point of pinching her skin to make her stop, which she did, while the shoplifter screeched "Yeeeeow!" The two of them remained on the staircase, staring at each other while Lilly yelled "Don't do that!" Not the most intimidating call to action, but it was all Lilly could think of saying at the spur of the moment.

"Way to go, Lill!" Vivian said as she continued to hold the receiver while she waited for the police to answer. Lilly grabbed the women's arm and brought her back to where Vivian was standing. All was fine for about eight seconds until the woman yanked the phone from Vivian's hand while Lilly clasped the woman's ear and pinched it until she drew blood. "Yeeeeooooowww!" She screamed again while Vivian grabbed the woman's arms and yanked them behind her back. As she was squirming which felt like an eternity, Mr. Sand and two security men came fleeting downstairs and took the young woman away.

"That was a doozie," Mildred commented.

"I will never listen to Frank Sinatra again," Lilly announced as Vivian sat on the floor gasping for breath.

All It Takes Is One

Vivian had a train to catch, and it wasn't the locomotive kind.

"Sunderland's isn't the only game in town!" Vivian squealed as she tapped her hand on Mr. Sand looked confused while he chewed the tuna sandwich that Vivian brought from home for them to share.

"I could try and sell the Travel Set to other stores!" Vivian announced as Mr. Sand shook his head beaming. "Good, right?" Vivian asked, while searching for approval.

"So right," Mr. Sand said. "Go to it!" He added.

"I can't believe I'm saying this—but I need to forgo those lunches at Beauty's. I need the time to sell this baby," Vivian announced as if she was turning down a party invitation—a party that she really wanted to attend, with a great friend and delicious food.

"Do what you have to do, my darling," Mr. Sand reassured her as he patted her on the shoulder.

Vivian began to work every Saturday so that one day off a week was allocated to calling every department store and small shop listed in the phone book to tell them about the Travel Set, in the hope that they could manufacture it and sell it in their stores.

She began at 9 a.m. sharp and hogged the home telephone for the entire day. This, of course, did not please Miriam, but thankfully it was only once a week. And of course, Miriam was not giving up her dream for her daughter, finding a husband and becoming a housewife and mother. As Vivian had her list of companies and retail stores by her side in a designated notebook and dialed, Miriam quietly prayed that a nice young Jewish executive would fall in love with her daughter's sweet voice and ask her out on a date.

What Vivian heard on the receiving end was not what she, her mother or anyone else expected. After a charming introduction of who she was, where she worked and what she wanted to create, the responses went something like this:

"Oh, I've heard of you! Why don't you come sell lipsticks for us instead?"

"Hey, that's super-duper neat, sweetheart, but I can't afford to create something like that Right now. Why don't you give me a call this time, next year?

"Why are you wasting your time working at Sunderland's? You really should settle down and get married."

And the worst: "You're so cute!"

Out of all the comments that was heard on the receiving line, Vivian loathed that one the most. Even though it sounded sweet and didn't mean any harm, it felt degrading. Cute were babies, puppies, and anything miniature —and she was not any of those things. It seemed as if her enthusiasm shadowed the smart, sophisticated, and wise woman that she was.

Making those phone calls was no picnic either as it was the exact opposite of working at Sunderland's, where Vivian was continuously surrounded by customers who hung on to every word she said. It was lonely and was as boring as watching baseball on TV with her father. As she sat at her kitchen table, she choose a store from the telephone book where she reached the main secretary and asked the name and number for every sales manager that would take her call. Then she would take notes from the responses, followed by a good cry in between each rejection.

Whenever Vivian had a difficult encounter with a customer, Mr. Sand and Lilly were right by her side, for support. And Vivian reciprocated as well, which made a huge difference for their morale. They were a team and it felt comforting to know that after each of them were through with the customer from hell, they would have a good laugh about it in the staff lunchroom.

At the kitchen table, where Vivian made her phone calls, any type of support system was nil.

There were no laughs after she had a conversation that made her want to strangle the sales person she was talking to, into a slow and painful death. No encouraging support to pick up the phone to keep going, promising a cookie from the lunch counter as a reward. Nobody cared, but Vivian herself. Her parents cared, but in a different way.

"Why are you spending your day off working so hard?"

Vivian had been sharing fashion advice since she could talk. The Travel Set was a fantastic idea that women all over the world needed to have. All it required was for one person to take her seriously. Just one.

But then life got in the way.

Marsha got engaged and with this announcement, the world just stopped. At least under the roof where Vivian and her family lived. After Miriam grieved the death of her parents from the Holocaust, that stole a part of her heart, and crushed her faith in humanity, Miriam was left angry and distraught. Taking months to break free from the trance that her parents were gone and years to accept the reality that one man could create such propaganda to try and wipe out an entire race, for no reason at all. The guilt for leaving Europe while her stubborn parents stayed behind weighed heavily on her existence. Thinking she should have remained with her parents so she could have taken care of them. Done something. No, she had to flee like she was being chased by a monster. Which she really was.

A simcha like a marriage was the perfect medicine to give her hope for the future and to bring her joy.

And if anyone was going to be in charge of choosing the flowers, buying this dress, matching this nail color to that tablecloth it was going to be Vivian, who took on the role like a duck to water. Obviously.

"And maybe you'll meet someone . . . soon," her mother said over a whisper, which her daughter heard loud and clear like a foghorn.

"Oh mother . . . ," Que eye roll. Some things still didn't change.

And then more life got in the way, and the weekly Wednesday phone calls began to decline.

A new product line came in and Elaine wanted Vivian to manage it, which included all the perks that any salesgirl would dream of. A raise, more bags of samples, invitations to catered 3-course meal lunches at the company's headquarters were regularly attended where they taught all the cosmeticians the entire line, with a warm welcome to go shopping in their supply room. It was a free for all to take anything they wanted, which made Vivian as happy as a child in a candy store. Taking home two large grocery bags of potions and lotions were huge perks—one for each hand! However, the responsibility for overseeing the line and the opportunity to teach what she learned to all who would listen at the department store made Vivian's phone calls to sales managers insignificant.

Any human being who would walk through Sunderland's double green hunter doors to work or shop would flock to hear what Vivian had to say about the products that she represented. Even the boring businessmen—who raised their eyebrows while they waltzed into the boardroom with their pipes and cigars in hand, were eager to learn a few things.

Hmph—so now you are listening to me, Vivian would privately mumbled to herself after they applauded her presentation on the proper way to use a certain product to wash one's face. It was clear that everyone loved to listen to Vivian preach about a product as she did so with great enthusiasm and authenticity, as her whole face would light up like a vase full of fresh flowers.

These presentations were all in the boardroom before the store would open, using the very same table that she presented on with her Travel Set. Although now, she didn't have to prove anything. All she had to do was talk about what she loved. And the response was the opposite of what those boring businessmen did on that dreadful day. The opposite of how she was treated as a child in her classroom. If only her angry teacher with the scuffed shoes and rippped stockings could have witnessed all of the applause and appreciation. The colleagues and her devoted customers who took her seriously and looked up to her. Vivian felt that her job was perfect. She got to still work in sales, which she adored and oversee a whole new line. The best of both worlds. With this new perspective, she placed her Travel Set on hold.

Lilly: That Day

Several days later, That Day started out as a typical day. But That Day will be remembered—a lesson for anyone that would listen.

As Lilly's alarm clock went off at 6:00 a.m., she hit the off button as quickly as possible.

There was no way on God's green earth that anyone was going to spoil her precious morning time. It was Saturday, and her children usually slept in until at least nine. Lilly adored this time to herself, just like when she was a child. How she loved to savor her first cup of coffee and a Montreal bagel, toasted, schmeared with cream cheese and topped with smoked salmon, a squirt of lemon, a sliced tomato and a few strands of red onion.

After stretching her arms out to the sides and swirling her neck around a few times followed by a generous sigh, she got up from her bed and walked to the bathroom to take a long, hot shower and lather her body with Yardley English Lavender Soap, as the scent was calming, while carrying gentle ingredients as it didn't irritate her skin the way the Palmolive did. After she finished, she gently patted her body with a towel to keep it slightly moist so that it would absorb her generous dollop of Ponds body cream, which she massaged all over her body and face—a luxurious ritual that she reserved just for Saturdays, when the morning routine wasn't interrupted by getting her three kids out the door and on their way to school. After she zipped up her dress and brushed her hair, she tidied up her room and went downstairs to the kitchen, where she passed by a window.

It was still dark outside, but that didn't bother her in the least bit as she looked forward to seeing the sunrise, that would occur momentarily. Lilly descended her steps and reached the front entry of her home. With great force, she opened the front door and a blast of cold wind blew into her face. "Whoa!" she said just above a whisper as she bent down to pick up the paper. She closed the front door and glanced at the front page as she walked into the kitchen. It was November 1952.

"Will you look at that—news about the Korean War," Lilly said with a heavy sigh, Lilly skimmed the article and went straight to the fashion section. She had her priorities and war of any kind was not one of them.

Because Saturday was *the* shopping day, Lilly wanted to be ready. Who was wearing what and how was it worn? "It" being clothes, makeup, and hair. If you were going to work the sales floor, you had to know the full scoop that was displayed in the newspapers, magazines and on TV. Lilly was always on the lookout as that was what Vivian always encouraged her to do.

Lilly was over the moon and quite relieved that she had such a fantastic ally and friend in her corner, who not only taught her the ropes, but, most importantly, always had her back. Unbeknownst to Lilly, she was going to need Vivian more than ever that day.

Brightness appeared in her peripheral vision which lifted her head away from the paper. Ah, the sun is starting to rise! Lilly said to herself as front door window had a strong beam of sunlight coming through it. With her coffee cup in hand, Lilly walked quickly to the living room window where one could watch the sun's morning debut with a more generous view. Coffee and a sunrise—the best, she thought to herself as she walked back to get her breakfast so that she could eat while watching the show.

After her last bite and sip Lilly washed her breakfast dishes and went upstairs to her bathroom to brush her teeth. As she was applying her lipstick, the doorbell rang.

"Oy—shhh!" she said on instinct, as she was afraid to wake the children. She flew downstairs and opened the door to greet her mother, who didn't have to work at her store that day.

"Sorry, I'm late!"

"You're not late. It's okay. They're still sleeping."

"Oh, good. Now I can watch them sleep a little. They're so delicious!"

"Oh, by the way, they plan on going tobogganing with their friends today."

"I'll make sure they have hot chocolate when they return . . . with marshmallows."

Lilly smiled; she knew that her kids were in great care.

As her mother took off her coat, she inspected her daughter's outfit by giving her the once over. "My, you look nice," she said in a warm tone.

"Oh, this? Thanks!" Lilly said as she looked down at her skirt. "This skirt is by Cherie—a new Canadian designer! Can you believe it?" Lilly announced proudly.

"Cherie? As in *the* Cherie? The designer from Chatelaine Magazine?"

"Tha's the one!"

"Well excuse me, fancy lady!"

"Mother," Lilly said as she rolled her eyes and waved her hand and laughed and thought about how she became the proud owner of the skirt that she wanted to be buried in.

Only the chosen few knew that the Cherie skirt that she was wearing was slightly damaged. The top button fell off somewhere in the store and no one could find it. There was quite a story behind how she became its proud owner.

Lilly had only been working at Sunderland's for a couple of months, which meant that every day still felt like the first day: new, unfamiliar, and panic mode challenging.

"WHO left the storage room open?"

"WHY aren't you selling more shoes?"

"WHY aren't you selling more shoes?"

Questions like these, especially the last two, were constantly directed at the shoe salespeople, but mostly at Lilly, who'd run her fingers through her hair and exhaled forcefully every time they were. But then, there were times when situations such as the following happened, which made her job feel like a party.

"Look what I have!" Mr. Sand sang in front of Vivian and Lilly one Monday evening, just before closing.

"Gasp!" Vivian took a deep breath in as she held her hand to her mouth. "It can't be!" she added.

"Oh, yes, it is! Presenting a Cherie skirt!" Mr. Sand said, smiling and swinging the skirt in the air.

Lilly's face crinkled in thought. "What's the big deal? I don't understand. It's just a black skirt."

"Darling, don't do that to your face—so bad for the forehead lines," Vivian suggested.

Lilly relaxed her face and witnessed the elegant camaraderie dance between Vivian and Mr. Sand. "And . . . for crying out loud, this, my friend, is not just a skirt. I mean, this beauty," Vivian breathlessly said.

"The craftsmanship," Mr. Sand Said.

"The details," Vivian added.

"So simple," Mr. Sand said.

"My gosh, it's like a trophy," Lilly commented.

"Yes! That's it—bingo!" Vivian agreed and turned to Mr. Sand. "Sigh . . . I've got to have it. How much?"

"Fifty," Mr. Sand said matter-of-factly.

"Fifty dollars? That's it. I'm officially going to flip my lid."

"Nifty, isn't it?"

"That is the steal of a lifetime!" Vivian announced with her fist in the air, as she very well knew that a Cherie skirt usually sold for around $250—a price that only the chosen few could afford, and with her salary, even with her employee discount, she was not one of them, even though she tried to dress the part as much as she could. Lilly's eyes bulged as her head tilted back while feeling intrigued and entertained by all the hoopla over this simple black skirt.

"No, wait. What's wrong with it?" Vivian asked.

"Right on the mark, as usual," Mr. Sand said.

"I figured. Too good to be true," Vivian said, sighing.

"The top button fell off! I looked high and low. I even crawled around on my hands and knees, but I can't find it. But it's at the top and it's black like the material, so no one will notice," Mr. Sand said.

"That's all?"

"Yep."

"Ok," Vivian thought as she held her hand to her chin and slowly turned her head to look at Lilly. "I want you to have it."

"Me?"

"Yes, you. It's time."

Lilly walked over to Mr. Sand, took the skirt from his hands, and held it to her waist. The texture of the material felt thick and sturdy, as it was made of tweed, which naturally had a slight pattern to it. The quality was impeccable compared to most of the skirts and slacks she wore every day, which wrinkled at the slightest bend. This skirt felt even better than the one that Vivian gave her on her first day. As she raised the skirt to her eye level, she envisioned each blouse that hung in her closet and some sweaters too—they all seemed to go nicely together, which therefore made the original assumption of a simple black skirt was now thrown out the window.

This skirt was exquisite, and the thought of owning it made her shiver with excitement. "Even if it's 50 dollars, I still can't afford it."

"Of course, you can! This skirt will take you everywhere: to the fanciest restaurants to anywhere that raises eyebrows, with the right accessories, and makeup of course," Vivian said.

"Sorry, I can't. I've got three mouths to feed!" Lilly said.

"It will look so smart on you," Mr. Sand said as Lilly shook her head.

"I can't stand it. You've got to have it. It's taken care of," Mr. Sand said as he winked at Vivian. Lilly's mouth fell open.

"Darling, what did I say about stretching your mouth like that?" Vivian scolded.

Back to Lilly's front entrance way, as she was saying goodbye to her mother as she left for work.

"Mom, I gotta run. The kids love this new cereal. It's in the pantry."

"Mom guilt got to you again. I tell you, it's in our genes. What's wrong with a little bagel and lox with a schmear of cream cheese?"

"Bye, Mother!" Lilly said as she put on her coat.

"Is that Cherie too?"

The wind blasted through as she ventured to her bus stop. Lilly wrapped her scarf around her head and hunched over to protect herself, especially her hair, as she didn't want to ruin her hairdo, thanks to her new Solomon Harper rollers that she got at half price because due to one measly damaged roller. Lilly didn't care that the 19 rollers heated up perfectly instead of 20. Plus, her employee discount made them almost free. Working at Sunderland's had some great perks.

Lilly thought about the recent conversation over hair routines with Vivian at the coffee shop the other day. Mr. Sand sat quietly, listening to the girl's chatter and being amused as ever.

"Can't do the electric rollers—my hair is too fine. The minute I take them out, my hair looks like I stuck my finger in the electric socket, where only three strands of hair get shocked, while the rest play dead. It's homemade cloth strips for me. Works like a charm since day one!"

"Nah, the hot rollers, for me as it makes my course hair less frizzy."

"Oh, put some olive oil on the ends of your hair after you shampoo."

"Really . . . okay, but I'm still using my rollers."

"Yeah, that's fine, just put it on the night before you wash your hair then set it—your hair will feel like silk—you'll thank me!"

"You better thank her before I toss a salad on your head!" Mr. Sand chuckled as he pushed his hair back with his hands.

"Ha—good one, Mr. Sand!" Lilly joked back while waving her hand in the air.

Lilly laughed at the memory as she climbed onto the bus that brought her right in front of Sunderland's. She couldn't wait to show Vivian and Mr. Sand what she decided to pair her Cherie skirt with. Taking care of how she presented herself at Sunderland's was Lilly's way of saying thank you to them. Those two helped her get back on her feet after the mess her ex had left her with. No one had ever been so kind and caring to her.

The giggling didn't stop, until other passengers took notice; then she quickly composed herself to think of something serious, like what she saw on the front page of the paper that morning about the Korean war. That put a damper on her giggles. And fast.

Retail stores began appearing in the bus windows, which was Lilly's cue to stand up and leave. As soon as the department store came into view, she saw the crowd of Saturday shoppers lined up to get in. It was 9:30, and she had fifteen minutes to get to the store, grab her second cup of coffee, and zoom to the shoe department, where she was stationed to work.

At 9:52, she was ready and waiting by the winter boots display.

"Uh, Lilly?" a co-worker named Marion said as she motioned an outline of her lips while walking toward her.

"Oh, my lipstick! I forgot to bring it to reapply. Damn that coffee and cookies!" Lilly admitted.

"Yes, but they are worth it! I know. Something magical about them. . . Here, take mine!"

Marion quickly threw her a tube of lipstick in the air, and Lilly caught it on the first try.

"Great pitch!" Lilly said.

"Great catch," Marion joked.

Lilly opened the tube walked over to the mirror that hung on a beam in the middle of the shoe department, that enabled customers to view the shoes that they were trying on in full view. As she carefully applied a coat, she put the cap back on and raised her hand over her head, like a baseball player and pitched it back at her. "Whoo-hoo-hoo, coming at ya!"

"Ladies, my goodness! This is not a baseball field," Mr. Sand hollered from across the hall as he was putting racks of dresses on display. The girls giggled and apologized.

"By the way, great skirt!" Marion added.

"Thanks . . . you can borrow it anytime. It's Cherie!" Lilly replied, swaying her hips from side to side.

"Really? Well, then, I may take you up on that," Marion said to Lilly, her face lighting up as if she had won the jackpot at the roulette table in Las Vegas.

"Hey, Lill!" Vivian hollered and waved from the cosmetics department one flight below.

Lilly walked over to the banister, where she could see her friend, and waved back.

Vivian mimed eating. Lilly nodded and held up three fingers and joined her index finger and thumb together, which was code for accepting to eat lunch together later that day.

Lilly: That Day

Minutes later, the department store bell rang, the front doors swung open, and eager shoppers spilled in like ants heading to their colony. Lilly loved to watch this scene every morning; it gave her such a thrill. It was so exciting to see all these people who were happy to be at Sunderland's to browse around shop. Especially if they were searching for the perfect pair of shoes.

Lilly's children were well taken care of. A fun lunch date with Vivian was in a few hours. And damn, she looked Cherie-good! That Day was clearly starting on the right foot, until a certain customer arrived.

"Oh, hello!" said a woman with shoulder-length strawberry-blonde hair that was perfectly curled at the bottom. She was wearing a double breasted light blue wool coat with a matching knit hat, while holding hands with a young girl, who had the exact same-colored hair. Lilly assumed she was her daughter.

"Hello there, may I help you?" Lilly asked.

"Yes, you may," she said. She looked down at her daughter and smiled, then smiled at Lilly.

"What are you looking for?" Lilly asked.

"A lovely pair of shoes."

"Well, that's a given, here at Sunderland's."

The two women had a little laugh.

"Is this your daughter?" Lilly asked.

"Yes. Her name is Patty. Say hello, Patty."

"Hello," Patty said as she curtsied.

"You don't have to be so formal here, Patty," Lilly said as Patty looked down to the floor from shyness.

"Ok, let's get down to business. Perhaps you can tell me about the outfit that you will be wearing with the lovely pair of shoes that I will help you find."

"Oh, yes, that would help, wouldn't it?"

Lilly nodded, showing her teeth.

"A simple cream knit dress, with a round neck and pleats at the bottom," the woman said as she illustrated her description with her hands.

"That's easy as pie! Let's have some fun here," Lilly said as she motioned for the woman and Patty to follow her to the designer shoe selection, where a rainbow of colors and styles were displayed on dark cherry-wood shelves.

"You can go with any color or style. Oooh, like this beautiful red pump with this adorable booowww! Will you look at this? Oh my . . . pardon me, I do get a little carried away here," Lilly giggled as she reached for the shoe and turned around with a giddy grin. The woman and Patty giggled along with her.

"You're funny!" Patty said, still giggling.

"Oh, that is lovely! Isn't it, sweetheart?" The woman warmly said to Patty, who agreed by nodding and smiling.

"Wonderful. I will go and get your size," Lilly announced.

"Six and a half," the woman said, in a completely different tone, which was stern and unfriendly. Lilly quickly registered this new and unfamiliar mood that popped a hole into her bubbly enthusiasm and took it down a couple of notches. She thought that perhaps she got a little too excited about the shoes, and some people didn't like that, as they were more reserved. "Six and a half, in the red. Very well. I'll be just a moment." Lilly slowly turned her back and walked briskly to the storage room.

As she was searching for the pair of shoes, she wondered what was going on. Besides the fact that Lilly's enthusiasm may have been a little too rich for her liking, perhaps the woman's breakfast wasn't sitting right in her stomach, and she suddenly developed a bout of gas. Yes, gas was it. Gas can make anyone slightly cranky at a moment's notice and wondered if she had any Alka-Seltzer around.

Moments later, Lilly returned with a shoe box and opened it up.

"A lovely six-and-a-half red heel with an adorable bow for you!" So much for turning down the enthusiasm. She couldn't help it as the red heel was just delicious and required an appropriate swoon.

"Red? I never said red."

"Pardon me?" Lilly asked, suspiciously.

"You must have misunderstood. I said green. A green pump, please."

"Oh dear, my apologies. I must have heard wrong. Luckily, this shoe also comes in green, and I will find it for you," Lilly said as she placed the red shoes back in their box and tucked it under her arm.

"And I'm a size seven. Not six and a half."

"Oh, sorry about that too," Lilly replied as she turned around and walked back to the storage room, feeling slightly flustered. She knew what she had heard in the first place—size six and a half—and she knew the woman was excited about the red shoe. But, then again, maybe she was mistaken and maybe she really needed to find that Alka-Seltzer. Lilly shook off her doubts and carried on with her duties. As soon as she found the size seven shoe, with the adorable bow in green, she returned to her customer.

"Ta-daaah!" Lilly proudly said as she opened the box to reveal the customer's wishes.

"I thought I said red. Size six and a half."

The little girl began to giggle and placed her hand over her mouth.

"Shhh," her mother quickly said to Patty as she squeezed her little hand and grinned as if she had a secret.

Lilly's face fell as her gut instincts told her that something was wrong but didn't know what—and she knew it wasn't gas and she also knew that it wasn't her excitement over a beautiful pair of shoes.

"We seem to be having a miscommunication here," Lilly said.

"No, we aren't. You are not understanding me," the woman's voice rose, and Lilly felt the blood rush to her face while her pulse speeded up, but she tried to remain calm and decided to begin again.

"Okay, let's start at the beginning. What color and size would you like?"

"A size six-and-a-half red pump!" the woman sternly said.

Lilly thought that maybe she was the problem and needed a hearing aid. But she shook her head, as she knew what she heard loud and clear and had an inkling as to what was going on, but to make sure, some time to think all this through needed to be bought. Lilly turned to the woman and her daughter, Patty.

"Before I get your shoes, why don't you both sit down on our benches. They are so comfortable, just like your living room couch at home. May I get you a cup of coffee? We are known for the best cup of coffee in the city, and the cookies here are divine!"

Patty's face lit up like a candle.

"That would be lovely," the woman said.

"Very well then. Give me a moment," Lilly said as she marched in the direction of the coffee shop, stopping abruptly at Vivian's counter.

"Coffee. Cookie. Now," Lilly said under her breath.

"Mme. Tremblay, cover for me," Vivian said as she walked around her counter to meet her friend.

Lilly and Vivian walked together down the department store aisle as Lilly brought Vivian up to speed.

"So, am I crazy or what? Should I go for a hearing test?" Lilly said as she paid for a coffee and two cookies.

"No," Vivian said quietly.

"Then?" Lilly said impatiently.

"Just do your job."

"What? Then I'm running around like a lunatic."

"I know."

Lilly scrunched her eyes.

"Darling..."

"Never mind my face right now. What's going on?" Lilly protested.

"You're being played, just in a different way then how I was—which was 'Don't say Oy, Vivian.'" Vivian said.

Lilly stared straight ahead, remembering their telephone conversation only a few months ago.

"They're just having some fun. Don't worry—it will stop. Soon."

"When?"

"I don't know. Welcome to the aftermath. They didn't get us physically here in Canada, but they sure are getting us in other ways," Vivian whispered.

Lilly shook her head.

"I can't believe this.... How did this woman even know I was Jewish?"

"Who knows... You eventually get used to it, like I did. It's part of our life," Vivian said as she gently squeezed Lilly's arm and motioned that they both should get back to work.

"It's not fair, Viv."

"No, it's not," Vivian said as Lilly walked up the stairs to the shoe department, while she went back to her post at the Revlon counter. However, even though it was a Saturday, and the store was packed, Vivian kept an eye and an ear on standby, as she knew there was going to be trouble.

Just as Lilly climbed the last few steps to arrive at the shoe department, she was feeling as if she was on a merry-go-round, desperately wanting to get off. On one hand, she was reassured that she wasn't going crazy or losing her hearing, but on the other hand, keeping one's race a secret seemed ridiculously unfair. In addition, feelings of familiarity had risen. Where He called her an imbecile for not placing the ketchup on the dinner table, although this time, she could not escape to her bedroom to cry. And there were no flowers or perfume waiting to apologize with. It was up to Lilly to defend herself.

As she approached the pair, she quickly closed her eyes and prayed for help, an idea, anything to get her out of this mess. And then she saw her friend and colleague Marion.

"Well, that sure took a long time!" the woman complained.

"Mmm, cookies!" Patty squealed as she tore open the bag and shoved one in her mouth, while she moaned "mmmmm."

"They are good, Patty. I had one this morning, and you know what? I ruined my Lipstick," Lilly said while the woman stared straight ahead while Lilly continued.

"And you know what happened next? My friend and co-worker Marion noticed that my lipstick was all off after I ate my cookie!"

Patty tilted her head and nodded while chewing her cookie.

"I looked just awful. Can you imagine me without lipstick? Just a plain, skin-colored mouth?

How boring, right?"

Patty nodded and was concerned for the void that Lilly felt.

"Marion was so nice. She threw me her lipstick, just like a baseball player! And I caught it on the first try! That was fun," Lilly grasped her hands and smiled like a woman in a TV commercial. Patty clapped her hands and opened her mouth wide, showing her partially chewed up cookie in her mouth.

"I think I should thank her. Wouldn't that be the right thing to do?" Lilly sweetly said, smiling to herself, knowing that she had a plan. And it was good. She couldn't wait to execute it.

The little girl nodded her head as her mother sat next her, watching every move.

"Oh, Marion? Can you please come join us?" Lilly asked in the politest manner, and Marion quickly came over. "I want to take the time to thank you for lending me your lipstick today."

"Oh, you're welcome, Lill! It was nothing," Marion said.

"Yes, and I also wanted to thank you for covering for me during Rosh Hashanah, a couple of months ago, the Jewish New Year."

"Of course. Such a pleasure."

The woman's eyes did not blink.

"I would like to return the favor by working on Christmas Eve."

"What? Are you serious? You will?" Marion's eyes were as bright as Christmas lights.

"I don't celebrate it, so it would be my pleasure to come in and work your shift," Lilly said proudly.

Patty watched both women converse with amusement and also witnessed her mother's mouth fall wide open. Lilly didn't want to tell her to close it. Let her ruin her complexion.

With all the courage Lilly could foster, she began her inquisition, albeit it with a shaky voice as she was scared out of her mind, but it had to be done as there was no way that this awful woman was going to make a fool out of her for simply being Jewish.

"So, let's get back to business here, and Marion, maybe you can help me. Tell me, madame.

What size and color shoe would you like to try on today?"

"Size six and a half. Red," the woman said quietly without any emotion and almost robotic- like.

"Six and a half. Red. With the adorable bow at the back?" Lilly asked. The woman nodded.

"Oh, I love those shoes. You've got great taste, madame," Marion said.

"She does," Lilly agreed.

"Very well. Marion, will you help me find these shoes?" Lilly asked.

"Certainly," Marion said.

The two women walked off to the storage room. As soon as they were alone, Marion began to question Lilly, "What's going on?"

Lilly nodded and squeezed Marion's shoulders. She closed her eyes and let a tear roll down her cheek.

"I don't understand," Marion said.

Lilly began to breathe hard.

"Lill, You all right?" Vivian's voice was heard coming into the storeroom.

"Viv!" Lilly reached for her friend and grasped her shoulders. "I can't."

"Yes, you can. I've been watching you. You're doing great. Keep going."

"No, I can't."

"Yes, you can. You're almost there. Go. Go out there and face her. Don't let her win!"

"What's going on?" Marion asked.

"Nothing but a little antisemitism," Lilly said in a sarcastic manner to Marion as she wiped away a tear and inhaled a deep breath.

"Whaaat? I didn't witness anything like that."

"Trust me on this one," Lilly quickly said while Marion shook her head.

"Impossible. She wasn't wearing a swastika or anything."

"You don't need to wear a Nazi uniform to be racist!" Vivian yelled.

"Breathe. Breathe. Go," "Okay," Lilly said as she raised her head, wiped her eyes, grabbed the pair of shoes that the lady wanted and turned to Marion and shook her shoulders around to release any ounce of stress that would leave her body. "Follow me."

"Are you still going to cover me for Christmas Eve?" Marion asked.

"Oh, for God sakes, yes!" Lilly said in an annoyed manner as the two women walked back to the shoe department and Vivian returned to the top of the staircase, watching.

The woman stood up to greet Lilly and Marion.

"Do you have my shoes?"

"I have your shoes; I always had your shoes," Lilly said.

Lilly: That Day

"Whatever do you mean?" the woman innocently asked.

"Don't play that game with me," Lilly sternly said as Marion watched in amazement.

"Why don't you just go away?" The woman asked.

"Madame!" Marion said.

"Dirty Jew!" Patty shrieked with glee.

"Oh, my goodness. You weren't kidding," Marion said.

Everyone in the shoe department stopped what they were doing and stared.

"Where did you hear that, young lady?" Marion asked in disbelief.

"My momma," Patty proudly said.

The woman turned a few shades of red and nervously laughed "Children—they're so funny."

Lilly was fuming inside but tried her best to remain calm, as she couldn't believe what occurred and what she was managing to do.

The morning at Beauty's with the Jewish nose comments was a real awakening—but this experience took the grand prize. She was being verbally abused for the sole reason of being Jewish and it infuriated her. But she had to put those emotions away, in order to gather her composure as best as she could, as she had something important to say. Despite her best efforts, her voice became shaky again, but she didn't care as she was determined speak.

"Now, you listen to me. I am here to find you, and anyone who asks me, for the perfect, loveliest pair of shoes. It doesn't matter where I come from or what color or religion I am. I am here to do my job, and I will do it the best that I know how. And, most importantly, I will certainly not go away. Why should I? I did nothing wrong."

"Maybe you shouldn't work here. I mean, you have no business wearing a Cherie skirt!" she screamed.

"Oh, yes, she does!" Mr. Sand's voice appeared from the aisle. All the shoppers stopped talking and stared. "I think you and your daughter should go shopping somewhere else," he added.

"I might indeed do that," the woman said as she grabbed her daughter's hand to leave the department store.

"But they have the best cookies here," Patty sadly said, walking away. "And the nicest ladies too...."

"Maybe one day your mother will appreciate that, or at least you will," Lilly said.

Mr. Sand quickly walked over to Lilly and told her to take a coffee break.

"No, I'm ok."

"You sure? I mean, you just went through a lot."

"I don't need to. I feel good. Stronger."

The two of them stood for a few moments together and Vivian joined them from the staircase.

"I can't believe that just happened. It was surreal. I will never let anyone mistreat me just because of my race," Lilly said.

"Me neither," Vivian said as she held on to Lilly's hand.

***

Lilly was really getting into the swing of things in the shoe department, especially after that mother and daughter disgusting duo that she handled so well, which was a blessing in disguise because Lilly found her voice. Besides having the courage to leave her husband, that was the first time she really stood up for herself, which opened a whole new world of confidence. She was a quick study and proved it in her sales records and before long, Lilly began to train new employees on the sales floor and took charge of the cleaning initiation in the basement that unfortunately had to be done, but Lilly gave plenty of notice on how to dress for the part and to offer breaks to come upstairs to the main floor, or to take a walk around the block every few hours, as not to feel so claustrophobic.

Mr. Sand remained in his sales management job for years, as he was quite content and enjoyed witnessing Vivian and Lilly excel in their positions. His work as a mentor did not go unnoticed and after several years, he received a promotion to buyer that included plenty of travel with all the perks that came with it. Including Fashion week in Paris and New York and meeting all the famous designers. Being the generous man that he was, handfuls of gifts were brought home to Vivian and Lilly, and they reciprocated by taking him out for dinner to catch up on all the Sunderland's gossip.

Vivian—1953

"Oh my God—I'm going to be thirty!" Exclaimed Vivian one day while she fixed her hair in a nearby mirror.

"In two years," Lilly reassured her friend.

"I know, but it's creeping up like tarantula," Vivian whimpered.

"And it's gonna bite you in the *tuchas*!" Lilly joked.

A few years have passed while Vivian and Lilly continued to work at Sunderland's and were still going strong. Thanks to a customer, who Vivian complained of her aching back and feet, a gift of the Royal Canadian Airforce 5BX Plan for Physical fitness workbook was sent to her that contained and explained an assortment of exercises. No gym or special equipment was needed and could be done in the middle of her living room, in the apartment she rented, as it was time to move into her own abode. She also quit smoking as the nicotine permeated her clothes and hair. She rarely drank alcohol, as she read somewhere that it caused premature aging. As she passed by a nearby mirror, she got a look at herself and nodded with approval. She felt great, looked good and was damn proud of it.

The opportunity to work in the clothing department, that she wanted so badly when she first begun somehow faded away from her agenda, which became completely fine, as she realized that she was exactly where she needed to be. She was happy working, coming

Vivian—1953

home, taking care of herself, and taking the train to Florida every couple of months to visit her parents.

Head of Sales and Cosmetics Buyer was now Vivian's role which entitled her to go on buying trips and conferences and to continue to have meetings in that very same boardroom where she presented her Travel Set and had taught the first line she ever represented, and the many other lines she oversaw. As Elaine told her as she pushed her new Sunderland's contract in front of her nose for her to sign, "If you're good—they will notice you—and honey, you're good!"

Recognition from Elaine was Vivian's bloodline. She needed positive feedback like that to keep her going because when she would enter that boardroom, the same twinge would still be felt in her stomach after all those years. She still thought about it. It never left her mind. Sometimes she would dream about it and report the details to Vivian and Mr. Sand the next morning.

"It was never meant to be," Lilly said, that felt like a punch in the stomach, and made Vivian wonder why Lilly would say such a thing. It may have been the truth, but it still hurt.

"What do you mean it wasn't meant to be?" Vivian blurted out, crossing her arms and frowning.

"You gave it your best shot," Mr. Sand said as he rested his hand on her shoulder. He was trying to place a flower on Lilly's comment, that didn't work at all, as far as Vivian was concerned, as it felt like he placed a rose on a pile of shit.

When new employees entered the store for training, they still had to pass the cleaning and inventory initiation task, although it was no longer in the basement. Vivian had decided that enough was enough and people shouldn't be sent to work in the cold damp basement on their first week. All inventory was moved to the new stockroom that was located on the main floor. But, of course, the new employees still had the look of dread after being asked to clean and organize the shelves of products from top to bottom—that did not change.

"Oh, come on now; we all did it," Vivian would say.

"Do I have to?" the new employee pleaded.

"Oh, heck, I will buy you a coffee and a cookie when you are done."

With that, the new employee's eyes would glow as Vivian shook her head and thought how good these kids have it today but came to the realization that maybe she had it too tough. Wouldn't it have been so lovely if someone were as patient and kind when she began her position? It was up to her to break the pattern and she was up to the task.

But what about her devoted customers? Even though her new title came with exciting opportunities and challenges, for Vivian, she loved nothing more than returning to her roots to help someone find the perfect shade of lipstick. Serving the public was the "why" of her job because in the end it was all about the customer and making them feel beautiful. I addition, conversations about each product that was sold or didn't sell revealed more to Vivian than any sales record on paper, which led to more information that she sent back to the companies. How she loved that part of her job. So, she made it happen.

Vivian would make sure that she was in the store at least twice a week and there were plenty of women who just wanted to be served by her, despite the other salesgirls that worked the floor. So, they would call the department store ahead of time to make an appointment with the famous lipstick girl, and special one-on-one time would be granted, escorting her customer around the cosmetics department to complete their beauty regime. Vivian loved every minute of it and so did her customers.

* * *

Life at the department store carried on much in this manner, until Mme. Tremblay began to winter in Florida.

Vivian—1953

Elaine retired.

Mr. Sand was busy traveling, and only came into the store once a week and Lilly was selling up a storm in the shoe department and was eventually promoted to manager.

When you worked in a department store many years, the staff at Sunderland's got to witness the circle of life. Not many families followed this pattern. But when it did, there was nothing like it, as far as Vivian was concerned, experiencing this highlight took the grand prize.

It began with the giggling teenager who wanted to purchase a bottle of nail polish, back in the late 1930s, before Vivian began to work at Sunderland's. Mme. Tremblay was working at the cosmetic counter and the young girl entered the department store with her friends and turned to Mme. Tremblay while looking down on the ground because she didn't know where to begin as there were at least 20 beaming bright colors sitting in little bottles, all stacked together, staring right at her. From the moment that she was in Mme. Tremblay's care, patience and trust was expertly built, which lured her to return. Someone was listening to what she needed and resulted to more purchases. To buy a cream or a powder. Maybe a perfume. Mme. Tremblay knew her skin, her habits and what was best for this girl.

A few years later, she came back and only wanted to see Mme. Tremblay. She bought her first foundation because she was noticing that she wanted to even out her skin tone. She trusted her taste and knew that she wouldn't let her leave the store looking like a clown.

Before long, she ran into the store to announce to Mme. Tremblay and the new girl, Vivian and all that would listen that she was getting married! She brought her mother into the store.

"This is the famous Mme. Tremblay!" Her mother exclaimed, and before long, she completely understood what her daughter had been talking about at the dinner table. Together, they stood at the cosmetic counter, while Vivian watched and learned, and they both choose how they were going to put on their makeup for the big day. Vivian became well acquainted with this young woman that day, and the bride's mother returned six months later to buy what she bought for her daughter's wedding, because it ran out and she still wanted to look her best.

Right after her honeymoon, mother and daughter returned to Sunderland's to show the pictures that were taken and to let them know how beautiful and natural the makeup looked.

"Compliments were non-stop! They couldn't get over how great I looked!"

Before long, the young giggly girl who first bought the nail polish to Mme. Tremblay in the 1930s returned to Sunderland's as a wife and mother with her baby. Years later, when Mme. Tremblay was no longer there, and Vivian took over, the young mother returned with her daughter in tow, who was six years old, who gazed up at her mother who choose a new compact. And when she grew up, the mother brought the daughter in to buy her first nail polish, which Vivian helped her purchase.

And then the mother returned to the department store with her teenage daughter and her elderly mother and the three of them not only bought makeup together but had lunch in the coffee shop. Three generations had been served by Mme. Tremblay and Vivian at Sunderland's. A rare but treasured event that went far beyond the ringa ding ding of the cash register. Situations like these were the meat of the shopping industry. It kept the industry going. It kept people's jobs. But above all, the returning of customers from each generation built trust, which was the heart of a sales person's goal.

Little did Vivian know that another mother and daughter duo would return to Sunderland's.

Vivian—1953

The reunion began with a young woman who came into the store, who seemed to be in her mid-twenties, with strawberry blond hair that curled ever so perfectly on the bottom. She needed some help purchase some makeup to go with an outfit.

That Girl

All walks of life would walk into Sunderland's. You never knew who you were going to get. They could either be a complete pleasure to deal with that would make you think that all humans are beautiful, generous creatures as you dance in the center of the department store aisle to sing *That's Amore*.

There were of course customers that were an absolute nightmare that would make you think that all humans were evil cynical monsters. Placed on earth to make you and everyone miserable, that provoked the desire to run home, hide under the covers and never come out.

These types of customers were not forgotten.

For all the rest who were in between became a blur and seemed to intertwine with each other. It wasn't surprising that fragments of conversations and subconscious feelings would pop into their minds as they picked up certain merchandise, or even show up in their dreams.

Regardless, it was amazing which situations were selectively remained implanted in their minds.

The day Cassandra Johnson came into the store, Vivian was busy putting samples away under the counter and tidying up loose bills. Even though it was more just a few years ago, as soon as Cassandra walked up to the counter, she brought in the same aura when Mrs. Linton came in, which was an aura of confidence. That day was forever etched in her mind, played repeatedly like a broken record. Then again, the aura that Cassandra brought into the store also had a sister that felt cold, and bitter. Was it from another customer that she served? Vivian wasn't sure, but it felt very familiar.

"Hi, I would like some help please," Cassandra asked.

"What can I do for you?"

"I'm going to a wedding, and I would like some makeup."

"What color is your dress?"

"White."

"Easy peasy! With a face like yours, we can do anything! Where shall we begin? Your eyes? Foundation? A face cream perhaps?" Vivian said breathlessly, as this type of opportunity to build the look from scratch was something that she still looked forward to doing after all these years, as to her, it was as exciting as an artist receiving a blank canvas to paint on.

"The wedding will be out of town, so I would like to have it all in a . . . in a . . ."

Cassandra was trying to explain what she was looking for but couldn't get the words out. She was waving her hands while talking and making a square with her hands in the air. "Um . . . you know, a bunch of key cosmetics that are all put together and organized in one spot," she said while Vivian stared straight ahead as if she saw a ghost. Cassandra stopped talking and looked concerned. "Are you alright, ma'am?" Vivian was in a trance and took a deep breath, holding on to her counter for balance.

"Oh, me? Yes, I'm fine," Vivian said, while looking around.

"Well, do you have that sort of thing?"

"I'm afraid not."

"Well, why don't you get one?" Cassandra asked while Vivian began to laugh.

"I already tried."

"NO!"

"Oh, yes."

"What happened?"

After a loud sigh with an added *oy*, as Vivian was done hiding who she was, she told her the whole story from beginning to end, which felt as if the vast amount of water that had been held up by a damn was finally released. How wonderful it felt to tell the Travel Set story to a person who wanted one herself and understood that it was needed.

"You must have worked so hard on your presentation," Cassandra said softly, looking down at her fingernails and then slowly looking up at Vivian.

"I did!"

"I am telling you—me and every woman in this city needs that Travel Set! I mean, it just makes sense! You are one smart mademoiselle!" she exclaimed while pointing with her index finger.

"Yeah, well, that was a while ago, and I put it to bed."

"Why?"

"Well, I got more responsibilities at work, and life got in the way..."

"Shame. I think the whole country should have it!"

"You think so?" Vivian asked, full of hope.

"I know so! Even beyond Canada—every woman in the world should have something like that." The girl said with great triumph as Vivian was hypnotized with her vision. She still couldn't understand how the staff at Sunderland's didn't want to take the risk and create the product for her—or anyone else for that matter.

"Would you believe that to this day, nobody has something like that?" Vivian informed her new fan.

"I really want one."

"Tell me about it!" Vivian said as she slammed her hand on the counter, as if she was putting a stamp of approval for how crucial she believed it was. Cassandra looked at Vivian, and a gentle smile grew across her face, slowly revealing her teeth that had a light-yellow tinge to them, which didn't seem to go with the rest of her appearance and added a dash of concern on Vivian's conscience but not enough to change her pace.

"You know, I have an aunt in New York that buys stuff like this all the time for a chain of department stores!"

Vivian's heart sprang through her chest. The girl said the magic words that became a beacon of hope. "Really? Which ones? Neiman Marcus? Marshall Field's? Or what about Selfridges in London!"

"Yes! Those are the ones! All of them! I can introduce you," Cassandra said.

"You would?"

"Absolutely, it's a great idea, and I think she will go for it! She's coming into town tomorrow."

"Oh, wow . . . but wait, what's the catch?" Vivian asked, as she had a feeling this was all too good to be true.

"I get 20 percent of sales," Cassandra said as she crossed her arms.

"Deal!" Vivian held out her hand, and Cassandra shook it.

"Ok, I'll bring my aunt here tomorrow. All you must do is write me a description, draw the design, and leave it with us."

"That's all . . . wait—I should type it."

"Fine, type it. That's great."

"I can do that," Vivian said breathlessly, almost in a panic.

"I'll be back tomorrow."

"Wait - I don't even know your name!"

"It's Cassandra."

Vivian couldn't believe her luck. Finally! Her big break had arrived, and she was ecstatic. So what that it took a few years? She was busy working and climbing the ladder. These things needed to happen at their own pace. "Can I bring the drawings that I did a few years ago? They still look good."

"Of course, you kept the drawings you used—look how organized you are!" Cassandra said as she knew exactly how to swoon her opponent. Once you compliment Vivian on her organization and preparation skills, she followed you anywhere. Vivian felt as if she got a gold sticker on her school report and wondered if her elementary school teacher was still alive. How she wanted to show her how far she had come and what she invented!

"Oh, yes. There's one more thing," Cassandra added, casually.

"What? Anything. I'll do it."

"Bring 5,000 dollars with you. A certified check is fine, but cash works best."

"Five thousand? That's a lot of money!" Vivian raised her voice and placed her hands on her hips.

"Aye, aye, aye . . . shhh. Keep cool," Cassandra said with her hands in the air, pushing downwards as if Vivian was a noisy child. This gesture added to that dash of concern, but the Travel Set train was set on its tracks and was ready to go, full steam ahead and Vivian really wanted to be on board! But before she bought her ticket, some questions needed to be asked.

"Why so much?"

"You should see the production costs! But don't worry, you'll get it back ten-fold!" Cassandra said, which kicked that doubt to the curb, but Vivian was still not convinced yet and wanted to buy more time. The next day was too soon to jump on that train with a stipulation like that.

"Let me think about it."

"You want to strike while the iron is hot! Trust me, you don't want to miss this opportunity, honey!" Cassandra said, and with those last few words, Vivian nodded to seal the deal and both ladies made a date to meet back at the store the following day at closing time with Cassandra's aunt in tow.

Thrilled out of her mind, she zoomed up to the shoe department and grabbed Lilly's arm and dumped the entire past twenty minutes on her.

"No. No. No."

"What do you mean no? This is my chance!"

"I can smell a rat, Viv."

"You're wrong. This is great opportunity. She's got contacts!"

"Really? I don't know, it seems too good to be true. And it's too fast!" Lilly said, as Vivian slouched in disappointment. *Oh, come on, listen to me!* Vivian pleaded in her mind.

"You just don't believe in me, that's it," Vivian said, crossing her arms and feeling frustrated.

"That's not fair—I do so believe in you! Look, let me get back to work. We'll go out for dinner after work, that will calm your nerves."

"I don't want to go out for dinner!" Vivian hollered that echoed throughout the department store while the customers stopped to look at Vivian, as she bowed down and went back to the cosmetics department.

Later that night, as the two ladies ate dinner at a corner restaurant down the street, Vivian reiterated the conversation she had with Cassandra once again and Lilly's reaction resembled a storm: a few moments of silence, followed by thrashes of wind and hail.

"Five thousand dollars? You will do no such thing!" Lilly said in a loud whisper.

"But I'm giving her only twenty percent!" Vivian protested.

"Over my dead body!" Lilly added.

"And I'll get the money back, ten-fold! I'm going to be rich!"

"Really? And you believe her?" Lilly was now yelling, as this was not the Vivian she knew. She wasn't making sense, not thinking straight and making poor decisions. It was as if she was obsessed with the Travel Set and couldn't think rationally. What was going on with her, Lilly thought.

"Why not?"

"If you give one red penny to this Cassandra person, you'll be sorry!" Lilly yelled while pointing her finger at Vivian. "Honey, that's at least six months of your salary; you've worked so hard for that."

"It's my money, and I will do what I want with it," Vivian yelled as she got up from the table and ran to her car. she started the ignition and then turned it off as she thought how weird it was it that Cassandra and Lilly both used honey as term of endearment, but Lilly's felt real. No, I won't be talked out of this opportunity. This is my chance! Vivian thought to herself as she turned on the ignition again and drove away, pushing down all feelings of doubt. She needed this victory. And wanted it so badly.

***

The next day, Vivian scooped up her presentation materials from her closet, and took them with her to work. As she was putting them away in the boardroom for safe keeping, she ran into Lilly who was passing by.

"Haven't seen those boards in a few years," Lilly commented. "Yeah, the Bristol board faded a little, and the pictures are a tad old, but the message is still the same," Vivian said as she straightened her headband.

"If you want to do this, go ahead. It's your money," Lilly said.

"Thanks. I have a good feeling about this."

"Wait, you know, maybe you should talk to Mr. Sand."

"He's away this week. Too late," Vivian said as she walked to her counter, leaving Lilly standing there as she waited a full five minutes before she was able to move.

On her lunch hour, Vivian went to her bank and ordered a certified check for 5,000 dollars, a huge chunk of her savings, which she put in an envelope and placed it at the bottom of her purse.

At 5:00 p.m., Cassandra met Vivian exactly where they were speaking the day before.

"Where is your aunt?" Vivian asked as she handed Cassandra the envelope, while she checked inside to make sure it was there.

"Oh, she couldn't make it." Vivian's heart sank to the floor as she knew something wasn't right. But it was too late, as Cassandra was walking away toward the front doors, and Vivian began to panic. She needed to stop her, but how? Two words left her lips.

"Frank Sinatra," Vivian whispered.

"Frank Sinatra?" Mr. Sand repeated as Vivian swung her head around to see Mr. Sand standing there in shock.

"Mr. Sand, what are you doing here?"

"Lilly called me. Luckily, my last tradeshow was cancelled so I was home. What's going on?"

"I've been ripped off!" Vivian yelled and grabbed Mr. Sand's hand and they both ran to the front doors to track down Cassandra. "Lilly!" Vivian yelled to the shoe department as she was at the front doors.

"I'm coming!" Lilly yelled as she left her customer with a pair of shoes in her hand and zoomed to catch up, but used the service side door to get outside, where she ran into Cassandra and dug her hands into her arms as if she caught a slippery fish. "Ooowww!" Cassandra yelled.

"Keep screaming and I call the police," Lilly threatened as she brought her back into the store. Once inside, the interrogation began.

"Security!" Lilly yelled as soon as she pushed the big solid brass doors open, holding on to Cassandra.

"No, Lilly—I got this," Vivian said.

"No, you don't," Lilly said as she and Mr. Sand held on to Cassandra's arm tighter, as she didn't put up a fight to escape, but remained calm in their hands.

"SECURITY! FRANK SINATRA" Mr. Sand yelled. "What is taking so long?" he asked nervously while customers began to talk and walk over to see all the commotion.

"Let me handle this, I know what I'm doing!" Vivian yelled, but Lilly just wanted to make this Cassandra person disappear.

"Security!" Lilly yelled once again, but no one was coming. No one was ever coming to help her, as she learned years ago, except Vivian. With her newfound voice and strength, she had to do something fast.

Flashbacks popped up in her mind that fueled her ammunition. The shoplifter who she pounced on in the basement. Running into Marie Ste. Claire and her friend in the grocery store. The delivery man who pinched her behind at her mother's store. Rage began to rise and she needed to put it somewhere.

While screaming, Lilly jumped on top of Cassandra, and both fell onto the cold linoleum floor where they wrestled and yelled. Rolling to the left and right with thrashes and screams in between. Lilly tried to reach to pinch Cassandra's ear, just as she did years ago to the shop lifter, but Cassandra's grasp on Lilly's arms was too tight. Mr. Sand jumped in and fell on top of both women, where the body of his weight managed to stabilize the brawl. Vivian stood motionless upon the wrestling match, while she contemplated what to do. Jump in? Run to her counter to call the police or scream to play Frank Sinatra again? It was too late for Vivian to do anything as all the yelling and screaming finally caught a security guard's attention, and he came running.

"Finally!" Mr. Sand yelled.

"Grab the purse, Vivian!" Lilly yelled, but Vivian didn't move.

"Grab it! Take it! Lilly yelled again, but to no avail, Vivian continued to stand motionless, while a customer went to grab it and held on to it.

The security guard took hold of Cassandra by putting her in handcuffs, and Lilly began to put everything together.

"Your hair..."

"It runs in my family."

"It was you that day. With your mother. The shoes."

"That was my mother, but I wasn't with her, as she was with my younger sister, and by the way, your check is not in my purse," Cassandra announced, as Lilly, Vivian and Mr. Sand's jaws dropped. Complexion comments were obviously disregarded.

* * *

All the customers who were at Sunderland's that day was witnessing an action-packed real-live fight, right before their eyes. Many had seen a fight in a playground, a sports field or a at a bar, but never like this—two grown women fighting like two screaming cats with the bonus of an extra large screaming cat on the department store floor as an encore.

"This is better than television," a young boy said to his mother, who nodded in agreement and couldn't wait to tell her sister what she saw. All eyes were on the players in front of the cosmetics counter, where Vivian stood on her feet for hours at a time, helping thousands of customers feel pretty and taken care of. Where Lilly worked and learned that she could do whatever she put her mind to, including finding her voice. Where Mr. Sand first discovered Vivian so many years ago. An eager young teenager who couldn't wait to be surrounded by beautiful things all day and every day. Who blossomed into a saleswoman that went beyond anyone's expectations, including her own.

"Hello again," said a woman from behind the crowd, who was the lady that tormented Lilly from that day several years ago.

"You," Lilly said, gazing at her opponent who, looked the same, but a few years older. She had a few more grey hairs and eyes that read anger.

"Me," the woman said. Lilly, Vivian and Mr. Sand's blood began to boil as they knew very well who this woman was as they could never forget that face that was attached to a soul that wanted to abuse Lilly for no other reason than for being Jewish.

"I asked you not to come back into the store again," Mr. Sand said.

"Well, I took a few years off. I thought that was good enough."

"Hand it over," Lilly said as Vivian stood there motionless.

"Are you kidding?"

"No, I'm not," Lilly threatened.

"Oh, what are you going to do to me? Call your man over here—like he's going to do anything—he may break a nail," the woman said while she waved her hand in a feminine way, mocking the fact that Mr. Sand was gay. "Don't you dare talk to Mr. Sand that way," Vivian blurted out, feeling like an egg in boiling water, about to burst out of its shell. Mr. Sand rested his hand on Vivian's shoulder, which meant to calm her, but didn't.

The security guard reached for his walkie-talkie and asked for back up, while the woman pushed away the crowd and ran down the aisle to the front doors and vanished.

"Mom!" Cassandra yelled.

"It's over," Mr. Sand said. Vivian turned around to look at him with a face that had fallen to her knees.

"I got it." I knew she wouldn't put the check in her purse. While we were wrestling, I reached into her bra and got it. Lilly proudly said as she waved the checkin the air and brought it down to eye level and ripped it into pieces and threw it up in the air like confetti.

That Girl

"Bravo, Lilly! You saved the day!" Mr. Sand clapped his hands while the crowd cheered and ran up to Vivian to hug her. Thrilled that she didn't lose her money, she was relieved and ecstatic. Although as Lilly came over to be by her side, Vivian was relieved indeed, but didn't smile.

I Need a Moment

That afternoon had pounded Vivian to the ground. It was as if someone placed both hands on her shoulders and kept them there so she couldn't move.

She was appalled at what happened. How could she fall for that mother and daughter devil duo? She couldn't believe that she took out all that money—the exorbitant amount of $5,000 for what? Just to get an introduction to all the major department stores in hope that the Travel Set would get produced? Looking back on her behavior, Vivian realized that she was not thinking straight. Lilly was right all along, and she couldn't stand it.

Vivian imagined how rich she was going to be with the long list of things she wanted to buy. Beginning with a country home for her parents, a new living room set and of course several designer pieces and jewelry. The treasured yet materialistic items were what she craved, but what she really desired for was the recognition. For everyone to know that Vivian Steiner created the Travel Set. To prove to anyone that ever doubted her ability to succeed was wrong. Take that Bonbons. The bloody teacher's ruler. The "why aren't you married?" and "you're so cute!" comments and shove them all up your asses. I did it, you bastards! She so desperately wanted to say.

I Need a Moment

As her victory daydreams poofed like fairy dust and she just wanted to cry in shame.

"Where was my mind? What was I thinking?" she said to herself. Out loud. And everywhere—from in the shower, while she shaved her legs, to her parents on the phone in Florida, to sales reps and to customers while she was applying lipstick on them. This created quite a stir among the public, but most women didn't care—they just wanted to have five minutes with the famous Vivian so they could buy the latest product and apply it properly. Although Mr. Sand did care.

"Dear, please keep your commentary to yourself. You made a mistake; your friend saved the day, and all is well. Can't you just move on?" Mr. Sand asked.

Vivian nodded but could not move on and decided to take a leave of absence from the corporate part of her job so that she could spend time doing what she truly loved, selling cosmetics to customers. It was a simple routine that she could do in her sleep. It was repetitive at times, but it humbled her, which helped for a little while.

The feeling of remorse was so great that there were times when she awoke in the mornings and could not move her head left or right, as it was stiff from tension. Being the stubborn girl that she was, she tried to force her head to turn, which led to a deep cry of agony, followed by her head collapsing in her hands as she sobbed.

Marsha, who lived nearby moved into Vivian's apartment with her, as she knew her sister was not in good shape and needed support, even though she repeatedly refused. "No way, Marsh—forget it. I'm fine."

"You're not—Move," Marsha announced, with her suitcase in hand at her front door as she marched to her guest room.

"When will this stop?" Vivian asked Marsha one morning as she was buttering her toast in her kitchen?

Marsha walked to the cupboard to get a glass.

"Just make it stop," Vivian pleaded.

"I can't. I wish I could," Marsha said as she poured some water from the faucet into the glass and handed it to her sister, while Vivian looked up at the ceiling to look for answers.

"Maybe you shouldn't go in today."

"I must. It's my job."

"But look at you—your eyes have been two red tomatoes for the past two weeks. Why can't you ask for a vacation? Time off?"

"I already told you a million times—I can't."

"But you are not at your best. You suffered a loss. You need time to heal."

"I need to be at work. I've committed to this job, and people are depending on me," Vivian said, as she took a sip from the glass of water. "It's the only think I know how to do well," she added as she walked to the kitchen table to eat her breakfast.

"What do you mean it's the only thing you know how to do well?" Marsha asked as a small crack from her past was exposed, and it burned like a fresh paper cut.

* * *

The ride to work that morning in her car was stressful as there was so much traffic. At a traffic light, she gazed at her polished red nails. The beautiful color gave her a lift of happiness, even if it was for a few short moments. She then flipped her hand over to reveal her palms. The scars were long gone, but the memory of over twenty years ago was still crystal clear in her mind and still hurt. "Oh damn," Vivian whispered as the tears began to fill her eyes. She vowed not to go there, but her mind was lost, and she was feeling as vulnerable as ever, from the brief conversation that she had with Marsha that morning.

If only her teachers could see her now. Ladies from all over Montreal were lining up patiently in order to meet her and get her advice. She didn't need the Travel Set to realize her worth. Or did she? Her head began to spin as doubt quickly rushed into her mind. Maybe her teachers were right—maybe she really was stupid. Why would she trust someone she hardly knew with $5,000? She gripped the steering wheel so tight, her knuckles seemed as if they were going to break through her skin. She still couldn't believe that she succumbed to Cassandra. And her mother.

She stopped her car right in front of Sunderland's and saw the lineup of women outside. She knew they were all for her as word got out that she was back at the store full time as a salesgirl once again. As she left her parked car in the employee parking lot and walked toward the front entrance several ladies walked up to her.

"Vivian! Did the new color come in yet?" a woman yelled.

"Viv! Vivian! Oh, my gosh—there she is! You look fabulous today!" another lady yelled.

"I'll see you inside," was all she could manage to say back and walked into the department store full steam ahead.

Lilly was at her counter, waiting for her.

"What are you doing here?" Vivian asked.

"Want a coffee?" Lilly asked sweetly.

"I guess."

"You guess? Come on, Viv. You love the coffee here. And how about some cookies?" Lilly sang swinging the bag the cookies came in.

"Lilly, I'm not six!"

"Alright! Geepers . . . what's with you?"

Vivian took out her lipstick and reapplied it even though it didn't need reapplying.

"How are you doing today?" Mr. Sand said as he walked toward the counter.

"Morning, I'm fine thanks. . ."

"Sure," Mr. Sand said sarcastically.

"Geez—will everyone just leave me alone?" Vivian said while startling Mr. Sand.

"You're not okay, are you?"

"I said I was fine. I am fine," Vivian said as she picked up the lipstick tray and began to clean it.

"Viv, you haven't done that in years. There are other associates who will clean the trays," Vivian stopped cleaning.

"I got it, go," Mr. Sand reassured her and gave a look that she knew so well because after over 10 years of working together, Vivian could almost read Mr. Sand's mind.

Vivian walked to the basement of the department store as quickly as her kitten heels would take her. It was there, where she had once counted nail polishes to earn her keep, that she let her guard down. No one was counting, organizing, or cleaning nail polishes or shoes there anymore, as they moved the inventory to a new room on the main floor. The basement was now where old display counters, advertisements and store signs were stored. Vivian took an old garbage can, turned it upside down, and sat on the base to cry near a large poster of Elizabeth Taylor. As she gazed at her perfect smile and velvet eyes, she wondered if she ever got scammed by a stranger and then saved by her best friend and then felt awful after. She shook her head and thought probably not. Nobody would screw with Liz.

Sometimes an associate would follow Vivian downstairs and would get her a glass of water and sit with her, and she would tell them what happened on that frightful afternoon. It was some story.

When fifteen minutes would pass, she then would compose herself, fix her makeup, brush her hair, and return to work. Lilly would be waiting, asking if she could do anything for her friend. Get her a cup of coffee, a cookie? Take her shift.

"But you don't know anything about these lines!" Vivian would say, as it was just an excuse as she knew Lilly would be completely fine working her counter.

"I could learn!" Lilly defended.

"Sure—you could do anything," Vivian said sarcastically.

"That's not fair."

"Is it?"

"Why can't you let me help you?"

"You already did."

Lilly's Man

The idea of getting married again, let alone meeting someone, never entered Lilly's mind. She had been married once before and had her kids, so what was the point? Companionship? Who had the time while working over forty hours a week? Keeping a roof over her children's heads and food on the table was her priority. Besides, she was turning thirty. *Who would want to date an old broad like me?* she had thought.

But there he was, buying a vacuum cleaner for his home at the famous Sunderland's Department Store on a Saturday afternoon, just before closing. Lilly never visited the fourth floor at Sunderland's, where they sold household appliances. There was no reason to unless one of her appliances also needed replacing. And it did, according to her mother.

"Oy! The filth on your carpets!" her mother said one day while she was visiting.

"I'll get around to it, Ma!"

"There is such a thick layer of schmutz here! I can scoop it up with a knife and schmear it on a St. Viateur bagel!"

"Eeewww, Ma!"

"Every time I come here, it gets worse and worse! Go and get a new vacuum cleaner today! I insist!" her mother cried as she put her hand on her hip and shot her a look that Lilly knew too well.

"All right," Lilly obediently agreed.

"Go and get it, or she'll have your head on a platter!" Mr. Sand jokingly said as he passed by Lilly's shoe department before he left for the day. Lilly had filled Mr. Sand and Vivian in on the carpet shmutz on a bagel fiasco over coffee that morning before the store opened and of course, roars of laughter followed that story, which made Lilly feel hopeful that Vivian was getting back to her usual self.

"Oh, right—I almost forgot!" Lilly said amid putting away a box of shoes.

"Go and please your mother," Vivian giggled in the ladies' room after their lunch break while they reapplied their lipsticks and face powder.

"Yeah, yeah, I'll go!" Lilly announced with her hands up in the air, feeling relieved as her assumptions that morning was turning out to be true.

Armed with as much will power as she could muster, Lilly was determined to walk to her destination and not be distracted. "Don't look, Lil! Don't look!" She whispered to herself as she picked up the pace as quickly as her heels would take her. But what was she preventing herself from seeing?

Shall we begin with the perfume counter that resided just to the left of the shoe department where she worked? She knew that her mission had to be accomplished before the store closed, so there was no time for any dilly-dallying with Sunderland's selective perfume collection, displayed on an antique silver tray that was imported from Paris, so it was said. So, she diligently refrained from reaching for one of the elegant glass bottles to spritz an enticing but unknown new fragrance on her wrist and the nape of her neck. Of course, her favorite scent was on display, the iconic Guerlain's Shalimar. Lilly was a proud owner of her very own bottle at home, as the distributor accidentally delivered an extra sample bottle, and Vivian snatched it for her before anyone else got their hands on it. It amazed her how much Vivian thought of her when it came to things like that. Always putting other people first and of course, pleasing them.

The next glass showcase housed the seasonal accessories. During wintertime, they had the softest and coziest wool scares, hats and gloves that would elevate any dull wool winter coat to face Montreal's bitterly cold winters, with style. Lilly was known for that look as she took advantage of her employee discount for those purchase. Then again, on the other side of the coin, there were hats and gloves that were embellished with a fur trim that of course matched perfectly with the chosen fur coat du jour.

As Lilly walked down the aisles, she remembered the time when she first started to work at Sunderland's where she daydreamed of elegance and status by means of being the proud owner of some fur. And it didn't even have to be a full coat, just some accessories. Yes, she tried to mix elegance with practicality, but it didn't work as it looked as if she was wearing a fur stole with a pair of dungarees. With the ambition of being the fashionista that Vivian was, Lilly put on her wool coat, that was handed down from her sister, that had a small tear in the inside seem that she meant to mend, but never got around to it, along with the fur accessories, she twirled around like a model for Vivian and Mr. Sand. And they responded with sour faces and shook their heads.

"Stick with the wool gloves and scarf," Vivian suggested as Lilly's face fell to the floor.

"Aw . . . you'll wear a fur someday!" Mr. Sand cheerfully said.

But when? Lilly thought, as she wondered what it would feel like to wear a fur coat. To waltz into a room and slowly let it fall off her shoulders and wait for a certain gentleman to take it from her as she sat down to dinner. She watched countless women enter

Sunderland's in their furs. Their head was held high, they threw their shoulders back and looked so elegant and sure of themselves. These women were filled with confidence. During that time in her life, she wanted to feel that way, too.

One morning, from afar, as she was cleaning the shoe shelves, she counted six minks and four foxes that all came in at the same time. And once, by accident, as she was showing a pair of shoes to a customer, she was within inches of a brand new, floor length black mink coat. A first to be so close to a coat like that and before she knew it, her hand gently made contact and gently caressed the luxuriousness. It almost took her breath away and was thankful that her customer didn't hear her sigh so heavy. Yes, Sunderland's sold fur coats. Yes, she very well could touch, caress, and bury her face in any fur coat that was displayed on the showroom floor. But she didn't dare. What kind of nincompoop would behave that way in public?

But that was years ago. Lilly placed that pipedream away on a shelf, as it didn't really matter anymore as she thought that perception weighed more than possessions.

Back to Lilly's destination: the fourth floor of Sunderland's! There were only two displays of merchandise before she reached the escalator, and with a sigh of relief, Lilly held onto the banister as she reached the appliance floor to buy a new vacuum cleaner.

Little did she know what was in store for her.

"Come here often?" was all he could think of to say to the most beautiful woman he had ever seen holding a brand-new vacuum cleaner by her side. Even if the pick-up line was overused like an old towel, Lilly didn't care. Not in the least. As she stared at this man, she thought of releasing her grasp of the vacuum cleaner, letting it fall onto the floor and then luring him to where the washing machines were displayed. As she loved the spin cycle. But she composed herself and answered his question.

"Yes and no," Lilly said, trying to tone down the smile that made her cheeks burn. Feeling completely careless for not refreshing her Shalimar from the customer display that she just passed by minutes ago, as the perfume that she put on before she left the house that morning usually faded by her afternoon coffee break. Wondering if her deodorant was working as she felt a droplet of sweat that was making its way down her back.

He waited. She gazed at the washing machines and then shook her head to focus on the situation at hand.

"Yes, I come here often because I work in the shoe department, but no, I don't come to the fourth floor. Ever. Unless, well, I need something like this," Lilly said, motioning to her purchase, as she was still hanging on to the vacuum cleaner. She never dropped it on the floor and walked hand in hand with the enticing stranger to the washing machines, but held on to that daydream for a little while longer while she smiled at the nice, handsome man.

Ever so discreetly, Lilly carefully moved her eyes to his hands, in search of a wedding band, and lo and behold, she could not find any trace of gold or silver. Relief washed through her, and she felt a rush of excitement that made the burn of her cheeks bleed to the rest of her body.

Please Don't Go

After a courtship of two years—followed by many different variations of *well?* and their reply of *what's the rush?*—they were engaged.

"But why do you have to leave just because you're getting married?" Vivian pleaded, after Lilly had shared her thoughts of leaving Sunderland's.

How could she? After being promoted to head shoe buyer, which gave her the opportunity to travel to Italy every season, attend all the fashion shows, with Mr. Sand and, of course, she brought home a pair or two for her old' pal Vivian.

"Bring home this one and this one. You know my size," Vivian would say as she looked through the upcoming catalogs. And, of course, Lilly would ask Vivian for samples when she attended cosmetic conferences in New York every spring.

"Do not even THINK of coming home without the biggest bottle that you can find of Lancôme's Nutrix. I don't care if you have to wrestle the sales rep to the ground," Lilly would demand.

"Read you loud and clear," Vivian would reply, while Lilly took that response to heart, thinking that she wasn't able to reciprocate. As she wasn't able to read Vivian loud and clear at all and she wanted to.

* * *

The Most Amazing Department Store

A few years had passed and with time, the whole Travel Set experience didn't make Vivian want to hide in the storage room as often, where she would talk to fashion icons on old cosmetic billboards. Yes, the memory still stung, but it wasn't brought up as often.

"Let it lie," Mr. Sand advised.

"But I want to talk about it," Lilly pleaded to Mr. Sand as they walked around the block one day during a coffee break.

"I don't think Vivian wants to open up that can of worms—as there is more in there than she can face," Mr. Sand said as Lilly lingered on the idiom and stopped walking.

"There's something there. And I want to know what it is."

"Let me see what I can dig up," Mr. Sand said to Lilly, as he placed his hand her on the back, even though he had no clue how he was going to poke at the blister that needed antibiotics (a martini would do) and a bandage, but he had to try. The next day, before opening, Mr. Sand, Vivian and Lilly were having coffee, waiting for a shipment to arrive for the shoe department.

"I have news," Vivian announced, while Lilly and Mr. Sand were all ears. "Would you believe that dynamic duo of demons were connected to a Neo-Nazi group?"

"No!" Mr. Sand said.

"Yes sir, the mother was an unidentified spy that was assigned to the department store for the first occurrence with Lilly, and then heard about my failed attempt with the Travel Set through a customer," Vivian said as Lilly sat there motionless, except for her blinking eyes.

"I did tell every human being who walked into Sunderland's that was served at my counter," Vivian admitted.

"And where is she today?" Lilly asked.

"She got fined. That was all. Daughter too," Vivian said.

"I hope for a million dollars," Mr. Sand joked.

"Who knows," Vivian said. Lilly placed her hand on Vivian's.

Please Don't Go

* * *

Back to the subject at hand, that was filled with questions like these that continued to circle Vivian's mind. How could Lilly leave? Didn't she enjoy her time with Vivian at Sunderland's lunch counter, where they would reminisce and gossip before their shifts began, drinking their coffee and devouring Sunderland's famous cookies?

"There is no reason why I must work. He's a periodontist and does very well," Lilly said.

"Oh. My. God. Eleanor Roosevelt would slap you."

"Let her."

"Don't go, Lil."

"I want to."

Lilly now had a choice. She no longer had the stress of putting food on the table and paying house bills. She could work at Sunderland's because she wanted to and because she was good at her job.

But she chose to leave. She loved her career; being a shoe buyer was not only fun but empowering. It reminded her of her school days where she would put in the hard work and receive an award for it—that beautiful letter A written in red. It was her stamp of approval that told her she was smart, worthwhile, and accountable.

And so, Lilly took that wisdom with her to Sunderland's. Every step that was taken before she bought a line was carefully thought out through research and by listening to her gut. She knew her customers; she knew which shoes would sell the moment she saw them. And most of the time, she was right. But, sometimes, she was wrong, and she was able to own that mistake.

Not like someone else she knew.

"This line of skincare should be flying off the shelves. Customers just don't get it yet," Vivian said one afternoon.

"Look, you made a mistake," Lilly pointed out. "It's okay. Move on and learn from it and stop buying that line."

"I did not make a mistake. I never make mistakes," Vivian had replied in a huff before she turned on her heel and walked away.

These moments were becoming more frequent and traveled into their personal lives. The time they spent together made Lilly clench her teeth. The criticism from Vivian was not constructive; it was hurtful, didn't make sense, and bothered Lilly, and she didn't know how to put a stop to it, although she tried. It was if Vivian was trying to erase what happened that afternoon by telling Lilly that she knew what was best.

"Viv, I will wear my pants this way," Lilly defended one afternoon in front of the ladies' room mirror.

"But that's so last year."

"But what does it matter? Pants don't expire like milk."

It wasn't just the fashion criticism. Lilly knew that Mr. Sand was right. Lilly really wanted to get that can opener to let those worms free, but Vivian was hiding the can opener. Even the manual one.

"Viv, we need to talk about it."

"Talk about what? Everything's fine." But they weren't fine, as both were carrying around feelings the size of boulders.

"Did you see the latest issue of *Vogue*? They are carrying the shoes you just bought for the store!" Vivian said, trying to add more sugar to the fruit that turned sour. Lilly shook her head, forbidding herself to the continued chatter that didn't go anywhere. After almost ten years of working at Sunderland's, it was time for a change. It was time for Lilly to leave.

"But why?" Vivian asked.

"I already told you why."

"But I'm here," Vivian protested.

"I'm not moving out of Montreal. We can still see each other," Lilly said, hoping that maybe with time, Vivian would be more transparent. Maybe they could talk about it.

Vivian's face fell as she knew in her heart that this wouldn't happen. How could it when she was hiding behind her veil of lipstick?

1982

Almost thirty years had passed since Lilly left Sunderland's, and there wasn't a time where she didn't miss that part of her life. What she accomplished in the ten years she worked there amazed her. Lilly knew she was smart, and she knew she had chutzpah, but her divorce lingered like a dark cloud, which followed her around everywhere she went. Working at Sunderland's allowed some light to shine through as it re-opened the door to her strengths, encouraging her to walk into challenges and face them head on.

But damn that Vivian. Even after all these years. Lilly hated leaving "it" alone—letting it lie, just like Mr. Sand suggested. She was still itching to get to the bottom of it, but didn't know how, or did she even want to try?

In the mid-1950s, on Lilly's wedding day, when the band was wrapping up their electrical cords and the waiters were sweeping the floors, the three of them, Mr. Sand, Vivian and Lilly stood in a corner of the dance floor, holding hands, promising each other that they would have dinner once a week together—forever. And thankfully, this promise was kept, while Lilly became a housewife and Vivian and Mr. Sand continued to work at Sunderland's.

One evening, during their weekly dinner dates, Mr. Sand didn't look well. He had a horrible cough and a stuffed-up nose.

1982

"This cold won't go away!" Mr. Sand said as he sipped his martini. But if you would ask what was really bothering him, it wasn't his cold, but the tension between the two ladies, as it was as thick as the two-inch steak that he just ordered.

"That's it, you're taking the day off tomorrow and I'm bringing you my matza ball soup."

Lilly said as she sipped her white wine. Vivian nodded her head.

"Meh," Mr. Sand said.

"What you need is plenty of liquids and rest," Vivian said.

"Oh, you girls. Always taking care of me," Mr. Sand said as he blew his nose.

"When you're busy taking care of customers and doing your job, so many things pass you by," Vivian said.

"Most things, but not all," Mr. Sand said.

Lilly looked up for more. "What do you mean?"

"Things aren't always what they appear to be," Mr. Sand said softly as Vivian glared at him, while she absorbed the cards that she was dealt with. Nobody except her parents and Marsha knew of the abuse that she went through when she was a little girl. She vowed that nobody had to hear about that dreadful part of her life and told herself to forget them and move on and be nothing but perfect. But of course, she spoiled that image after she was rejected by her business proposal and then get scammed by two anti-Semitic thieves.

Why burden anyone with those sad and dreadful experiences? What was the point?

But there was a point, as she could have solved all of what was between Lilly and her over one simple conversation. No matter how close two people may seem, no matter what they have in common, or how many laughs they share, something between them still could be missing.

To have that conversation, they would have to create a safe space to listen, to not judge and be kind. So simple yet so difficult because before each of them could let their guard down, a mutual understanding of trust and empathy had to have been present, which was not apparent.

"You have taken care of us. We both wouldn't be here if it wasn't for you," Vivian said to Mr. Sand while smiling at Lilly, who returned the smile and a voice that screamed to Vivian, *Let me in!*

Visiting Hours

Lilly sat by Mr. Sand's hospital bed and held his hand. She was visiting him every Tuesday afternoon for the past month, when living at home was no longer feasible. She knew Vivian wouldn't be there, as Tuesdays was her standing manicure appointment. It was as obvious as a nail polish chip that Lilly was avoiding her.

"Why can't you see her point of view?" Mr. Sand asked Lilly.

"Point of view? Mr. Sand, do you know how she treated me? After I saved the day?"

"Whoa whoa whoa there."

"She made me feel worthless."

Mr. Sand gave her a disapproving look. "Let's take a moment and look at the whole story—I mean the whole thing—from beginning to end."

"Be my guest."

"Ok. Here we have Vivian Steiner. Sales associate extraordinaire who put her heart and soul into her job. Created a product that didn't make it off the ground. And, to top it all off, she got scammed by two anti-Semitic thieves."

"Right."

"Then we have you—Lilly Krovchick, a divorcé. When *no one*

got divorced—I have to add, because my dear, that took guts like nobody's business."

"Thank you," Lilly said as pushed her hair off her shoulders.

"Mother of three. Worked her way up in the shoe department and got married and left Sunderland's."

"Exactly. So, what did I do? Why am I being punished? I didn't take her dreams away. In fact, I tried to help her."

"I want you to look closer at Vivian's story. Is that all? Why do you think she couldn't accept your help?"

"I don't know!"

"Neither do I. But we must find out why."

"There's that can of worms again! Why can't you just tell me?"

"I don't know myself, my dearie!"

"Oh, come on!" Lilly screamed as Mr. Sand shook his face, as it fell.

"Why can certain people cope and not others? Why couldn't she accept your help. I also want you to think about all the good that took place. And another thing—why are you weighing your friendship on this shit—oh my, pardon my French," Mr. Sand said in a strained voice, as it took an effort to speak, especially with emotionally filled words. He reached out to hold her hand and hoped that he would be able to see the day that his two friends would make amends before he would pass. Lilly held Mr. Sand's hand as he wrestled with his heavy eye lids. She knew she had to say something to Vivian.

"I can't go with the both of you not speaking. I just can't."

"Mr. Sand, don't say that," Lilly said in a panic as she squeezed his hands, while the doctor on call entered the room.

"How are you doing, Mr. Sand?" he asked while giving a warm gaze at his patient, nodding to Vivian to greet her and then reaching for the clipboard that hung on the foot of his bed to study it.

"As fine as I'll ever be," Mr. Sand said with a heavy sigh. "I just have some unfinished business to deal with." Lilly's face fell to the ground while she played with the strap of her purse.

"Will you excuse us, for just for a moment?" the doctor asked. Lilly nodded her head reached over to Mr. Sand and gave him a hug.

"I'll be back in a few days," Lilly said and left, while the doctor sat down on the side of Mr. Sand's bed. He looked deep into his eyes, paused, and gave a gentle smile. His warm presence made Mr. Sand feel at ease while spoke in a soft tone, just above a whisper as he shared what was going on with his bloodwork and how to remain as comfortable as possible. Mr. Sand took in the information as best as he could, but he was obviously distracted. A knock at the door was heard.

"Surprise!" Geraldine, Lilly's thirteen-year-old granddaughter announced as Mr. Sand's face lit up like a birthday cake. "I thought I would pop by and say hello."

"Aw, you just missed your grandma!" Mr. Sand said as he stretched his arms wide while Geraldine bent down to hug him.

"How's my favorite Sand Man?" Geraldine said as she planted a kiss on his cheek. Mr. Sand had been a part of Lilly's family since the day Geraldine was born. A frequent guest at their Shabbat table and all of Geraldine's birthday parties—where he would give her the best presents as he always knew what she liked.

"I'll leave you two alone. But I will be back," the doctor said.

"Bye Doc!" Geraldine said while shooing him out of the room.

"Bye, doc? You have such . . ."

"Chutzpah?"

Mr. Sand shook his head, very well knowing that his little friend was becoming more like her grandma by the minute. What will she think of next, he thought? If anything, she better start thinking fast, as time was ticking on his watch.

"Sand man—it's the grandmas. There's trouble."

"How did you know?"

"I wasn't born yesterday."

"That's for sure."

"It's this tension. You can feel it every time my grandmother mentions Vivian. Such a yucky feeling," Geraldine said as she leaned on the bed handle, which placed a seed in Mr. Sand's mind, but wanted to continue prompting.

"What are you saying?" he added while Geraldine stood up and placed her hands on her hips, hoping she could shine some light on the situation, as he knew she was wise for her age.

"What do ladies do to feel better?"

"Shop," Mr. Sand said matter-of-factly.

"Working with ladies who shop for so many years is one tough job. If you can figure that out, you can do anything," Geraldine said with a smile and a wink. "I'll see you later," she said.

"Hey, where are you going? You call that a visit?" he asked.

"It's quality, not quantity!" Geraldine said as she skipped out of the room. Then she came back in to pop her head in the doorway. "Oh, relax . . . I'm just going to pee. Want anything from the cafeteria?"

Mr. Sand smiled as he shook his head. As soon as Geraldine left, Mr. Sand reached over to his telephone and phoned Geraldine's mother Corrine to share what was on his mind. Nothing was going to stop him to get this message to his girls, not even death.

***

As Lilly walked back to her car in the hospital parking lot, she knew that she had to open that can of worms at some point. But when? When would she be ready? Would she ever? And how?

Three months later, Mr. Sand passed away.

Lilly: Shiva Schmoozing

It was the room that gave her the most comfort and pleasure, in her whole house. Lilly's living room was so aesthetically pleasing that it warmed her heart with happiness every time she opened the wooden framed glass doors and stepped onto the plush area rug. Art hung on the walls with decorative frames that was skillfully curated. The furniture was chosen from antique stores with an array of trinkets that were collected from travels abroad. But the most significant piece that stood in the far end of the room that Lilly treasured was her mother's couch. Reupholstered in a chocolate velour fabric that accentuated the wallpaper perfectly.

Lilly stood in the corner of her favorite hideaway. When they moved in many years ago and the children were teenagers, she warned them with a death wish if they dared to enter. God forbid a can of Coke would spill on the carpet or a baseball would make its way through an oil painting.

Out of all the rooms in her home, she spent the most time here, reading, writing, and enjoying the latest issue of *Vogue*, along with a delicious and nerve-calming glass of red wine.

Of course, before Lilly moved in, just after she got married, she received an offer from Vivian to help her decorate it. To choose the carpet, wallpaper, and some other accessories. She accepted, as they were still on relatively good terms and the tension was not as thick as the steak Mr. Sand ordered that night at the restaurant, more like deli, sliced very thin.

"That wallpaper! My gosh—those fuchsia peonies are as big as beach balls!" she recalled telling Vivian as they sat together looking through a catalog of wallpaper patterns as thick as two telephone books.

"Darling . . . trust me, you won't regret it. It's a classic. Besides, the wallpaper will highlight your mother's stunning couch, as they aren't made like that anymore—hang on to that masterpiece!"

"You don't mind helping me pick out a few things for the house?" Lilly asked after she agreed on the pink peonies and slammed the catalog closed, hoping this project would allow them to talk about . . . things.

"To quote the youngsters, I get my kicks out of this stuff! Encouraging you to paste these delicious pink peonies on your walls is pure bliss! Please, please let me do this—it makes me so happy."

The conversation was as crystal clear in her mind as if it happened the other day. It always amazed her how much talent Vivian had and how willing she was to help Lilly, but that was as far as it went.

"Grandma, Vivian is here to see you," Geraldine said.

Lilly paused and leaned in toward the front door, where she heard a voice that was as familiar as an old song.

"Tell her I'm in here. Let her schmooze with whomever is hanging out in the hallway," Lilly said. She needed time to compose herself. As she placed her hand to her chest, she thought of the last time she saw Vivian, as it was years. Before she could figure that question out, thoughts and questions bounced around in her head. What was she doing here? Why did she come? Why now? Lilly wasn't ready. No, she was. No, she wasn't. All this *mishigas* was making Lilly's head spin.

Lilly: Shiva Schmoozing

"Wait a minute—wait a minute, Lil!" she said to herself, and lately, she was talking to herself more and more during that time of mourning. Vivian is here to pay her respects because you just lost your God-damn husband, you nitwit! Passing away just months after Mr. Sand. A sudden diagnosis that didn't cause him to suffer, for long.

Although Lilly quit years ago, this time was the ideal time. No, the perfect time for a cigarette. What she would give for a deep inhalation of that bad-ass but oh—so delicious carcinogenic stick, dressed in a coat of white armor that gave her the perfect amount of dopamine to calm her right down. She wasn't surprised that she needed this type of pacification. It was a silly thought. Giggling to herself, she could just see the response to her lighting up.

"Mother—what the fuck are you doing?" her middle son would ask, who had a habit of planting the F-bomb on occasion. Okay, frequently.

As she learned from quitting smoking, there was a replacement for the disease-inducing habit to manage her stress, so off to the bodily self-caring she grew accustomed to. No time for any rigorous exercise such as a power walk, but the massaging of temples would suffice. Off went her fingers to her temples as she began to massage them, trying to quiet the noise from the hallway that the visitors from the Shiva gathered.

A hand squeezed her shoulder, and Lilly looked up to see her son—the middle one that would have sworn like a sailor if she would have lit up a cigarette.

"Mom, you looked beautiful that day," he said, while pointing to the wedding picture that was surrounded by other framed photographs.

"Thank you."

"Are you hungry?"

"I ate."

Lilly didn't like to lie to her children, but she wasn't hungry.

"Well, I better go and greet Vivian...," Lilly said to her son, as she put on a smile, and shoved the problem to the back corner of her mind, if that was at all possible, and it wasn't because it kept creeping back up, where it met a knot of nervousness that twisted in her stomach. Damn those questions that popped in her head. Lilly tried to think about all what Vivian did for her for so many years. Where was the good? Think about that, Lil, Focus! She thought to herself.

Lilly walked to the front door with clenched fists as she tried to breathe deeply to calm herself. No such luck there, as the pounding of her heart trumped any breathing technique that was recently learned at her late husband's hospice.

As she got closer, that familiar scent that brought her back to when they both worked at Sunderland's when they greeted each other in the mornings reached her nose, when they shared that first cup of coffee before their shift began, along with all the dreams and aspirations they wanted, especially that one dream and moment that ruined everything.

Even though Lilly learned to finally bring her shoulders back and hold her head high that presented the confidence that she had earned, without the help of any furs, that day was a challenge to follow through with that appearance, as her present sorrow kept her head down, which her slumped shoulders carried.

And there they were—those patent-leather, high-heeled shoes that Vivian was famous for wearing, which never went out of style. Lilly thought that she would figure out how she would feel if she saw her in person, but to no avail, that didn't happen, and she was conflicted as ever.

Lilly's eyes widened as she followed the shoes, up to the skirt, blouse, and famous strand of pearls. She held her smile and gathered her strength to greet her old friend in a cheerful way. She had to at least try.

"Hi Vivian!" Lilly said with a bright smile.

"Darling! You know how feel about you stretching your jaw like that!"

Out of habit, Lilly closed her mouth quickly and tried to figure out when she had begun to avoid her friend.

"Hello, my old friend!" Vivian cried while opening her arms. Lilly had no choice but to go in and hug back and the two ladies embraced and continued to hold each other as they began to speak.

"Who are you calling old?" Lilly joked. Ah, she was able to crack a joke, have a little fun. This was good, Lilly thought, and Geraldine laughed.

"Ah, the famous Vivian—your partner in crime where you guys told all those Jew-haters off!" Geraldine proudly stated. Lilly's eyes bulged as she reacted to the sting of her grandchild's question. She brought her hand to her mouth, as a flood of memories tested her tolerance. She had shared these stories with her family, knowing that they were important lessons, even though at the time, all that she had wanted was to dig a hole in the department store floor, crawl under it, and die. How she had gotten through those times, she had no idea. Yes, she did. Vivian was there. Coaching her. Reassuring her. Being there for her. This was the good that she was looking for, which brought her hope. It was just the very last incident that broke the bond between Lilly and Vivian that was still lingering to that day.

Vivian looked at Lilly, smiled without showing her teeth and decided to share some quick advice with the young. "Anti-Semites, dear . . . you should use that term. A more formal, respected term."

Geraldine nodded, as Lilly reached out to hold her hand, which gave her some extra strength to keep going and to take one for the team. If she knew her friend, this would work beautifully. And it did.

"Vivian—you look fabulous!"

"Oh . . . stop!"

"No, I won't"

"Ok, don't," Vivian giggled but suddenly felt awful about it as she knew that this was not the time and place to be so happy and to gush over superficial things, even though Lilly did say she looked fabulous. But maybe she shouldn't have taken the compliment? This was a Shiva, for God Sakes. Time to switch gears and be there for the mourner. Be attentive and to listen. Let the mourner initiate the conversation. She heard that this was how you were supposed to behave at a Shiva visit. Or was she supposed to be happy? Sad? Offer a tissue? Vivian had no idea how to act.

"I'm so sorry to hear about your loss," Vivian blurted out, as she knew that she had to say that line at some point.

"Thank you. It's a relief he is no longer suffering, but I feel like I lost my right arm."

"I can't even imagine," Vivian sighed with relief that the conversation became very Shiva-like. All good now, and proper.

"Twenty-five wonderful years . . . well, twenty-four . . ." Lilly said as they both walked toward the living room.

"Oh, those peonies!" Vivian remarked. There you go again with the superficial shit, will you just shut up? Vivian thought to herself.

"They are still fantastic!"

"I told you!" Vivian said because it was true! Ah, where does it say that you can't talk about pretty things while having a Shiva visit? At this point, Vivian decided to throw all the rules out the window and just relax. Lilly sat down on a Shiva chair while Vivian sat next to her on her mother's couch, and their two heads immediately connected in conversation.

Clusters of visitors continued to stand scattered around the house. One by one, Lilly's children checked up on their mother to see if she was okay, especially her daughter, Corrine, the mother of Geraldine, who knew almost every detail of her time at Sunderland's

Lilly: Shiva Schmoozing

with Vivian. But so did Geraldine, as she picked up on everything like a sponge.

Geraldine walked up to the two ladies, watching them converse. Her head moved from side to side like a tennis match.

The ladies gabbed and gossiped like they were two teenagers. Topics ranged from the latest styles in pants:

"Why are they coming back? Never looked good on anyone who ate more than a grape!"

To politics:

"*Why* is he in charge?"

Travel experiences:

"Someone should have explained 'clothing optional' to you."

Geraldine became bored of the conversation, and decided to go and find her mother, Corrine, who was in the kitchen.

"I have decided that Vivian is a bitch."

"She's not a bitch; she's just direct."

"She's a bitch."

"You know that Bubbe worked at Sunderland's with Vivian for years. That's where she met Popa. She said it was one of the best times of her life."

"Yeah, I know—but what's the deal with them?" Geraldine questioned, wanting to learn more than what she already knew, if that was possible.

"After Bubbe stopped working, I guess they kind of lost touch." Like her mother, Corrine also didn't like lying to her children, but in this case, she was. Several years ago, her mother confided in Corrine and told her all about the Travel Set, the burglars, the cat fight on the department store floor, and asked her daughter to keep the story to herself.

"I don't blame her; she's a real bitch."

Corrine gave Geraldine a stern look and said, "Did you say something to annoy her?"

"Maybe . . . you know, Bubbe isn't the same."

"What do you mean?"

"She's not Bubbe in there," Geraldine said as she pointed toward the living room. "Something is different. She's not herself."

"Aw, Bubbe is just sad. She just lost her husband."

"Yeah, but there's something else" Geraldine said as she looked down to the kitchen floor.

Corrine agreed with her daughter, as she didn't know either. Mr. Sand called Corrine from his hospital bed, just before he passed and spoke about Lilly and Vivian's time at Sunderland's. How special their relationship was, and that it was spoiled for the wrong reasons. They had to get to the bottom of it. But when? How?

"Look what I have!" Vivian reached into her purse to pull out a very familiar white paper bag.

"You didn't!"

"I did!"

"I'll take one," Lilly said as she reached into the bag to get herself a cookie, then held it up close to study it and sighed. "It's amazing how this one little cookie can bring you back in time." Lilly closed her eyes and inhaled the aroma that the cookie carried and took a small bite.

"I know."

"Tell you a secret," Vivian said, as Lilly's eyes lit up. "These cookies—they have a secret ingredient—passionflower! It's a natural alternative to valium."

"Well, I'll be—that explains everything".

"It sure does."

"Ah, what the heck," Lilly said as chewed the soft buttery goodness, that gave her that rush of euphoria once again, trying to take a deep breath to nurse the pang in her chest.

"You betcha!" Vivian smiled and nodded, trying to do the same thing.

Lilly's Granddaughter Geraldine

Embrace the unexpected that helps you see what you can't.

Geraldine didn't even own a watch, but she knew what time it was. The same thing happened every morning at 10:30, and she wondered if anyone heard it. It was her stomach, and it was growling: she needed a snack. She stared at the clock on the wall. Finally, it rang, and Geraldine sprang out of her desk in search of the brown bag that had what she needed.

Elated that she had her snack in hand, Geraldine went outside to the playground while she munched and enjoyed every bite of her Ritz Crackers. She felt the oily remnants of them on her fingers, which she planned to savor afterwards in the most discreet way. Licking your fingers, as she was told, was not the finest act of etiquette, but the devouring had to be done. The idea of washing away the minute crumbs that still carried such immense flavor down the school washroom sink was as wasteful as tossing out perfectly good leftovers that taste far better the next day.

Geraldine looked around to make sure no one was watching and slowly turned to a wall in the playground and began to strategically lick the remains of the crackers from her fingers. She stopped a few times, walked to a different wall, and licked again. When all was done, a feeling of satisfaction and calm washed through her, and she thought about what to do next.

Someone tapped her shoulder.

"Want to play?" the Queen Leader (QL) asked, who was holding the coveted tool of the season—the Chinese Jump Rope. Such a racist name to call the toy, but that was what it was called at the time. With fierce green eyes, and a toothless grin, she stared at Geraldine as if she was her next meal.

Geraldine's caramel eyes glistened as she felt honored, excited, and wanted to go but was still nursing the scrape on her knee from her accident the other day. It was still red, slightly inflamed, and needed a Band-Aid, as a protective scab had not formed yet. Her fall was no one's fault but hers. How was she to know that the rope was in her way as she walked back to the classroom?

It crossed her mind that the rope could have been placed in her path on purpose, but she dismissed the thought because she so wanted to be QL's friend, and the girls she hung out with.

She wanted to be friends with *them* as they looked like they were having so much fun at recess. The latest games were played. Laughter that was so intense, some collapsed on the floor, while they held their stomachs. The boys chased them around. Gerladine witnessed from afar as it was more entertaining than what was on TV that night.

The word on the street was that they had the best sleepovers with movie-style popcorn that was served in a special media room. Even though Geraldine had no idea what a media room was, she still wanted to go. She wondered if they served Ritz Crackers in that special media room and what would happen if she licked her fingers afterwards? She thought about it and decided that she would probably excuse herself and go to the washroom to continue her ritual.

Full of hope, Geraldine nodded "yes" and followed QL and her posse as they walked with pride to a secluded area of the playground like a pack. Geraldine felt proud because she was there with THEM. Maybe they were testing her, she thought. Maybe they had suddenly realized that she was a smart kid and was fun to be with, and they would be kind. QL reached out to hold Geraldine's hand when she asked her to come and play their game, which was such a comforting gesture, Geraldine thought.

They picked a spot on the playground to set up. Everyone was in position.

Two girls held the rope between both of their legs, and a generous space was created to play. The spectators were standing by, and Geraldine waited to begin, as she courageously volunteered to go first.

Chinese jump rope was played by either jumping in, out, or on a stationary rope that completed a jumping pattern. A circular elastic rope was placed around two sets of legs that were spread apart where there was plenty of room for the player to perform a jump pattern. The challenges arose when the player progressed to the next level as the rope got placed above the knees and they had to jump higher. When it was placed around the ankles, which was the first level, anyone—well most anyone—can do it. If the player touched the rope with a body part or missed a step, they were considered "out".

Geraldine had confidence that she could do this, as she had done it many times before with Ellie and Michelle, her friends at school since day one. Quiet like her. Reserved like her. But she wanted to be with THEM, and this was why Geraldine was there with QL and her gang.

Geraldine took a deep breath and jumped inside the rope with ease and then followed the rest of the pattern—out, side, side, on.

"Out!" they all yelled in unison.

She knew that was going to happen, as it always did. Every time Geraldine played with them.

"But I didn't make a mistake!" Geraldine pleaded, looking confused but knowing very well she was talking to a wall, as these girls knew what they were doing. She hoped maybe this time would be different.

"Yes, you did! We all saw," QL said, grinning, this time showing her teeth.

Geraldine bowed her head down in defeat. She knew that she was right but couldn't say how, as she didn't know how to say it. Geraldine bit her lower lip until she tasted metal while she took the bait and stood by the side and watched the rest progress to more difficult jumping techniques and levels. She studied their faces. Each player was focused and took deep breaths before they began their turn. Some made a deep inhaling sound as they jumped, and others filled their cheeks with air and blew it out with force. Long hair was either swept up in a ponytail or hung loose while being tucked behind the ears. You could see their strands of hair bounce all over the place. Even yards away. How Geraldine wanted to show them she could do that all that, too.

All who were around the game watched each player's moves carefully, but there was always one or two girls who looked around the playground and saw what else was going on.

Geraldine watched everybody all the time and was dreading when her turn would come up again. Why was she still there, taking the bait? The hope of acceptance into their group was a given, but also, she wanted to prove that they were wrong. That she was not out and never was. And she also wanted them to know that she was a nice person and fun to be with. Why couldn't they see that?

"Your turn."

After shaking her head to wake up to stimulate her focus, she gathered her strength and gave a response that was hard to do but needed to be done.

"I'll pass."

"It's your turn!"

"No."

"Why?"

"You keep saying I'm out, but I know I'm not."

"Ok, ok—this time, we'll really watch carefully!" said QL, who grabbed a chunk of her long red hair and slung it to her back.

Geraldine narrowed her eyes as she recognized that QL slung her hair like that every time she got nervous, especially before the French exams, where she would also cry as well. Geraldine twitched her mouth while she wondered why she was suddenly nervous.

QL glanced at her sidekick, who nodded with approval. Sidekick (SK) followed her every move. She had kinky, curly black hair, wore mostly black, and made sure everyone knew that she was in possession of eighty-nine pairs, and counting, of the hippest, coolest running shoes. She never wore the same pair twice. "You have THE BEST shoes!" someone would say, and SK would beam and respond, "I know."

Determined to hold onto a gleam of hope that they wanted to play with Geraldine and be her friend, she agreed to continue to play. Even though a suspicion was felt as something was going on that did not feel right.

QL and SK stood across from each other with the thick elastic band wrapped around their ankles, while they waited for Geraldine to begin. She walked slowly up to the court and stood on one side, then took a deep breath to focus on her move, as she thought about where the best place to aim her first jump would be and where she should land. When Geraldine looked up to QL and SK, she saw QL smiling at the crowd around them and SK who looked straight ahead at the court, as she tapped her fingers on her thigh.

Geraldine gathered all her strength and took a big breath before she jumped as high as she could in the air, while she maneuvered her legs exactly to land smack in the middle of the rope and softly on her feet. The rope did not budge. Not a single elastic hair was out of place. The rope looked frozen, as if it was left outside in the Arctic overnight. Geraldine stood proudly in the middle of the rope, waiting for the verdict. This time, two spoke at once.

She should have known better.

"Out!" they all sang together.

Beauty's 2.0

On the Sunday morning, two weeks after the Shiva visit, where the conversation flowed like a steady stream with a huge tree branch stuck in the current, Vivian and Lilly made a date to have breakfast at Beauty's—their favorite old hangout.

Was Lilly nervous to be with Vivian without her family around? And without Mr. Sand?

Yes.

Vivian was just as nervous, if not more.

Nevertheless, both women placed their hesitation, anger and hurtful feelings aside and committed to the date.

It had been years since they stepped into the famous restaurant that had a similar lineup of those who wanted to meet with Vivian at Sunderland's. Long. Around the block long. Of course, the girls were smart and decided to go early, before anyone with a hangover from the Saturday night before, wanted a freshly squeezed orange juice. At around 7:30 AM, Vivian stepped into her Chevrolet, as her mother's car, the pink powder puff was long gone. In the driver's seat, she pulled down the mirror on her car's visor, to make sure that her foundation hadn't fallen into her creases. No such luck; it fell. She shrugged and added a giggle as she turned on the ignition and drove the fifteen minutes to Lilly's home.

While Lilly was waiting by her window, she thought about the game she would play in her mind called "alternate universe" and think of what would happen if Vivian's Travel Set worked out. There was no scamming, nor a need for any intervention of attacking the Johnson women on the department store floor. Would they still be friends? Would she be famous and rich? Would they still be friends?

These questions, especially the latter, kept repeating over and over in her head as she walked to Vivian's car as she saw it pull up in her driveway. It was fall, and the leaves had just turned. To the left of her driveway was a bright red tree. She stopped walking to admire the perfect cherry dark red color the tree wore and embraced the slight chill she felt at the back of her neck. She knew she wasn't the only one who would appreciate that stunning red hue as over the years, it was Mr. Sand and Vivian who taught her how to seek out and appreciate beauty, as it was everywhere.

There she was. Grinning with her trademark bright red lips and dyed jet-black hair neatly styled in a headband. Lilly got into the car, sat herself down, placed her purse in her lap, and faced Vivian.

"For sixty-five, we look pretty damn good!" Vivian announced.

Lilly shook her head and smiled at her friend. It felt good to be with her and she had an internal desire to start this friendship again.

Over to Beauty's where they were the first ones to walk in. As soon as they both sat down, they ordered the usual. A bagel, lox and cream cheese with tomato and onion, with coffee, of course. Diving right into conversation, about where they used to sit in the restaurant, their days at Sunderland's and where to spend the winter. After breakfast, they shared a bowl of their favorite, rice pudding, and began to speak of Mr. Sand which completely changed the course of the pleasant past hour.

"It was a lovely funeral," Vivian said.

And then it happened. Without warning, Lilly's response burst out of her mouth in an angry tone. The idea of starting the friendship again was not off to a good start.

"How can you call it lovely?"

"Because it was," Vivian said as she stared at Lilly in shock.

"I wouldn't use that word, even if I did attend," Lilly said with a sour face.

"Why didn't you come?" Vivian quickly asked.

Lilly looked to the left, as she didn't know where to begin. She did know one thing, her breakfast was not sitting well in her stomach, and wondered if she was going to be sick. Maybe it was the lox, she thought. No more finding the good or giving one for the team. The bandage was off, and the air was stinging the deep scrape.

"Lill?" Vivian asked.

Lilly looked straight ahead at Vivian and tried to keep her cool by taking deep breaths as she collected her thoughts because the rage was getting the best of her. She reached for a glass of water and took a sip. She didn't want to just yell; she wanted to scream her head off and yell "*Why couldn't you let me in?*" But she kept quiet, for now as Vivian stirred the pot with her ceremonious manner that was really getting on Lilly's nerves.

"Oh, no"—Vivian waved her polished red fingernail in the air—"there's more to it. What's going on?" Vivian probed, but to no avail; Lilly wasn't budging. "Why didn't you come to the funeral?"

"I don't like funerals," Lilly said a flat out lie. Lilly wrestled to let her anger out, to tell Vivian how she really felt. Just say it! Say it! She screamed inside her head. Vivian rolled her eyes.

"Oh my God. Who does?" Vivian said with her arms out wide. "You didn't have to leave Sunderland's, you know," Vivian said. It was if she reached into her purse to pull out a box of matches. Slowly taking out a single match.

"I can't get into this now," Lilly shot back, as that response was so much easier to say. That can of worms needed to be opened, but not now. Not at Beauty's. But when? she thought. That little match sure looked enticing. If Vivian wasn't going to strike it and place it under Lilly's *tuchas*, she was going to reach out and grab it out of her hand to do it herself. Just not yet.

"Why not?" Vivian prompted, striking the match.

"I just can't," Lilly said as she stared at the imaginary fire on the tip of the match. Place it over here. Over here. Insinuating the energy to the lower part of her body.

"Lilly, for God's sake, answer me—what is going on here? Why are you so upset? I said I was sorry!" Vivian said in a stern voice as the fire was now directly under Lilly's *tuchas* and the fire ignited into a blaze. All hell broke loose.

"How could you treat me that way?" Lilly yelled as the heat from the flames rose to her face as the pain drove her words. Her eyes grew as she drew in some breath. The hum of customers' conversation at Beauty's arrived at a complete halt. She took another deep breath and closed her eyes to deal with the rush of blood that made its way to her face. She felt overwhelmed as there was too much to say, and all Lilly could do was ask that first question and leave. And that's what she did.

"Treat you in what way?" Vivian blurted out.

"I tried to help you," Lilly softly said, while Vivian looked straight into Lilly's eyes as if she was stabbed in her heart as she was unable to go back to that painful experience that ripped her ego into shreds.

Lilly knew one thing for sure; she and Vivian had a wonderful friendship, filled with laughter, support, and love. But those things could only go so far when something goes very wrong. Vivian sat there, holding her coffee cup, feeling all the eyes that looked her way as Lilly got up from their table, left a $20 bill, and walked out of the restaurant to hail a taxi to take her home.

Geraldine

A few days after Vivian and Lilly went for breakfast, Corrine called her mother Lilly and shared that Geraldine was having a difficult time with friends at school and couldn't get through to her. "When you come over on Sunday, let her stay here for a while, you know how she loves to play with the shoes in my closet. That will get her talking," Lilly said to her daughter.

"I'm always out in this game that we play at recess," Geraldine whined to her grandmother as she sat on the floor of her closet and reached to the third shelf to pull out a silver high heeled number with a four-inch heel.

"Bubbe—how could you wear these? They are so hiiighhhhh!"

"I know . . . one time I did. Can't now. Go ahead, try them on!" Lilly said as she found the mate of the shoe, which made her think of her initiation days in the basement of Sunderland's—cleaning the shoe shelves, one by one, and finding the pair that went together. A giggle escaped her.

"What's so funny?" Geraldine asked.

"Oh, just a memory of working at Sunderland's."

"With Vivian?" Geraldine asked as she took off her socks and wiggled her foot into the narrow and dainty high-heeled shoe.

"Yup."

"They're pretty!" Geraldine said as she slowly stood up and hobbled to the mirror to check herself out.

"They sure are," Lilly said, as she walked toward where her granddaughter was standing in the mirror, held onto her shoulders and looked at their reflection. She loved spending time with her granddaughter. It was such a special time, and she cherished it.

"Why are you smiling so brightly, Bubbe?"

"I'm happy you're here," Lilly said as she closed her eyes and hugged her grandchild.

"I'm glad I'm here, too. I like it here."

"Why?" Lilly asked, hoping to dig into the soul of her granddaughter.

"I can just be myself. It's easy."

"That's a very important feeling to have," Lilly said while she turned to her shelves of shoes to see what else Geraldine could try on and to keep her from crying. "So, what's this about you always being out in this game you play at school?"

"Oh that—yeah, it's this stupid game at school. Everyone's playing it."

"Do all of your friends play it?"

"Not all."

"Do you like playing it?"

"I guess."

"Do you like playing it with your friends?"

"Which friends?"

"What do you mean which friends. The friends you have at school," Lilly asked, which really confused Geraldine because she wasn't sure who her real friends were.

***

Geraldine

Geraldine stood near the jump rope and the friend group that went with it and looked up at the two girls who held the rope militantly between their legs. Their hands were on their hips, and they were staring right at her, lips sealed and eyes glaring.

"GO!" another said, loudly.

Every eye felt like a dagger, and sadly, Geraldine was beginning to get used to the pain, but that wouldn't do. Someone was about to help her who didn't have the medicine she needed but the desire to get to the root of the problem—a far wiser solution for any type of pain.

"Hey, whatcha doin'?" a familiar voice said behind her back.

Geraldine quickly turned around and saw her science class partner, who was a whole head and shoulders smaller than Geraldine. She was carrying a glass jar with a mosquito in it.

Mosquito Girl (MG) instigated way too much misbehaving during class, which was usually welcomed, like a dive in the lake on a steaming hot day, especially after Geraldine's usual recess sessions.

Geraldine had a front row seat to witness this mighty force in action, who had a keen eye for justice and a voice that made so much sense. Whether she challenged their teacher—"Are you sure you are right about that theory?"—or saw someone step out of line—"You can't leave your garbage on the floor like that! What were you, brought up in a barn?"—her wise words and challenges were shared with all who would listen and those who wouldn't. Yes, there were a handful of heads that would turn away, but that was their loss. Geraldine admired and almost envied MG's presence, hoping one day to be able to dig deep into matters that meant so much to her and fearlessly educate the world, just like she did.

"You've got to see what this little guy does! Come with me!" MG said as she held her jar tight. Although she was as serious as a surgeon with the things that mattered most to her, there was such a playful side to her that Geraldine loved, that made her feel comfortable and allowed her to be herself.

MG was smiling from ear to ear, encouraging Geraldine to come with her. And she did.

"Hey, where are you going?" Queen Leader (QL) asked while Geraldine began to walk away, wondering why she even cared. QL was clearly not her friend but her toy that she liked to bash around. Geraldine looked at MG and asked for direction with her eyes, which, miraculously, she completely understood.

"Why are you giving a second of your energy to these clowns?"

"They're not clowns—they're cool."

"Really? Do cool people make you feel like shit? Tell you are out of a game when you are clearly not—and I have seen you play—you are not out," MG said with gusto. As harsh as her comment was, it was the truth that made Geraldine realize what a real friend was and gave her full permission to walk away.

***

Later that week, Lilly took Geraldine to Sunderland's to buy a pair of shoes for a party. From working there all those years, Lilly was still entitled to a discount, along with a fruit cake that was delivered to her home every Mother's Day. The only requirement was that Lilly had to be present to purchase the item, which suited Lilly just fine, as the opportunity to shop with her granddaughter was a special time for them both. But Vivian would be there, and she would have to face her. Again. The ladies have not spoken since their breakfast date nearly a month ago, which made Lilly's stomach turn upside down as soon as she approached the marble tiles that housed the hunter green-framed glass doors.

As soon as they entered the store, Geraldine spotted Vivian right away and waved and looked up at her grandmother to lead the way. She knew there was tension between them, as she felt her Bubbe's anxiousness on their way downtown.

"How are you, ladies? Vivian asked as she leaned on her glass counter.

"We're here to buy a pair of shoes for a party!" Geraldine proudly announced.

"Exciting! Well, it's a good thing you have your Bubbe with you. She knows her stuff—even though she doesn't work here anymore."

"You bet she knows her stuff. My Bubbe knows everything."

"Really!" Vivian said as she rested her elbows on the counter and placed her face on her hands so she could be at Geraldine's eye level.

"Well, not everything," Geraldine admitted.

"What kind of things does she know?" Vivian asked as she walked around her counter to walk them to the shoe department.

"Like what a friend really is," Geraldine answered.

"And what's that sweetheart?" Vivian asked.

"Someone who loves you exactly how you are. No matter what . . . I learned that from my new friend at school and from your friend."

"What friend of mine are you talking about, dear?" Lilly asked.

"Mr. Sand."

"Mr. Sand passed away, darling," Vivian said.

"I know. He called my mom just before he died to tell her that."

* * *

What do you know? The next day, just before lunch, an invitation to play Chinese jump rope was given once again.

"No," Geraldine replied, armed with her newfound knowledge and power.

At dinner that evening, another invitation came by phone.

"No," Geraldine said to the receiver and then banged down. Corrine gave her daughter a concerned look. "Ah, she deserved it," Geraldine said as Corrine watched her daughter walk back to

The Most Amazing Department Store

her seat at the dinner table in amazement. This was a
new side to Geraldine that was filled with confidence, and
proud.

And one more, by a note in class. Geraldine wrote in
fancy cursive, just because she could.

This went on for weeks, and Geraldine didn't understand
they were not getting the message. The following day, as
minding her own business, hanging around with Ellie
and MG on the playground, QL entered their territory,
Chinese jump rope in her hand, swinging it, and snapping
the drug that Geraldine savored. And still wanted.

"What? What are you doing?" MG yelled, feeling furious
she could go back there, But Geraldine didn't hear her, off to
QL for more torture because that was what it was. That
she knew.

"No. No. I'm coming with you," MG said to deter her,
followed the girls to their part of land. She was on a mission,
this was a goodie. There was no way that her friend was
be treated like garbage if she had anything to say about it, and
goodness, did she ever.

The thick and firm elastic was pulled tight around their
legs. Geraldine stood beside the rope and paused as if strat-
egizing her next move. She gazed at the length of rope, and
looked up at all that was around her. She spotted MG looking
straight at her and mouthed, "No."

Geraldine stopped. She finally felt the negative energy of the
girls that made her feel awful and wanted no part of it. "I'm
outta here," she said as she briskly walked away from them.
MG followed. She really wanted to continue playing to prove
them wrong, but she didn't need to.

The day after school, Geraldine went to go visit her mother
as she needed to tell her what she had done. It was awkward,

Epilogue

As you reach for the stately department store front doors and step onto the place that you adore, you walk with purpose down the aisle. Once again, delighted you are here. In this beautiful place, with beautiful things.

The fragrance counter has caught your eye, and you stop in your tracks. Wait a minute—did you see that one advertised recently? Your eyes grow like flowers as you reach for the uniquely designed glass bottle and gently press the automizer to release a miniature shower of a scent that immediately makes you sneeze.

"Oh darling, that isn't for you!" says a salesperson. "Here, let me show you some others. But first, inhale this." The salesperson gently says this while a jar of coffee beans is placed under your nose to clear your nasal passageways. And before long, you will have found the fragrance that has lifted your spirits and celebrated you.

The same goes for the skirt to wear to that meeting. The scarf that will not only raise the dial on the style meter but will keep you warm. Don't forget about the shoes to complete your outfit, which you will wear again and again. And hand it down to someone special.

These treasures could be found on your own, but it is much more productive. Much more meaningful and downright fun to have some help, especially from someone who works at the department store and knows the store like the back of her hand. But then again, so do you.

Help from someone who welcomes you into their world and is kind, patient, and listens. Refrains from judgment. Traits that very few own but earned with the passage of time, as painful as it was. Count yourself lucky if you encounter someone like this. However, if a salesperson found someone like this to work with, that's especially lucky.

What glistened and sparkled in an elegant department store, such as Sunderland's, were two women who not only found their voices but also found each other, which is the most amazing thing of all.

ACKNOWLEDGEMENTS

Thank you to Kleenex tissues. You are doing a great job of absorbing my tears of joy as I write this.

It takes a village to raise a child, and it also takes a village to publish a book. Welcome to my list of Most Amazing of Humans. The roster of people that helped me to get this book into your hands. I hope you enjoyed it as much as I enjoyed writing it.

To Amy Laura Jones, OMG . . . I'm writing my acknowledgments, just like you said I would! Thank you for coaching me through my first draft and encouraging me to run with it.

Thank you, Lisa Borden. You are my sounding board, my confidante, and my friend. You know exactly when I need to kick some ass.

Thank you, Yael Greenwood for reading the first draft, and for being the real friend that you are. You were so right, and I am grateful for you and for your honesty.

Michael Leo Donovan, it has been over 30 years since I last stepped into your classroom, but your teachings are forever engrained in my mind. Thank you for helping me to see the talent that I did not know I had.

Thank you to my dear friends and to my 'frenemies's. You know who you are, and you all matter in your own special way. You were each placed in my path for a reason. Thank you for showing me who you are, and for giving me such great material to work with.

Thank you to all the obstacles and challenges that have shown up in my life thus far. These too were placed in my life for a reason.

Even that 10-foot nail polish shelf that I had to clean from top to bottom when I was 17-years old.

Deanna McFadden, everyone told me how amazing you are, but I didn't realize how true that was until we started working together. You let me drive, while gently suggesting when I should make certain turns. Thank you for your patience, your expertise, and your vision.

Rebecca Eckler, thank you for believing in me, my work, and my purpose. I am grateful for your (and Rowan's) very first accolade from my debut novel to where we are today.

A special shout out to Melvin Eldinger who was there.

Thank you, Adrienne Gold Davis for being the best Torah teacher. Ever.

Thank you to my loving parents, Evie and Morrie Neiss, for sharing Montreal's Jewish history with me. You both have taught me more than you know.

To Auntie Dorey and Dad, thank you for sharing pieces of your mother's story, especially those on which this novel is loosely based.

Carrie, My PB, spiritual advisor and best sister I could ever ask for. Thank you for digging deep with me and listening.

Kiddies! Josh, thank you for your superb proof-reading and for tolerating my stubbornness. Adam, your many "check-ins" to see how I was doing meant more than you know. Liv, how I love your strong voice, your "Yay, Mom!" cheers. Thank you for bringing home that piece of information that has now become this novel.

To Gordie, my beautiful husband, partner in crime and favourite person in the world. You have seen it all, and still want more. How lucky am I?